Praise for the Novels of Marta Perry

"What a joy it is to read Marta Perry's novels! . . . Everything a reader could want—strong, well-defined characters; beautiful, realistic settings; and a thought-provoking plot. Readers of Amish fiction will surely be waiting anxiously for her next book."

—Shelley Shepard Gray, *New York Times* bestselling author of the Sisters of the Heart series

"A born storyteller, Marta Perry skillfully weaves the past and present in a heart-stirring tale of love and forgiveness."

—Susan Meissner, bestselling author of *The Last Year of the War*

"Sure to appeal to fans of Beverly Lewis."

—*Library Journal*

"Perry carefully balances the traditional life of the Amish with the contemporary world in an accessible, intriguing fashion."   —*Publishers Weekly* (starred review)

"Perry crafts characters with compassion, yet with insecurities that make them relatable."   —RT Book Reviews

"[Perry] has once again captured my heart with the gentle wisdom and heartfelt faith of the Amish community."

—Fresh Fiction

A
Springtime
Heart

MARTA PERRY

JOVE
New York

A JOVE BOOK
Published by Berkley
An imprint of Penguin Random House LLC
penguinrandomhouse.com

Copyright © 2020 by Martha Johnson
Excerpt from *A Christmas Home* by Marta Perry copyright © 2019 by Martha Johnson
Penguin Random House supports copyright. Copyright fuels creativity, encourages
diverse voices, promotes free speech, and creates a vibrant culture. Thank you for buying
an authorized edition of this book and for complying with copyright laws by not
reproducing, scanning, or distributing any part of it in any form without permission.
You are supporting writers and allowing Penguin Random House to continue to
publish books for every reader.

A JOVE BOOK, BERKLEY, and the BERKLEY & B colophon
are registered trademarks of Penguin Random House LLC.

ISBN: 9781984803214

First Edition: July 2020

Printed in the United States of America
1   3   5   7   9   10   8   6   4   2

Cover art: Photo of woman by Claudio Dogar-Marinesco
Cover design by Sarah Oberrender

CHAPTER ONE

A glance at the schoolroom clock told Dorcas Beiler that her scholars' recess was almost over. She stepped back outside, where the schoolyard seemed overwhelmed with the sights and smells of springtime in Promise Glen, Pennsylvania. The land around her woke with the spirit of new life, with the bulbs they'd planted along the porch bursting open. Certainly her scholars felt the change. They'd been rambunctious all day, and she could only hope that recess had worn off a little of their excess energy.

Dorcas reminded herself that she was too old to experience spring as the children did. But even with her schooldays long behind her, a sense of restlessness stirred, lifted its head, and had to be pushed back down again.

It had been one thing to give in to that longing when she'd been a heedless teenager looking for something beyond the confines of Amish life. It had been dangerous enough then. Now it would be a disaster. She was an adult now, an old maid at twenty-five, and the respected teacher of the Orchard Hill Amish school. This was her life, and it suited her just fine.

Reaching up, she caught the bell rope and pulled. The sound brought a quick glance from Anna Stoltzfus, her teenage helper, who flagged down the boys she'd been pitching to in a pickup softball game. Anna was quick to respond—the boys not so eager.

Of course, Anna was probably dreaming of having a school of her own one day, while the boys' thoughts were on their game. Dorcas smiled, noticing the older girls watching as the boys jogged in from the field, pushing and jostling one another. No doubt the girls were reacting to spring in a very different way, if their sidelong glances at the boys were any indication.

Her younger scholars were the first to reach the door, their faces touched by the sun as they smiled up at her, eyes bright, hair clinging damply to their foreheads. Then came some of the older ones. Esther Fisher bounced to a stop in front of her, smile flashing, her blue eyes lit with excitement.

"Teacher Dorcas, have you heard?" Her voice lifted on the words, but she didn't wait for a response. "My brother Thomas is home at last!"

Dorcas stood very still, not letting herself think. Fortunately Esther rushed on to corner someone else with her good news. She couldn't know, thank the good Lord, that it wasn't exactly good news for her teacher. Upsetting, even frightening, yes. Good, no.

The habits of the past seven years as a teacher asserted themselves. Whatever her personal problems, she didn't bring them into the classroom. Fixing what she hoped was a pleasant smile on her face, Dorcas focused on getting her scholars settled, returning to her desk, and setting them to work on their spelling words.

"Spelling bee starts in fifteen minutes," she warned at a faint buzz of sound. "You'd best concentrate now, ain't so?"

Silence fell. Dorcas exchanged a smile with Anna, and they started at opposite sides of the schoolroom to walk up and down the rows of desks, alert for anyone having problems or giving in to the temptation to pester his or her neighbor.

Dorcas had started with the youngest children, and she paused between the six-year-old Raber twins, Matthew and Mark, the stepchildren of her dear friend Sarah Yoder, now Raber. If anyone was likely to have trouble settling to work, it would probably be Matthew. In fact, as she stepped past him, Matthew looked up, his mouth forming an *Oh* of surprise.

"Teacher," he whispered. "I forgot."

Suppressing a smile, she whispered in return, "What did you forget, Matthew?"

"Mammi says will you stop on your way home if you have time? She has a surprise for you. It's—"

"Shhh." His brother nudged him. "It's a secret. Remember?"

"You mustn't tell me then," she said quickly. "Get working on your words, now."

Dorcas moved on, wondering. Could Sarah have heard that Thomas Fisher was back from the relatives in Ohio, where he'd been sent when they were teenagers? Sarah knew something about the relationship between Dorcas and Thomas, but thankfully not everything. No one knew that, except for her. And Thomas, of course.

Feeling as if she were sweeping crumbs from the floor, Dorcas whisked the pesky memories from her mind. She had to start the spelling bee.

The afternoon went on its usual course, and aside from an inability to concentrate, Dorcas flattered herself that no one would guess she felt as if she'd been butted by her brother's irritable billy goat.

By the time all the spellers had been congratulated, she felt as if she had become, if not settled, at least right-side-up again. She picked up the copy of *Little House in the Big Woods*, which lay on her desk, ensuring instant silence as her scholars anticipated the chapter she'd read to them today. Safe in the adventures of Mary and Laura, they would all, including her, forget everything else.

The hands of the clock reached three, and Dorcas finished the paragraph and closed the book. Her twenty-four scholars waited silently until she smiled at them and then gave the nod that meant they were dismissed.

That, she decided, was something young Anna had yet to master. When the girl had figured out how to control the classroom with a look, Dorcas would be convinced she had the makings of a teacher.

As usual, she and Anna fell in behind the children, who, grabbing lunch boxes and sweaters, headed for the door, chattering loudly.

"Did you hear?" Anna, her usually shy face filled with curiosity, repeated Esther's question. "Thomas Fisher is back in Promise Glen."

"Yah, Esther told me." She managed a smile that she hoped looked normal. "I'm sure his family is wonderful glad."

Anna nodded, but she still had a question in her pale blue eyes. "Yah. But folks are saying his daad won't be so happy. I guess it's extra hard for a minister of the church to have a son go wrong."

So that was what people thought of it, at least according to Anna, who was something like a third cousin to Thomas in the tangle of family relationships among the Amish. Not knowing what Minister Lucas Fisher might be thinking, she wouldn't comment. But it would be a sad thing if Thomas returned and didn't receive the welcome usually accorded to a prodigal son.

Not, of course, that Thomas had run away from the church. As far as anyone knew, he'd been faithful in attendance with his aunt and uncle out in Ohio.

Her mind still wrestling with the question, Dorcas stepped outside in the wake of the children, blinking for a moment in the bright sunlight. Then her vision cleared, and she saw the masculine figure leaning negligently against the porch post, the sunlight glinting on his auburn hair, his dark blue eyes lit by teasing laughter at the sight of her.

Not only was Thomas Fisher back in Promise Glen, but he was here, at her school. She took a deep breath, trying not to stare. He'd been a boy when he left, all gangly arms and legs that he didn't seem to know what to do with. But he was a man now, with a man's sturdy frame and hard muscles.

He pushed himself away from the post with a single, fluid movement and came toward her, somehow giving the impression that he was laughing at her. If he was, she could be sure that, in some ways, Thomas hadn't changed a bit.

The only question was what she was going to do about him.

THOMAS MOVED TOWARD Dorcas, wondering at the changes in her. He'd known when he'd offered to pick up his little sister that he would see Dorcas. Maybe that was even why he'd come, if he were honest with himself.

Curiosity, he thought firmly. Just curiosity. He'd found it hard to believe that the rebellious girl, up for any risk, taking any dare, had turned into something so staid as a teacher.

Come to think of it, she didn't look all that staid. True, her rich brown hair was confined under her kapp, not flowing down her back as it had been the last time he'd seen her. He couldn't see the dimples that used to flash in her cheeks. He'd have to make her smile at him for that, and something told him it might not be easy to win a smile from this grown-up Dorcas.

Some things hadn't changed. Her skin still had the warm, peachy glow that had always intrigued him. She was taller than she'd been in her teens, still slim, but filling out her simple blue dress nicely.

All in all, Teacher Dorcas was a far cry from the old maid teacher he'd had when he went to school here.

Reaching her, he was pleased to find he had to look down at her. Dorcas tilted her head and gave him an unconvincing smile that didn't reach her eyes.

"Thomas. I heard from Esther you were back."

"It's been a long time, *Teacher* Dorcas." He said the title with a question in his voice, wondering how she would react.

The instant flicker of anger in her eyes told him she knew he was making fun of her.

"You still have the same temper, I see." He quirked an eyebrow, teasing.

"And you still haven't given up tormenting the girls, I see," she retorted. For a moment they were back in the schoolyard, and he might have been chasing her around and tugging at the strings of her kapp.

"Teasing, not tormenting." He couldn't help but grin. "And you always did rise to the bait, ain't so?"

"I thought I'd outgrown that weakness." Despite an obvious effort to contain it, she gave him a genuine smile.

He'd wanted to see those dimples again after all this time, just to see if they were as pretty as he remembered. They were; that was certain sure.

"I'm glad you didn't," he said lightly. "It brings back memories."

She sobered fast enough at that, her lips growing tight, and he wondered if she thought he'd meant something he didn't. But before he could come up with a way to assure her that the circumstances of his leaving were long since forgiven and forgotten, she'd gained control of herself.

"So what have you been doing now that you're all grown up?" she asked, sounding like an elderly great-aunt talking to a fourteen-year-old fresh out of school.

Teasing wasn't getting him anywhere, so maybe he'd best try sticking to facts. "Learning the construction business from my uncle—my mamm's bruder out in Ohio. Best thing I could have done," he added, hoping that would show he didn't bear a grudge. "Onkel James is a master craftsman, and he let me work alongside him just as if I was one of his boys."

Before he could go on, Esther emerged from a crowd of girls and grabbed his arm. "Aren't you ready to go yet? Mamm said she'd have a special snack when we got home."

"I expect it'll last until we get there," he told her.

"Not if Jonas and Adam get there first," she muttered rebelliously, making him look at her in surprise. That sassiness wasn't how he remembered his baby sister.

He let a slight frown appear. "I'm talking with Teacher Dorcas right now."

To give her credit, Esther looked ashamed. "I'm sorry, Teacher Dorcas."

The dimples appeared in Dorcas's cheeks again. Maybe she wasn't sorry to have their talk interrupted. "That's all right, Esther. I know it's exciting to have your big bruder back again."

Esther sparkled at the understanding tone, looking more like the little girl he remembered. "I'll wait. You go on talking."

He'd like to do just that, but it wouldn't be easy to say what he wanted when Esther was hanging heavily on his arm. When had she gotten so big? Things had changed while he'd been gone. People had changed, like it or not.

"That's all right." Dorcas looked just as glad to make an end to their conversation. "I see Matthew and Mark are waiting. They're going to walk partway home with me."

She nodded to a pair of small boys who were hanging from the porch railing much as his sister was hanging on his arm. He looked, then gave a double take.

"Twins?" He scoured his memory, not coming up with anything.

Dorcas's laugh was a low chuckle that made him want to hear it again. "They are the Raber twins. Their daad has a furniture-making business. He recently remarried to my friend Sarah. Remember Sarah Yoder?"

"How could I forget? She used to give me a disapproving look every time I got too close to you."

He didn't want to talk about the twins, whether they were Sarah's or not. He wanted to talk about Dorcas, and what had brought about such a change in her.

But it seemed pretty clear that Dorcas was ready to leave, besides the fact that it would be next to impossible to detach Esther from his arm, so anything they said, she'd hear.

"They live not far from us," Dorcas went on, taking a step back. "It was nice to see you, Thomas. Enjoy your stay, though I'm sure your uncle is eager to have you back with the summer construction season coming."

"Didn't I tell you?" he asked, a little annoyed that she was so eager to be rid of him. "I'm not going back. I'm going to start my own construction business right here in Promise Glen, so you'll see me often. You're not getting rid of me that easily."

He delayed just long enough to see the mixture of consternation and anger on her face. Then he headed straight toward the buggy. Or at least, that was what he'd intended. Esther was obviously determined to lead him right through a bunch of her friends, and they tugged him into a circuitous route of her own. Showing him off, he supposed. Going past the gauntlet of giggling young girls was even worse than confronting his teenage crush.

By the time they'd reached the buggy, he was feeling ashamed of the way he'd talked to Dorcas. What was he doing, letting himself fall back into old habits just because he was home again? Dorcas was right—he'd gotten too old for such teasing.

He glanced back, thinking he should apologize, but Dorcas, with a twin on either side of her, had already started down the lane that led toward the Beiler place. Apologies would have to wait until he could get her alone again. Not that she was likely to give him much chance of that. Even in the close-knit Amish community, a girl intent on avoiding a guy could manage to make it happen.

Esther had already clambered onto the buggy seat, so he swung up beside her and grasped the lines. He clucked to the mare, an old friend who'd been half grown when he left, and they started out the lane that led to the main road.

"Who's running the Beiler place now that Teacher Dorcas's daad is gone?" he asked.

He'd heard that William Beiler had passed not long after he'd gone out to Ohio. William had been sick most of that last year, now that Thomas came to think of it.

Esther shrugged, not much interested. "Levi and Lemuel, I guess. Mamm could tell you all about it. Thomas, now that you are home, will you teach me how to drive the family buggy? Daad keeps thinking the pony cart is enough for me, but I'm almost fourteen already."

"I don't think you can say you're almost fourteen when your birthday is still six months away," he said.

Her pointed chin set stubbornly. "I'm big enough. I'll bet you were driving long before you were my age. Just because I'm a girl . . ."

"A smart girl," he said. "Too smart to let Mamm hear you say you'll bet about anything. And I'm too smart to let you get me into trouble with Daad on my second day back."

Esther pouted for all of thirty seconds, and then her sunny nature reasserted itself. "Will you let me take the harness off when we get home? Please?"

"I will." He wanted to get the conversation back to Teacher Dorcas if he could. "So how are you doing in school? Only one more year to go after this, ain't so?"

She nodded. "It seems like forever," she muttered dramatically.

"It's not that bad, is it?" He glanced at her, and she blushed.

"I guess not. Teacher Dorcas does make it fun. Everybody likes her."

"Yah? Including some special guy maybe?"

Esther got the giggles. "Silly. I meant all the kids in school. And Teacher Dorcas doesn't have a come-calling friend. She's too old for that, and anyway, she's a maidal."

Maidal, he repeated silently. Old maid, in other words. He'd like to point out that she was the same age as he was, but he supposed that to his baby sister, he was old, too.

Well, old or not, he'd like to restore his friendship with Dorcas. But given what a bad start he'd made, that didn't seem likely.

DORCAS WALKED STEADILY toward the lane with the twins, determined not to look back. She tried to concentrate on what was in front of her, not on what had just happened.

You can't change the past. Her grandmother's favorite saying came back to her, comforting her. Grossmammi had lived with them while Dorcas was growing up, and she'd been very dear to her granddaughter. Dorcas still missed her more often than she'd have thought.

She smiled down at the boys, one walking on either side of her. Almost at the same moment, each one thrust his hand into hers. Funny how they seemed to know what the other was going to do, even without looking or speaking. Their hands were small, rather sticky, and definitely dirty, but they held hers so trustingly that her heart warmed.

In tribute to the mild spring, Sarah had switched them to their summer straw hats, and beneath the brims their fair hair clung damply to the napes of their necks. It was one of life's oddities that small boys could look so vulnerable and at the same time be as tough as leather, constantly running and falling and bouncing up again. They made her feel foolishly better, just by walking alongside her.

Not that their mode of progress could really be called walking. Matthew hopped on alternate feet, while Mark was skipping, humming a little tune of his own and stopping frequently to check the growth along the verge.

The lane led through a patch of woods and then ran along pastureland to the Raber place. The boys led her down the well-used path, and the sight of Sarah standing on the porch to greet them reminded her that according to the boys, Sarah had a surprise for her. She trusted the surprise wasn't that Thomas was back. She'd rather not talk about him, even to Sarah. Why was he back after all this time? Had she imagined that there was a threat in his words or his attitude, or was that her own guilty conscience? A shiver went through her.

Mark, always sensitive to others, looked up. "Are you cold, Teacher Dorcas? You can have my jacket."

"And mine," Matthew said quickly, not wanting to be left out.

"Denke, but I'm fine. We'll be inside in a minute, ain't

so? What do you think your mamm has for your after-school snack?"

That distracted them, and they raced on toward the house, greeting Sarah with shouts of "Mammi, Mammi," something she knew Sarah loved. As Dorcas mounted the porch, Sarah looked up from their hugs with a welcoming smile.

"Wilkom, Dorcas. I'm glad the boys remembered to tell you."

Sarah looked so happy and satisfied with her new role as wife and mother that Dorcas felt a pang of envy. Chasing it away, she hugged her friend. "I got your message. Matty says you have a surprise for me."

Sarah looked disconcerted for a moment but ushered her into the kitchen. "Tell you in a minute," she whispered, her voice masked by the exclamations of the boys, who'd discovered a plate of brownies on the table.

"Yah, yah, you can have brownies," she said to the boys. "I thought you could have a little picnic out on the porch, with brownies and lemonade, while I talk with Teacher Dorcas. All right?"

The picnic idea was enthusiastically received, and in a couple of minutes the boys had been settled out of earshot while Dorcas and Sarah sat down with their coffee and brownies at the kitchen table.

Dorcas took a sip of the hot, strong coffee. "Ah, just what I need after a long day of trying to deal with spring fever among my scholars. So what is this surprise of yours?"

Sarah blushed, smiling. "That was so silly. Matthew overheard us talking, and I had to tell him something. So anyway, I made a batch of snickerdoodles to send to school for a snack tomorrow, and so as far as the boys are concerned, that's the surprise."

"And it's a wonderful gut one." She could handle the

snickerdoodles, as long as the real surprise wasn't something about Thomas. What Sarah knew about her relationship with Thomas was bad enough, and even she didn't know everything.

"The secret is something I really wanted to tell you that the kinder don't know," Sarah said, and her blush deepened.

Dorcas looked at her blankly, not sure what to say. And then she realized that it was joy filling Sarah's face, joy that brought the flush to her cheeks and overflowed into a pleasure so deep that Dorcas could almost touch it.

"Sarah!" She nearly knocked over her coffee in her rush to get to her feet and embrace her friend. "Really? I'm so happy for you and Noah. When?"

"Late fall, I think. I haven't even talked to the midwife yet," Sarah said, laughing at herself. "But I'm so happy that I had to tell you."

"Ach, I can't find the words to say how glad I am for you. I'll keep it a secret as long as you want. But don't worry about the boys. They're going to be delighted to have a little sister or brother."

It took a few minutes for them to settle down again, but eventually they'd both relaxed and their chatter had returned to a normal level.

"I'm going to look up the crib quilt pattern my grossmammi loves," Dorcas said, knowing that the minute she started a baby quilt, speculation would begin among the women as to whose it would be. She hesitated, her thoughts churning up an image of Thomas. "It's silly, but I actually thought you might want to tell me that Thomas Fisher is back."

"Thomas? Really? I didn't know." Sarah's surprise was mixed with a tinge of apprehension. "I do hope it will go well with his daad. Thomas wasn't a bad boy, just a little wild, like lots of teenagers are."

"Including me, you mean," Dorcas added, managing a smile.

"Well, you did have me worried for a time," Sarah admitted, "especially when you went to some of those Englisch parties. Thank the gut Lord you didn't go to the one the police raided, or you might have been arrested, like Thomas."

All Dorcas could do was to try to mask her feelings. Everyone knew that Thomas's arrest had been the last straw as far as his father was concerned. As soon as his fine had been paid, Thomas had disappeared from the community, sent off to relatives in disgrace.

So how did Thomas feel about her now? She had gotten away, thanks to him. He had suffered for what happened, while for the Englisch kids it had been nothing but an embarrassing incident. And Dorcas hadn't suffered at all.

He had never told, she reminded herself. If he hadn't talked in all these years, he certain sure wouldn't talk now.

CHAPTER TWO

By the time Dorcas reached home, her mother was starting to set the table for supper. She took the plates firmly from her mother's hands.

"I'll do that. Where's Betsy?" Thinking that might sound critical of her sister-in-law, she hurried on. "She usually does the table when you're cooking."

"She's feeding young Will." Her mother's face glowed as it always did when she spoke of her first grandchild, just two months old and named for his grandfather. "He smiled when I talked to him today. I think he knows me."

"Of course he knows his grossmammi." She gave her mother a quick hug, knowing she'd joyfully do Betsy's work for her anytime in return for pulling Mamm out of the depression that had gripped her off and on since Daad's passing.

"I do think so." Mamm checked on the pot roast she had cooking on the back of the stove. "Such a bright little boppli."

Even with the distraction caused by her first grand-child, Mammi still looked twenty years older than she should. She had aged so much during Daad's long illness, and even more so after his passing.

At least spring was here at last. Mammi always perked up with the warmer days, maybe because she didn't get out much in the winter.

Dorcas shook off those thoughts while firmly blocking any tendency to dwell on her encounter with Thomas. The less said about that, the better, as far as she was concerned.

"I see the lettuce is coming up in the kitchen garden," she said, hoping to bring the smile back to her mother's face. Instead Mammi looked worried. "I hope I didn't plant it too soon. We could still get a frost. Maybe I should have waited. What do you think?"

Mammi had been given to having second thoughts about every little decision since Daadi's death, and her children had to reassure her constantly.

"I think it's worth planting early, even if we do get a frost. If the worst happens, I'll plant it again for you. And maybe we'll have it to eat earlier than anyone else. Think of that."

Mamm did smile at the suggestion, and a moment later Betsy came in from upstairs, distracting her entirely. "How is that sweet boy? He's getting bigger every day, ain't so?"

Betsy beamed with the praise for her son, looking as proud, Lemuel always said, as a peacock with two tails. But he never said that when his brother could hear him, of course. Levi was an equally proud daadi.

Dorcas finished the table. "Can I go up to see him? I won't disturb him."

"Oh, I'd rather you didn't." Betsy shook her head as if Dorcas had asked the impossible. "If he's disturbed, he won't get off to sleep again."

Fussy, Dorcas thought. *As if I didn't know enough not to disturb him.* But at a glance from her mother, she smiled. "Later, then."

"We're about ready," Mamm said. "Betsy, will you ring the bell?"

While her sister-in-law pulled the bell out on the back porch to call the boys to supper, Dorcas helped her mother to dish up. Once supper was over and the dishes done, she could escape to her room with the excuse that she had schoolwork to do.

And then she'd finally have the privacy to think about what had happened between her and Thomas. Privacy was not easily come by in a busy Amish household; that was certain sure.

In a few minutes, they were gathered around the table and silent prayers offered. Then the serving dishes began clattering around the table.

Betsy glanced at Levi. "What was happening in town today?"

He shrugged. "Nothing."

Dorcas could have told her that this was Levi's characteristic reply to any question. He had never been much of a talker. But Betsy was clearly not going to put up with that from her husband.

"You must have talked to someone." There was an edge to her voice that made Levi look up, startled, and Dorcas exchanged an amused look with her mother. Levi might have married the one woman who wouldn't let him get away with silence.

"I went to the harness shop, so I talked to Jacob Miller. He's doing fine." He hesitated, obviously trying to think of some other news to impart. "Oh, and he told me that Thomas Fisher is back home from Ohio." He glanced at Dorcas, a question on his face, and then seemed to decide not to ask it.

She didn't really have a choice, did she? The news that Thomas had visited the school today was probably spreading over the valley already.

"Yah, I saw him. He came to pick up Esther from school today. She's wonderful happy to have her big bruder back."

"That's nice," Mamm said. "Just think how happy his mother must be. She was telling me how well he's been doing working with her brother in his construction business."

Levi and Lemuel murmured agreement, although whether they agreed or just wanted to make Mamm happy, she didn't know. Maybe they were wondering, as she was, how glad the minister was to have his erring son home again.

"He was a special friend of yours, wasn't he, Dorcas?" Betsy looked at her with open curiosity.

"Just ordinary rumspringa stuff," she said easily, feeling as if Mamm had let out a sigh of relief at her response.

But Betsy wasn't finished yet. "From everything I heard, you had a narrow escape."

Silence fell, and everyone stared at her. Betsy, oblivious, looked up and suddenly realized she'd said something wrong.

"I mean . . . I mean . . . well, that you might have . . ." She sputtered off into silence.

"Have some more roast," Levi said, thrusting the platter at her.

Dorcas had been sure that someone would bring up her friendship with Thomas sooner or later, but she hadn't expected it to be right in her own family. Well, it was done. The chatter would go flying around the community and everyone would be buzzing, but then it would die out or be replaced with something else. She just had to keep her head.

"I heard that someone is buying the old Hanley place," Lemuel said, providing a distraction. "Maybe you'd best warn your scholars not to go getting in the way when the new folks are moving in."

"Englisch newcomers?" she asked.

He nodded. "Not from around here, so I heard. An older man was in the hardware store when Jacob was there, so Jacob heard him talking about moving in soon."

"It'll be nice to have someone in the house again."

Since the property in question bordered the school grounds, Dorcas had an interest in it. Maybe it would be good for her to call on the new people, since her scholars were likely to walk along the edge of their property in order to stay off the road. She wouldn't want to get off on the wrong foot with newcomers.

"Gut idea," Lemuel said. He hesitated, and it seemed to Dorcas that he had something more to say.

Dorcas raised her eyebrows, looking at him. "What? Would you rather do it, since you're on the school board?"

It wasn't usual to have an unmarried man on the school board, but Lemuel had been pushed in due to a dearth of other candidates and the fact that their daad had been a member for years.

"No, no, you'll do it best," he said quickly. But he'd paused, looking as if he had still more to say and didn't know how to do it. That was unusual for Lemuel, who unlike Levi, could talk to anyone, anywhere, on just about anything. She gave him a closer look.

"Okay, out with it. What's wrong?"

Everyone was looking at him now, and Lemuel shrugged, unhappy.

"Well, the fact is, there's been some talk. Not on the school board, I don't mean that, but just a couple of folks mentioning it to board members." His words petered out.

"And?" She frowned at him. "Tell me, whatever it is. If it's something about the school, I should know."

He grimaced. "I don't want you to get upset."

"I'll get really upset if you don't tell me," she pointed out, exasperated.

"Well, the thing is, some folks are saying we should give up the Orchard Hill school and combine with the Oak Creek Amish school." He blurted it out on a single breath, and then he fell silent, looking at her like a puppy who'd got into the garbage.

Nobody spoke for a moment, and then there was a chorus of voices, all talking at once. Dorcas made herself heard.

"Whatever for? Our school does a perfectly good job for the kinder. If this is about me . . ."

"No, no," he said as fast as he could. "It's about all those repairs we have to do, mostly. And the fact that we don't have all that many scholars right now, so there's a thought we could sell the property and come out ahead."

"That's foolishness," Mamm said, with more spirit than she'd shown about much of anything except the baby. "Where would little Will go to school? He couldn't walk all the way over to Oak Creek. And what would happen to your sister if they close the school?"

She was more amused than anything that Mamm had put her second behind little Will, who had years before starting school. But this was no laughing matter. Her teaching career would be over if they closed the school.

"I don't see why this is needed," Levi said, maybe moved by the mention of his son. "We always take care of the school repairs."

"Don't tell me," Lemuel said. "I agree. But I'm just repeating what some folks are saying. It's a shame we didn't get the work done over the winter. Everyone's so busy now with their farms that it'll be hard to find time to work on it. Besides, there's the cost of wood and shingles. That storm caused a lot of damage."

"The storm just happened a month ago," Dorcas pointed out, trying to stay calm. "So we couldn't have done the repairs last winter. It's nobody's fault that freak windstorm swept through."

Levi nodded. "We all had damage, not just the school."

They'd called the problem straight line winds, but it might as well have been a tornado, given the damage it had done.

"You're not going to vote to close the school, Lemuel."

Mamm frowned at him with a look as commanding as Daad's used to be.

"No, Mammi, for sure I won't, but I can't speak for the rest of the board. I just thought you . . . well, especially Dorcas, would want to know."

He looked so stressed that Dorcas couldn't help feeling sorry for him.

"There's nothing I can do, since I'm the teacher," she pointed out. "But I hope the rest of you will do your best."

"For sure," Levi said, and the others nodded. Even Betsy, distracted from her baby for once, agreed. "We'll talk to everybody we can. It's a foolish notion." For him, that was a long speech, and Dorcas appreciated it.

Her family would do what they could, and she didn't really believe most parents would want to send their young ones to the Oak Creek school. But somebody did, or they wouldn't be talking about it.

She resisted the temptation to ask Lemuel who it was, knowing that would put him in a difficult spot. But she knew she'd be looking around her classroom tomorrow, trying to figure out whose parents would want to see her school closed.

As if she didn't have enough to worry about, there was still the mystery of Thomas. Why on earth had he decided to come back now?

TRUE TO HIS word, Thomas let his little sister unharness the buggy horse, keeping a watchful eye on her as she moved around the mare easily. With a final pat she turned the mare into the paddock and returned to hang the harness on the appropriate peg and push the buggy back against the wall.

"Gut job," he said, and she responded with a smile that crinkled her cheeks.

He was frankly surprised at Esther's grown-up competence. He'd missed a lot in the past seven years. Funny that he hadn't realized how much while he'd been away. He'd thought that the frequent letters back and forth had kept all of them up to date, but there were things a person had to see for himself.

Had it worked the other way, too? Maybe the family was surprised at the man he was now. In the flurry of greetings and getting settled in his old room, he couldn't be sure, but he guessed he'd figure it out by the way they responded to him once they were past the first few awkward days.

Esther was hurrying on into the house, apparently intent on that after-school snack she'd talked about, but he didn't see anyone else around. A moment's thought gave him the answer. It was about milking time. They'd all be in the milking shed. He'd gotten out of the rhythm of life here.

He headed toward the milking shed behind the barn, wondering what kind of reception he'd get. Daad's greeting the previous day hadn't been quite what he'd hoped—certainly not the equal of Mammi's hugs and tears. Not that he'd expected outright enthusiasm. Daad wasn't one to show his feelings.

But Mamm had led him to believe that Daad was as eager to have him back as she was. Maybe she had overstated his reaction in her own enthusiasm to have her oldest son back. Or it might just be that it would take some time for him and Daad to relax with each other again.

Not that he'd ever felt that relaxed around his father, but he'd become used to the criticism after a few years. He'd heard that parents were usually stricter with the first child, but Daad had added on the additional burden of being a minister's son and expected him to be an example. Aside from Mammi, Esther was the only one who'd welcomed him back with enthusiasm. He had to smile, thinking of how eager she'd been to lead him right past her friends—showing him off, from what he could tell. Daad and his brothers seemed cautious. He tried to tell himself it wasn't all that surprising, given the time that had passed and the way they'd parted.

Well, he'd have to take this one step at a time; that was all. And he'd start by helping with the milking.

No one noticed him when he paused in the doorway, taking in the scene. Daad, Jonas, and Adam each sat on a milking stool, leaning against the warm flank of a cow, hands moving rhythmically. The scent of hay, the rush of milk into the metal pails—all of it was so familiar and yet strange . . . strange because he wasn't a part of it.

He stepped inside, making enough noise to ensure they'd look up. "Looks like I'm just back from the school in time. I'll grab a pail and get started."

Jonas, his next younger brother, frowned at him. "No need. We've got this."

"Like Daad always says, nothing like another pair of hands at milking time," Thomas said easily.

"We're almost done." No one could miss the tart tone in his brother's voice.

Thomas looked at Jonas with a sinking feeling. What had happened to Jonas, six years younger than he, always so eager to do whatever his big brother was doing? Seemed like that hero worship was long gone. He shouldn't be surprised, but he was left standing there feeling as if his little brother had thrown a bucket of cold water in his face.

Something rattled behind Thomas, and he turned to see Adam, the fifteen-year-old, holding out a bucket.

"Here you go." He grinned, freckled face flushing a little. "You can take the place next to me. I'll race you to see who can fill a bucket the fastest."

"You're on." Thomas couldn't help smiling in return,

grateful for any hint of a welcome. "But you ought to give me a head start since I'm so out of practice."

"Doesn't Onkel James have any dairy cows?" Adam asked, sounding surprised. Around here, most families had one or two, even if they didn't sell to a dairy.

"The whole family is so busy with the construction business that they get their milk from the next farm over. Even our cousin Alice works alongside the boys. You should see her shingling a roof."

Adam's expression said he wasn't so sure of that, but he shrugged. "Different, I guess. You're all working away from the farm, then."

"Yah, during construction season we were. If there was a big job on hand, we'd be gone until sunset."

It had taken Thomas a couple of minutes to find the rhythm, but then the milk began to flow. He relaxed into the process, liking the warmth of the creature and the placid way she accepted him.

"What jobs does James have coming up this summer?"

Thomas nearly lost his tempo in surprise. He hadn't realized that Daad had come up behind him. Well, if he'd wanted to check that Thomas knew what he was doing, he ought to be satisfied. After all, Daad was the one who'd taught him.

"They're working on some new houses that are going up a couple of miles down the road," he answered. "It was a big company from away that got the contract, but they subcontracted some of it to Onkel James. They're putting a lot of fancy houses on what used to be fine farmland."

Daad nodded slowly. "Yah. It's happening all over." His face tightened, if that was possible. "Hate to see good farmland lost."

"Onkel James feels that way, too," Thomas hurried to add, sensing a criticism. "But the houses are going up no matter how anybody feels about it. It'll get him more known among the Englisch and maybe bring him more work. He hopes so anyway."

Daad didn't say anything—just nodded and moved on, leaving no hint of how he felt. Well, at least they'd actually exchanged a few words without Mamm prompting them. Maybe that was progress.

Adam leaned sideways, tilting his milking stool to the edge of gravity, it seemed. "I'm surprised you wanted to leave. There's good money in construction work."

Thomas shrugged. "There'll be construction work here, I imagine. I'd like to get started on my own. Onkel James thought it was a good idea. I'll have to start with small jobs I can do on my own, but that's how any business builds."

He grinned as Adam's stool slipped under him, with his young brother saving himself only by a complicated acrobatic maneuver. "Take it easy. You'll scare the cow."

"Not Daisy." Adam patted the cow's hip. "Nothing ruffles her. Just keeps on producing no matter what." He glanced around. "Looks like we're the last ones done. That means we get to clean up."

"Sounds fine by me." Thomas got up, stretching. "I see the dairy herd is quite a bit bigger these days."

Adam nodded. "That's because of Jonas. Nothing will suit him better than to take on the farm from . . ." He stopped suddenly, turning red from his chin to the tips of his ears. "I mean . . ."

"That's okay," he said, wondering if that was the cause of Jonas's reluctance to let him help with the milking. Did Jonas imagine Thomas was going to try and oust him from the place he obviously wanted? "I'm interested in construction, not dairy farming. I just want to pull my weight while I'm here. Soon as I can pick up some business, you won't see me milking cows."

"If you do . . ." Once again Adam stopped in midstream, flushing again. Must be something about being fifteen that made boys constantly say the wrong thing.

"If I succeed, you mean?" He shrugged. "I won't know until I try, will I?"

Adam, maybe deciding he'd better stop talking, turned to hose off the cow. Thomas wouldn't ask the question in his mind, but he did wonder. Who had been doubting that he would find any work here? Adam wouldn't have come up with that on his own.

Was it Jonas? Or Daad?

That didn't hurt, did it? Why should he be hurt if Daad didn't think he'd have it in him to make a success of a business? But it did seem hard if Daad couldn't see beyond a few reckless years to the man he was now.

DORCAS RUSHED OUT the door early the next morning, headed for the school. This way, she'd be able to have a good look around at the damage to the stable. She'd been awake too much of the night, her worries bouncing back and forth between the school and the return of Thomas.

Grossmammi always said to give your troubles to God and stop fretting. She'd tried, so many times. She was pretty good at turning them over, but unfortunately, she promptly picked them up again.

It was always better to do something than to sit and worry. That was another of Grossmammi's favorite sayings. Since the weather had warmed up, she'd been walking to school, so she hadn't been using the stable. Still, that wasn't an excuse for not having looked over the damage herself. She should have thought of it sooner, so that she'd be prepared to talk about it instead of being taken by surprise, the way she had been yesterday.

One good thing about walking to school—she couldn't

help but cheer up when she saw the signs of spring all around her. The evergreens still wore their dark green coats, but against them, a haze of pale yellowish green surrounded the other trees, promising blossoms and leaves to come.

The air was crisp and still, especially this early, but her sweater was warm, and the sunlight filtering through the trees hinted that it would be another nice day. Her scholars would be happy, and so would she. Nobody liked it when they had to have indoor recess.

In sight of the school, Dorcas hurried her steps. Dropping her books and papers on the small porch, she headed for the stable.

There were two stalls in the front part of the building— one for the teacher and one for any parent who came to help. The one on the left seemed fine, just as she'd left it after the last use. The one on the right, though . . . She stepped inside it and looked more closely at the floor. It had been two days since they'd had rain, but a definite damp spot reflected the light coming in from the window.

That wasn't good. She looked up, trying to see where it was coming from, but the roof looked normal to her. Maybe . . .

"Are you looking for a sign?"

Dorcas jerked around at the sound of a voice behind her. Not just any voice—Thomas Fisher's.

"Sorry," he said quickly. "I didn't mean to startle you."

"I didn't expect anyone to be here this early, that's all." She tried to compose herself, reflecting that it had been years since Thomas left, and he had never caused her any trouble. So he wouldn't be likely to start now.

"I have some things to do in town for Mamm," Thomas said, "So I told Esther I'd drop her off as long as she didn't mind being early."

She looked past him, scanning the schoolyard. "Are you sure you didn't forget her?"

Thomas chuckled, low in his throat. "I said she could walk the mare around a little as long as she didn't go near the road. She's been itching to drive something bigger than the pony cart. Seems like it's a sore point that Adam started driving the family buggy when he was just a little older than she is now."

"That's what it's like to be the youngest. Believe me, I know. Mothers always try to hold on to their babies."

A corner of his mouth lifted. "Their babies don't often listen, do they?"

Was he hinting at her teenage episodes or not? If she could be sure, she'd confront him about it. But she couldn't, so there was no point in reminding him.

As she started to move, Thomas put out a hand to detain her. "Seriously, why were you staring so intently at the roof? Is there a problem?"

"See for yourself." She stepped back, making room for him to get into the stall.

He frowned at the floor and then knelt to put his palm on it, seeming to measure the wet expanse with his eye. Then, like her, he looked up.

"It's coming from somewhere up there, but I can't quite tell where. We had some damage in a storm about a month ago, but I guess I didn't realize how bad it was." The worry came and sat on her shoulder again.

"Better get the school board on the job to fix it." He was still staring at the ceiling, not at her. Maybe that's why she went on.

"They know. But at least one family is balking at the cost of what needs to be done. They're even talking about shutting down the Orchard Hill school and sending our scholars over to Oak Creek."

"What?" Thomas was hearteningly upset at the idea. "They can't do that. Our families have always gone here. Are there so few children now?"

"No, not really. It's a bit of a low year, but that happens. In a year or two, there will be more younger ones starting again."

He was looking at her face now, studying her expression, it seemed to her. It made her nervous, and she shrugged.

"Never mind. It's not your worry."

"You forget," he said. "My sister goes here. It is my worry, and I'd like to have a closer look."

Before she could stop him, he'd climbed up the stall bars. Reaching up to grab a crosspiece, he pulled himself up in a quick, easy movement. Then he was balancing on the two-by-four, surveying the roof.

"Thomas, don't." She put her hands up as if she could pull him back down again. "You'll fall."

He looked down at her, laughing. "You think so? I've been working construction for nearly seven years. You have to have a head for heights in my business."

"I'm sure you do, but please come down. I'm responsible, and if you get hurt, the board is sure to ask why I didn't stop you. Please."

"Since you asked me," he said. He swung himself down, hung by his hands for a second, and then dropped to the floor, inches away from her.

She gasped, reaching out for him. "Don't do that. Promise me. You scared me."

He smiled again, a little too close, a little too intimate, for comfort. "Like I said, since you asked me."

For a moment she couldn't move. She could only look at him, too aware of how close they were to each other.

Then the clamor of children's voices intruded, and she stepped away quickly. "I . . . I have to go."

She scurried out of the stable, well aware that she was blushing, and that Thomas would have seen it.

What was wrong with her? After all these years of being happy without a man in her life, why should she be ambushed by feelings now?

CHAPTER THREE

Dorcas could only be thankful that the next few days passed without trouble. No one mentioned moving the school—at least not in her hearing—and she didn't see Thomas again. Even Sunday happened to be the off-Sunday, when they didn't have worship in their community.

Instead, they had spent the day with one of her mother's many cousins, giving her a chance, if not to forget her troubles, at least to push them to the back of her mind. The second cousins who were her age were all married and many of them had young children.

After a raucous game of tag with the little ones, Dorcas headed for the nearest chair, out of breath. Her cousin Jenny handed her a paper cup of lemonade, laughing a little.

"Can't keep up with them?" she asked.

"I guess not." She gestured with the cup. "Denke. This is just what I need."

Jenny pulled a chair over next to her. "After spending all your days working with kinder, I'd think you'd want to get away from them on weekends. Instead you're entertaining them."

She smiled, shaking her head. "Not a chance. Besides, these are my kin. Amazing, isn't it?" She glanced around the crowd—nearly forty of them, she'd guess. "We're quite a mob when we all get together."

"That's what having big families will do." Jenny patted her belly lightly, her figure now the same shape as her round face. "You're getting behind, Dorcas. You'd best get started."

Knowing exactly what Jenny meant, she shook her head. "You have them. I think God means me just to teach them."

Jenny gave her a doubting look. "I don't think so. God gave you a lot of love to share . . . even more than you need for teaching, I think." She turned away to speak to one of her youngsters, but the sound of her words seemed to echo.

That memory slipped back to Dorcas as she stood on the school porch Monday morning, waiting for her scholars. Jenny meant well, but she didn't understand. Dorcas's scholars were enough for her. Not even those moments with Thomas could change that. She was certain sure.

A few of the younger children emerged from the path through the woods, followed in a moment by older sisters and brothers. The older ones accepted the responsibility of watching the younger, but that didn't mean they wanted to walk right alongside them, it seemed. The older girls had their heads together, giggling over something.

Another little group came hurrying down the lane, probably afraid they were missing something. And in another moment, she spotted the group that walked to school along the blacktop road. They'd turned into the driveway, but instead of walking, they were running.

Racing, she wondered, or just excited about something? Three or four of them rushed up to her, with Esther right in the forefront.

Good. That meant that Thomas hadn't driven Esther to school today, so she could feel comfortably sure she wasn't about to run into him.

Esther reached her, closely followed by several of the older ones. "Teacher, Teacher!" Their faces were alert, and one or two of them looked a bit frightened.

"What is it?" She looked from one to the other. "Catch your breath first, and then tell me."

Joseph Miller gulped and inhaled noisily. "They're moving in at the house." He turned, pointing down the drive to the small one-story house that stood facing the road, just next to the school drive.

"Yah, well, we knew someone would come in soon, ain't so? Englisch, aren't they?" The children certainly weren't this excited just because someone was moving in.

Esther nodded, having gotten control of herself. "Just one old man was all we saw. He's mean."

"Mean?" Surely, they couldn't have gotten into trouble already. She hadn't even had time to greet the newcomer yet. "Why do you say that?"

"He yelled at us." Several children nodded at Esther's vehement comment. "We weren't doing anything, but he yelled and told us to get out of the way of the movers."

"Were you in the way?"

"No!" Esther was imaginative and dramatic, but then, thirteen-year-old girls often were for little or no reason.

But Joseph backed her up, and he had no imagination at all. "We were just standing and watching them carry things in. They had a great big television."

That would have interested the young ones, she supposed. The important thing now was to smooth over the incident so that the children wouldn't build up the poor man into a monster.

"And then the man came out and started yelling at us," Joseph continued.

"It can be very hard for people to move, especially older people," she explained calmly. "He was probably afraid you'd get hurt. I'm sure the next time you see him, he'll feel better. And you be polite, all right?" She raised her voice. "Take your seats now, everyone. It's time we got busy."

The morning went on its usual routine, and Dorcas dismissed the possibly difficult neighbor from her mind. Most likely what she'd said would turn out to be true. It might have been disconcerting for the man to discover a clump of Amish children supervising his moving in.

She probably ought to call on him after school and welcome him. She'd intended to do it after he'd had a few days to settle in, but the scholars' accounts made it desirable to get in her visit immediately. It was just as important to calm the new neighbor as it was to calm the children.

The usual opening routine quieted everyone down, she was glad to see. Anna, in the back by the oldest scholars, settled them when they continued to talk in excited whispers.

Anna had become used to the school routine since she'd volunteered to help, and she was proving to be a valuable assistant. When they started on arithmetic, Anna automatically moved to the primary scholars she'd guided through arithmetic the previous week.

Dorcas smiled at her across the width of the room. She must remember to tell Anna's mother what a good job she was doing. Many sixteen-year-olds were too preoccupied by thoughts of the next singing and who might offer to take them home to focus on something like schoolwork, but Anna seemed to have a goal in mind—maybe a school of her own one day.

Catching a low buzz of talk, Dorcas moved along the aisle to where Esther was passing a paper to the girl next to her. Intercepting the paper, she frowned at them. "This is time for arithmetic, ain't so? Is this paper arithmetic?"

"No, Teacher," they mumbled in unison.

"Let's see what it is, then." She unfolded it to see Thomas Fisher's name looking up at her. After a startled instant, she realized that it was an advertising flyer for construction jobs. She looked at Esther, an eyebrow raised.

"I'm sorry, Teacher. I helped Thomas make some posters to put up in town. To get jobs with, I mean."

"I see that. It's a kind thing for you to do, but not when you're supposed to be working on arithmetic."

"I'm sorry." Esther said the right thing, but there was a slightly rebellious look on her face. Esther, Dorcas decided, would be worth keeping an eye on.

"Let's get to work, then." She started to take the paper away with her, then reconsidered and left it on the desk. She didn't need to be looking at it; that was certain sure.

Nevertheless, it had brought Thomas back into her mind, and now she'd have to chase him out again.

The sun was still shining at lunchtime, so Dorcas announced that they might take their lunches outside to eat before recess. The reminder was important, because otherwise they'd toss lunches on the picnic table and forget to eat them. Still, it was a pleasant break in the day, even though it meant an interrupted lunch for her and for Anna.

Outside, Dorcas managed to eat half of her sandwich before she had to send several of the younger boys back to finish their lunches. She turned to frown at Joseph, who had his bag poised to throw at one of his neighbors. Joseph turned the gesture into a stretch and put the bag in the trash can.

Dorcas had just headed back to her own lunch when she realized someone was approaching them from the road—an Englischer unknown to her. She stepped forward to meet him, catching Anna's eye. They'd had to practice what to do in case of a threat, something that would have been unthinkable just a few years ago. But the horrible rash of school shootings had made everyone nervous, and she'd had several meetings with the school board to work out their procedures. Already Anna moved in front of the children, ready to hustle them to cover at the slightest sign of trouble.

Reaching the visitor, Dorcas gave a tentative smile. The elderly man didn't look threatening, but he also didn't look friendly. He was probably in his late sixties, with a fringe of gray hair cut very short around a bald head, and a gaunt frame.

He didn't leave her in doubt for more than a moment about who he was or why he was here.

"Those kids of yours were trespassing on my property this morning." He glared at the nearest of the scholars. "They were getting in the way when I'm trying to move in."

Since he hadn't mentioned a wife, Dorcas suspected he was going to live there alone, and by the look of it, he wasn't going to be a very friendly neighbor.

"I'm very sorry, Mr. . . . ?" She spoke in her most peaceful tone.

"Haggerty," he answered. "Listen, that's my land, right up to the fence, and you better remember it. I don't put up with trespassers."

"I'm sorry," she tried again. "I'm sure the children didn't mean to disrupt your move. We've all been interested in who our new neighbor was going to be." *And how nice,* she added silently without much hope.

"I didn't move out here to have neighbors." It was almost a snarl. "I moved out here to get away from them. I have a right to privacy, and if you're in charge of this school, I expect you to see that I get it. That means no kids walking across my property."

Unfortunately, his property ran along the very narrow berm of the road, just on a curve, making walking on the gravel berm a risk. The image flew through her mind in less than the time it took to breathe.

"But Mr. Haggerty, it's difficult to walk along the berm just there because—"

"I don't care why. Just keep them off my land."

Before she could marshal any response, he'd turned and marched off. Anna, her face white and her eyes wide with shock, pressed close to her.

"That . . . that was awful. He scared me. And our scholars."

By the look of it, Anna was taking it harder than the youngsters were. At least they were intent on getting a maximum amount of play in their recess rather than complaining about the neighbor.

"I wouldn't worry about it." She patted Anna's arm. "I'm sure he'll cool off once he gets settled in." She tried to sound more hopeful than she felt. The last thing an Amish school needed was trouble with an Englisch neighbor.

Had she handled it badly? If only she could have made him listen to her . . .

But on second thought, she didn't see any way she could have made him do anything. She hated the thought, but if the matter didn't improve, she might have to take it to the school board for advice. They'd probably think . . . well, she didn't know what they'd think.

THOMAS, WALKING DOWN the business street of Promise Glen, had worked his way through his list of places to display his posters. Everyone had agreed to put it up, but no one had seemed overly hopeful as to results. Still, he had to start somewhere.

He approached the harness shop, sure that Jacob Miller

would agree to display one. After all, they'd been through school and their teen years together, when Jacob had joined him in more than one foolish prank. The fact that they hadn't seen in other in years didn't wipe out that early friendship, did it?

Sure enough, the instant Thomas stepped inside, Jacob was pounding him on the back, grinning.

"I thought it was about time I was seeing you. I hear you've come home to stay, ain't so?"

"Yah, if everything goes well." He stood back, surveying Jacob. "You grew up." The skinny kid who'd been all elbows and knees now topped him in height and probably in weight, too. And there was nothing wrong with the muscles he'd developed, either. The Amish tended not to be very big, and Jacob probably stood out in any crowd of them.

"I could say the same for you." Still smiling, Jacob gestured toward the back of the store. "Komm on back. There's a couple chairs by the machines."

The heavy-duty machines for sewing leather had a spot of their own in the back, with room for two workers at a time, if needed. They were powered by a belt that ran through a slot in the floor to the cellar below. He remembered being allowed to try one out when Jacob's father was running the shop. It had been a lot harder than it looked to handle the heavy leather and keep the stitching straight.

"Sorry to hear about your daad," Thomas said, feeling a little awkward to be expressing sympathy so long after the fact.

Jacob nodded, his open, friendly face darkening for a moment. "And Mamm not long after him. Still, she wouldn't have been happy here without him, I guess. Anyway, I had already started to run the store, so I continued. And here I am."

"I guess we've become the grown-ups, whether we want to be or not. But it does seem funny sometimes."

Thomas had managed to escape a lot through being away, but he'd found the changes that age brought to his parents too evident since he'd been back. Not that either of them was likely to admit to aging.

"Yah." Jacob shrugged. "Some days it feels pretty good, and some days not. I had a good business to step into, so I can't complain." He lifted an eyebrow, studying Thomas's face. "I hear you've been working construction. You like it?"

"Best thing I ever did. My onkel is one of the best, and he made sure I know enough to handle just about anything to do with building." He held out the poster. "That's what I'm doing today. Putting these up around town, hoping to drum up some business."

Jacob read it and nodded. "Fine idea."

Carrying the poster, Jacob went to the long bulletin board that carried notices about anything and everything. He moved some around, took three off entirely, and tacked Thomas's up right in the middle.

"There. And I'll talk it up to anybody who comes in. Hope it'll get you some business."

"Me, too. Denke." He wouldn't want to sound desperate, but he didn't like not having work on hand to do. It didn't seem right, not after working with his uncle, who was always booked up far ahead. "I don't have enough to keep me busy."

Jacob straddled the chair. "Seems like there'd be a lot to do this time of year on the farm."

"Yah, there is. It's funny not having Daad yelling at me to get it done." He shrugged, surprised at his own need to talk to someone about it. "But nobody seems eager to let me help. The young ones grew up while I was gone, I guess."

Jacob picked up a buckle and began toying with it. He

always had to have something to fiddle with, Thomas remembered. Still studying the buckle, he said, "I hear tell Jonas is a big help to your daad. Wants to be a farmer, ain't so?"

Thomas nodded ruefully. "He does, and that's fine with me. I sure don't want to take over the dairy farm. I just have to convince Jonas of it."

"A little jealous, is he?" The grown-up Jacob showed an insight that the awkward, enthusiastic boy never had.

"Yah. That's another reason why I need to get some work of my own—so he'll stop thinking I came back to take something away from him."

"Not so easy being the prodigal son, ain't so? I'll do my best to spread the word." Jacob frowned absently, looking at the poster. "It's too bad you've been away so long. People forget."

"It seems to me the problem is that they remember the wrong things. I'll have to convince them I'm not a heedless teenager any longer." He wasn't going to retreat, not now that he'd come home.

He rose, holding out his hand to Jacob. "Denke, Jacob. I appreciate it. And I'm glad to have somebody to talk to besides family."

Jacob grabbed his hand and then slapped his shoulder. "It's wonderful good to have you back." He grinned. "And not married. I'm tired of hearing people ask when I'm going to get serious and marry some girl. Now they can ask you, instead."

"Yah, I can see the question lurking in Mamm's eyes already. Nothing she'd like better than a houseful of grandchildren, I guess."

Jacob walked to the door with him. "Things will settle down. You'll see. As for that old story . . . even if they talk about it at first, there'll be something else to keep the tongues busy soon enough."

He nodded. He surely did hope Jacob was right.

Thomas stood for a moment on the sidewalk, thinking if there was anyplace else to put a poster. But it seemed he'd covered them all. Promise Glen hadn't changed much in the time he'd been gone, and he was in a mood to be glad of something that hadn't.

Climbing into the buggy, he headed for home, satisfied with his day's work. Not only had he started getting the word out about his business, but he'd spanned the years between them with Jacob. Remembering Jacob's grin made him smile. That, at least, was still there, though not as frequent as he remembered.

Jacob had always been relaxed and easygoing, taking things as they came. It was surely natural enough that he'd be a bit more serious now, having lost both his mother and his father just a couple of years ago. He probably should have asked about Jacob's younger sister, but he hadn't thought of it. Was Jacob responsible for her now? He'd have to ask Mamm about the family.

Well, however little his relationship with Jacob had changed, he couldn't say the same for his own family. Certainly not with Jonas and his prickly response to anything Thomas tried to do. And Esther had turned into an almost-teenager who perplexed him anew every day. Adam seemed the same easygoing kid he remembered, but he wasn't sure what was going on behind his relaxed exterior.

As for Daad—Thomas had been back nearly a week, and his father was still treating him as politely as if he were a stranger. A visitor he didn't know well. Maybe his mother had been wrong when she'd said Daad was ready for him. And maybe it was time he talked to her about it.

Fortunately, when he reached the house, he found his mother alone—in the kitchen, as always. "Thomas, gut. There's fresh coffee, and plenty of shoofly pie." She set the shoofly pie on the table as she spoke and turned to the coffeepot.

Thomas opened his mouth to say he didn't need anything, but then he closed it again. If he was going to talk to his mother about Daad, it might be easier done across the table.

"Only if you'll sit and have some, too."

Looking pleased that he wanted her, Mamm provided herself with coffee and took the chair across from him. She pushed the shoofly pie nearer to him. "Eat, eat. You could stand to put on some weight."

He took an obedient bite, knowing that feeding people was Mamm's way of showing love. "No, I couldn't." He patted his flat stomach. "I'm just fine the way I am. I wouldn't want to be hauling any more weight up any ladders."

Her eyes lit. "Did you find some work, then?"

"No, not yet. But I put up all the posters." He tried not to show his disappointment. "It'll come, I'm sure." He'd best be sure, or he'd end up skulking back to Ohio with his tail between his legs.

"I'm sure, too," she said, loyally. "Someone will see your posters and get in touch."

"I hope so." But this wasn't getting him where he wanted to be. "Mamm, I need to talk to you. About Daad."

Her eyes darkened with concern, but she tried for a light tone. "What about your daad? He's fine."

"Fine, yah. But you said he was ready for me to come back. But it doesn't seem like it to me."

"Ach, Thomas, what are you talking about? I'm sure your daad . . ."

Her voice trailed off, and she lowered her eyes, looking at her hands clasped on the table.

He reached across to put his hand over hers. "You know what I mean. He's too polite. It's like I'm a stranger."

She clasped his hand in both of hers, and he felt a pang

as he saw the blue veins standing out on their backs. Mammi took a deep breath.

"He did say all right when I talked to him about you coming back. I think he meant it, but once you were really here . . ."

"He had second thoughts, didn't he? Remembering how people talked before, and I suppose they're talking again now. So Daad's thinking about how much worse it would be if I messed up now."

Mammi didn't say anything for a moment, as if she realized it wouldn't do any good to keep insisting that everything would be fine. Keeping his hand in hers, she spoke softly. "Maybe you're right, Thomas. But I think it's just that he needs time to adjust to having you back as a grown man. You will give him time, won't you, Thomas? For me?"

His mother's eyes were glazed with tears, and he knew perfectly well he couldn't refuse her. He patted her hand. "It's all right, Mammi. I'll give it some more time."

But if nothing changed . . . well, he might not have any other choice but to leave.

DORCAS HADN'T FORGOTTEN the incident with Mr. Haggerty the next morning, and she went out on the porch early so that she could watch the children get past his house. When she spotted her scholars coming, she stepped down off the porch, ready to go to the rescue if they were interrupted.

But nothing happened. Obviously remembering her talk with them, they walked cautiously along the narrow berm in single file, not breaking into their usual chattering groups until they were coming down the drive.

Good. The tension that had gripped her relaxed. She'd best remind them every day for a bit, but surely the man would forget about it by the time he was settled. Most likely he was feeling a bit embarrassed already. The idea was comforting, and she encouraged herself to believe it.

To her further pleasure, or so she told herself, Thomas didn't drive his sister to school. Esther came trotting down the road, probably eager to catch up with her friends for a chat before the bell rang.

Dorcas didn't need to stand out here any longer. She went back inside the schoolroom to be sure that everything was set up for the morning's activities.

She couldn't hope to avoid Thomas for long, she told herself. For sure she'd see him at worship on Sunday, if not sooner. But each day that passed increased her confidence, allowing her to convince herself that she felt nothing at all about Thomas.

The school day started smoothly, but she was aware of a certain amount of restlessness in the room. It was familiar enough, since it happened every spring like clockwork. The nice days followed one another, and children longed to be outside, even if it meant work for them. They anticipated the end of the school year and talked about little else. As she told Anna, from here on out, their main job was to keep the scholars focused as much as possible, and it wouldn't be easy.

When the schoolroom clock approached three, she collected their attention. "It will soon be time to start working on our program for the end of school."

A stir passed through the room, as the scholars exchanged smiles and murmured their excitement. "Anna and I will begin planning the program this week, and once it's ready, there will be parts for some of you to learn. We'll be making posters and thinking of ways to show your parents what you've learned this year. If we're to put on a program for your families, it's important to concentrate and work hard on it. Ain't so?"

"Yah, Teacher Dorcas," they chorused.

A glance at the clock told her she'd timed it perfectly. "Those of you who walk along the road, be mindful of our neighbor's property. Dismissed."

With a babble of conversation, the classroom erupted as some rushed for the door while others gathered in small chattering groups, making their way out more slowly.

Dorcas followed the last few—the older girls, who were plying her with questions about the end-of-school program. Since she hadn't thought much about that, she wasn't prepared to answer.

"Enough, enough," she said finally, laughing a little. "We'll be working on planning this week. If you have ideas, write them down and give them to me tomorrow."

That diverted them, as she'd hoped. She saw the girls out and stepped onto the porch to tell them good-bye and greet any parents who were there.

It wasn't unusual to see a buggy or two pulled up in front of the school. What stopped her in her tracks was the sight of Thomas Fisher standing there talking to Abel Miller, the chairman of her school board.

Abel could have come to pick up Joseph, although he didn't usually. And Thomas could have come to pick up Esther. It might be perfectly innocent. But there was nothing for her to like about having her school board president deep in conversation with the man who knew her most closely guarded secret.

The thoughts flew through her mind in a fleeting second, and then she walked toward them, pasting a smile on her face that she hoped looked more genuine than it felt.

Abel caught sight of her. "Here's Teacher Dorcas." He nodded to her. "I was just catching up with Thomas. It's been a long time, ain't so?"

She managed to nod while he clapped Thomas on the back as if they were old friends.

"Are you picking up Joseph? I thought he came out already."

"Yah, I saw him. The boys are playing catch until I'm ready. I thought we should have a look at the stable and that old shed—just see how big a job it would be to fix it up."

He headed around the school building, seeming to assume Dorcas was coming, too. She hurried after him. Did he mean he wanted to start on the repairs? That would be one worry taken care of.

Thomas fell into step with her, and her frown didn't seem to discourage him. She could hardly tell him outright to go away, much as she'd like to.

Abel headed into the stable first, glancing at Dorcas. "Not driving your horse today?" he asked her.

"I usually bring the buggy just when the weather is bad. Plenty of times in the winter, but not much now unless it's pouring rain." She glanced around, wondering what his assessing gaze was telling him.

Dorcas felt an urge to rush into speech, but she kept a respectful silence, knowing that Abel was one to take his time making up his mind. One thing, though—once he decided, he'd follow it through. And he certain sure cared about the scholars, so he'd be fair.

"So where's the leak you spotted?"

Dorcas stared at him, at a loss for an answer. Then she realized he wasn't asking her. He was asking Thomas.

"Right up here." Thomas brushed past her. Once again, he climbed the stall bars, looking up at the roof.

Dorcas had a suddenly vivid image of his jumping down within inches of her, his face alight with laughter, and her unfortunate response.

She clamped her jaw tightly and forced the picture away.

Thomas was standing on top now, balancing easily and

pointing up at the section of roof above one stall. "Right up there. It's not bad, but I can see where the moisture has soaked in. And there's a small gap where the sunlight is coming through if you look closely enough."

What was going on? Had Thomas gone to the school board about the problem he'd seen? What business was it of his?

As if he'd read the question on her face, Abel filled her in. "You'll be glad to know that Thomas has made a fine offer to the school board. If we can supply the materials, he'll do all the needed repairs on the barn and the shed."

She felt quite sure she was gaping. "That . . . that's very generous of him." She had to say what the school board would expect from her. But if Thomas did this job of work, just what good had it done her to resolve to stay away from him? He'd be underfoot, disturbing her, every single day, most likely.

"Not as generous as all that." Thomas looked down at her from his high perch. "I'm trying to get a business started. Doing the work on the school building gives me a chance to show everyone what I can do."

Before she could think of a response, he swung himself down and dropped lightly to the floor. "Anyway, I want to help Teacher Dorcas. Doesn't everyone?" Mischief lit his eyes, and she knew he was laughing at her. He knew how uncomfortable he made her, and he was laughing about it.

She bit her tongue to keep from saying something sharp. Abel wouldn't understand, and the last thing she wanted was to make anyone think about her past relationship with Thomas.

"Do you think the whole roof will have to be replaced?" Abel asked, frowning up at it.

"I'd say not. Looks to me as if it's a fairly small section where some shingles came loose. But I'd go over the whole thing and make sure it's all sound. There's no point in doing a job halfway if anything else is bad."

He and Abel were talking over and around Dorcas as if she weren't there. Was she going to have any choice in the matter? Was she to be stuck with Thomas every day?

"What do you think, Teacher Dorcas?" Abel asked. "With the stable and shed repaired, that takes away the big complaint of those who think we can't afford to keep the school open."

So Abel knew about that, obviously. And he was asking her opinion. This was her chance. She could say she didn't think it was a good idea.

But she couldn't. Abel wouldn't understand. However much she might want to reject Thomas's offer, she couldn't, not without raising even more questions that she didn't want to answer.

And Thomas knew it. She could read it in his eyes.

Gritting her teeth, she tried to find a smile. "It's a fine idea. Denke, Thomas."

Abel accepted her words at face value. But Thomas . . . Thomas was watching her in a knowing way, the teasing mischief in his eyes, a quirk at the corner of his lips. He knew exactly what she really wanted to say. Like it or not, she was stuck with him.

CHAPTER FOUR

Dorcas's mind continued to spin around and around the problem as she walked home, trying to see what else she could have done. But there wasn't any way to prevent Thomas from taking on the job.

Her thoughts came suddenly to a dead stop. What was she thinking? Thomas had made it clear that this job was important to him in establishing his new business. Was she really so self-centered that she'd ignored his needs in favor of her own?

She stopped, staring down at the path as if she could see something written there. Thomas had sacrificed himself to get her away safely that night so many years ago. She had rushed off home, thankful to escape the police, who seemed to be everywhere.

What's more, she'd been frightened enough that she'd changed her ways. No more taking risks and sneaking into Englisch parties. No more lying about where she'd been.

Thanks to Thomas, she'd gotten off scot-free. And when she heard the next day that Thomas had been arrested, and learned the following day that he'd been sent away to his uncle in Ohio, had she even considered telling the truth?

She walked on, trying to remember the girl she'd been.

If she had thought of confessing the truth, she certain sure hadn't considered it seriously. She had thanked the Lord on her knees for keeping her safe, but she hadn't thanked Thomas.

Could she . . . did she dare to thank him now? Everything inside her cringed at the idea of talking about that time with Thomas. If he had forgotten about it, wasn't it better to let it alone?

That was the same way she'd reacted at the idea of telling the truth back then, she'd realized—rationalizing it to do nothing. But she wasn't a frightened girl now. She was an adult, and it was time she acted like one.

By the time Dorcas had reached the house, she knew she had no choice but to speak to Thomas about it. What she didn't know was how she was going to do it. Or when.

Walking into the kitchen meant immediately being swept up in putting supper on the table. Once again, Betsy wasn't there.

"I was hoping little Will might be awake when I got home." She set a heavy pottery bowl of chicken potpie on the table. "I haven't had a chance to hold him in days."

"It's a shame you have to miss so much, being out all day." Mamm wiped her hands on a dishcloth, her face lighting up as it always did when she thought of her grandson. "Ach, I think he's gained weight in just the last day. Such chubby cheeks as he's getting."

Dorcas couldn't help smiling in return. "Well, I'll have to make up for it on the weekend. If Betsy will let me. Sometimes I think she's trying to keep me away from him. Is she afraid I'll drop him?"

"That's the way it is with the first little one," Mamm said wisely. "I think every first-time mother gets fussy that way. I know I did with Lemuel, but then Levi followed so quickly that I couldn't do it again."

Dorcas tried to imagine her mother being overprotective of the almost-six-foot Lemuel. She couldn't.

"And here I thought it was because of my wild reputation," she said lightly.

"Nonsense," Mamm said firmly. "You never had any such thing."

A weight dropped on her without warning. Just as she'd never thanked Thomas, she'd never apologized to her mother.

"I hope not," she said, knowing it was what Mamm wanted to hear. "But I know I was . . . well, difficult when I was a teenager. And with Daadi so sick, too."

And now they were looking at each other with tears in their eyes, and she wished she'd left the whole subject alone.

"Ach, Dorcas, don't think that. It was a hard time for all of us."

"I didn't make it any easier," she murmured, blinking away the tears that clouded her vision. "I'm sorry, Mammi."

Her mother's arms closed around her. "And I'm sorry, too. You've always been a gut girl. I'm afraid I didn't pay enough attention to you, and that's a time when a girl needs her mother."

"No, no. It wasn't your fault." She hadn't wanted to make her mother feel guilty. That was the last thing she'd want to do.

Mammi drew back, wiping her eyes and trying to smile. "We're being foolish, ain't so? Crying about something long past. I'm ashamed of myself."

The thunder of boots on the porch announced that Lemuel and Levi were coming in for supper. That put an end to any confidences, and they hurried to finish getting the food on.

Betsy came in a few minutes later, announcing that

Will was asleep. "He looks so sweet all limp like a rag doll with his cheeks as pink as can be." She smiled at her own imagining.

"He's the sweetest baby I've ever seen," Mamm said.

"Maybe I can creep in and see him after supper," Dorcas suggested.

Betsy exchanged looks with Levi. "Maybe," she murmured, making Dorcas wonder what message had been given between them.

Changing the subject seemed a good idea. "Lemuel, you'll be glad to know one problem at the school is solved."

"Yah?" He paused to swallow a mouthful of potpie. "How's that?"

"Abel Miller stopped by after school to take look at what had to be done to the stable and shed. It turns out Thomas Fisher would like to do the repairs, so no one else will have to take time away from planting. That's gut, ain't so?"

"That's generous of him," Mamm said, quick to praise as she always was.

"If it's okay with Abel, it's okay with me," Lemuel said. "Hope he's not too busy with his business to get it finished soon, before that roof causes any more damage."

She hoped so, too. "That's one reason he offered to do it. He feels it will help with his business if folks see his work."

Levi nodded. "That's most likely true. I don't doubt it will, so long as he gets it done soon."

"You'll have all the parents at the school for the program the last day," Lemuel added. "If he can have a good bit of it done, that's a chance to show it off."

"But that means he'll be working there while school's still going on." Betsy was the only one to look as if she disapproved of the idea.

"That's not a problem. He'll be out back, and the scholars won't hear much." Dorcas gave a wry smile. "They'll drive him crazy with questions at recess if I give them a chance, though."

"I wouldn't think you'd want him there at the school all the time with you."

That was what Dorcas had been thinking, but how did Betsy know?

Betsy's talk flowed on. "I mean, think of his reputation. You wouldn't want folks to start talking. Isn't that right, Levi?"

The appeal left her husband gaping, showing only too well that he didn't know how to answer.

Dorcas found her temper fraying. She wouldn't say anything to Betsy, but if her brother dared to lecture her—

"That's foolish," Lemuel said bluntly. "Thomas is a grown man now. Nobody thinks about what any of us did when we were teenagers, and it's a gut thing, too, or we'd all be in trouble, ain't so?"

Levi grinned, obviously remembering, and then he sobered when he looked at his wife. "I don't think we need to worry," he mumbled, and Betsy clouded up at his lack of support.

Dorcas didn't know whether she was more annoyed or dismayed. She hadn't intended to cause any family strife. She didn't believe that other people would react to Thomas that way. She was just concerned about how *she* would.

FOR ABOUT THE first time since he'd returned to Promise Glen, Thomas felt as if he belonged when he reached home. He drove the buggy horse up to the barn without a second thought and hopped down to perform the familiar tasks of putting the harness away properly and tending to the gelding Daad had let him use for the time being.

He had a job to do, and it was one that held the promise

of a future back here where he belonged. Even though he wouldn't be earning, he had saved enough to carry him through until his business picked up. He wouldn't be living off Mammi and Daad.

Thanks to Dorcas. He smiled, mentally vowing to stop teasing her so much. The trouble was that she made it just too easy. He always had known what her every expression meant, and it seemed he still did.

But he had to treat this job in a professional manner, and that meant no teasing. Or at least, as little as he could get away with. It wouldn't be in his nature to turn solemn all of a sudden.

Seeing that the milking was still in progress, he walked through the barn to the milking shed. Once again, as he'd done all week, Jonas ignored him. His father gave him a short nod, and Adam thrust a milking stool in his direction.

With all of them working, the milking went quickly enough. When he carried his full pail back to the cooling tank, Jonas was just turning away from it. He reached out for the bucket Thomas held.

"I'll do it."

"No problem," Thomas said. "I can finish up."

Jonas still stood in the way, glaring at him. A pang went through Thomas. What had happened to the little brother he'd left behind?

Moving aside grudgingly, Jonas watched his every movement and then slammed the lid closed. "You don't need to help. We get along fine without you."

Thomas felt as if Jonas had slammed him, too. His temper simmered, but he wouldn't set it free. If there was going to be an open breach between the two of them, he wouldn't be the one who started it.

"I'm sure you did," he said mildly.

It didn't seem to matter what he said; Jonas didn't like

any of it. His fists clenched, and he looked about ready to explode.

"Jonas." Daad's voice cut through the tension. "Go and help your brother hose down."

Jonas didn't move for an instant. Then he turned and walked away without a word.

"Sorry." Thomas blew out a breath. "I guess Jonas would rather not see me around all day. He's about to get his wish. I've picked up a job repairing the shed and the stable at the schoolhouse."

If Daad was surprised, he didn't show it. "That storm last month did a lot of damage. I don't think the school board can pay much."

"Nothing, actually. I'm doing the labor, and they're supplying the lumber." He hesitated, unable to make out what his father thought of it. "I thought it'd be a way to show folks what I can do. Onkel James always says you should point to what you have done if you're trying to get new work."

Daad nodded, his expression easing. "I always did think James was a good man of business. Sounds like he taught you well."

Thomas hesitated, not wanting to push his luck too far, but encouraged by his father's reaction. It was true, so why not say it. "It was the best thing for me, heading out to Ohio." Maybe saying thanks would be going too far, so he left it at that. After all, it had been intended as punishment, not reward.

Daad didn't move for a second. Then he nodded again. "Gut." He seemed to think he'd said enough, and he headed back into the milking shed.

That almost sounded like approval. Or maybe he would just be glad to have Thomas out from underfoot.

He couldn't quite believe that, or maybe he didn't want to. Still, he supposed he could cause Daad more embarrassment out in public than he could at home, so Daad must trust him a little.

Heartened, he went on to the next chore, which happened to be fixing fence wire in one of the pastures. At least with Adam he could relax. Everything Adam thought showed on his face, and he seemed to take Thomas's return as a matter of course.

For a second he wondered if his little brother had taken his leaving the same way. Then he shook off the thought and set about stringing the new wire.

Adam seemed full of plans for the singing that was coming up on Sunday evening. But instead of looking forward to chatting up the girls, Adam seemed intent on what games they were going to play.

"Some of us guys wanted to play corner ball, but the girls didn't like that. They'd be afraid of getting messy." He said it in a contemptuous tone that showed what he thought of girls at this point.

"Sounds like you don't want to please the girls," Thomas said, pulling the wire taut.

Adam gaped at him. "Why would I want to please them? All they do is chatter and giggle every time we all get together. We'd have a better time without them."

"Just wait a year or so. You'll figure out the attraction of having a girl think you're pretty special."

"Not me," Adam said with emphasis. "Nobody's going to catch me settling down before I've had some fun." That seemed to remind him of something, and his hands slowed. "Listen, Thomas, how about finishing this for me? I'll do something for you in exchange."

He didn't mind, but he guessed he ought to find out what Adam planned. The boy wore an expression too innocent to be believed.

"You have a date?" He grinned at Adam's reaction.

"Never mind thinking up a convenient excuse. I've used them all in my time."

Adam shrugged, not looking at him. "I'm just going to meet a guy and hang out. That's all." Then he met Thomas's gaze, saw the doubt there, and smiled, eyes crinkling. "If you must know, he's Englisch. He's a friend of mine. We're not doing anything bad, but Daad wouldn't understand."

"And you figure I will, since I wasn't exactly a saint when I was your age. Right?"

"Right." He looked relieved. "You won't tell, will you?" He was already dropping things into the toolbox, taking Thomas's answer for granted.

"Hold on." Thomas thought fast. He didn't want to lose his relationship with Adam, but . . . "I'm not going to lie for you."

"You won't need to." Adam dismissed that with an airy gesture. "I'm meeting a friend, that's all. And I'll be home by sundown. Promise."

Given how early sundown still was, he didn't suppose there was much harm in it. Besides, what choice did he have?

There seemed nothing to do but nod agreement, but as Adam scooted, Thomas couldn't get rid of an uneasy feeling. He'd thought he understood his little brother. Seemed like he'd been wrong.

"WE'VE MADE A fine start on the program," Dorcas said the next afternoon. She and Anna had stayed at school to work on the spring program after the scholars had left.

Anna looked at the papers Dorcas had swept into a stack. "I never realized how much work goes into setting up something like this program. Do you think we're starting in time?"

"Oh, I think so. We can't drag on the practices for too long, or the scholars get bored and start doing worse instead of better. This is the hardest part, especially finding something that hasn't been done over and over. It was nice of Ruth Schutz over at the Oak Creek school to trade programs with me."

Ruth was a fine teacher, and she'd been a great help to Dorcas when she was just starting out. Still, that didn't mean Dorcas wanted to lose her scholars to the Oak Creek School.

When Anna continued to look doubtful, Dorcas had to chuckle. "Don't worry. It will come together. We don't want to start the scholars on it until we've worked it all out ourselves. They're starting to get spring fever already."

Anna nodded. "I've noticed it. I can't believe we behaved that badly when we were that age."

Dorcas chuckled. "You did, believe me."

Her helper responded by blushing. "Did you hear Esther today, bragging about how her bruder is going to rebuild the stable and the shed? She says he's going to let her help him."

"I hadn't heard that part." Dorcas felt a wave of concern at the idea. "I'll have to talk to Thomas about it. We certain sure don't want any of the scholars to get hurt on school grounds. Or anywhere else, for that matter, but we're responsible for them here."

"Esther isn't the most coordinated child, either," Anna said, and then looked as if she wondered whether she should have.

"All girls seem to be at that age. The boys will start getting awkward a little later, when they hit a growing spurt." She stuffed the papers into her bag, rising. "I'll need to go to the library to make copies of parts. Maybe I can do them all on Saturday, if we finish up tomorrow."

"Yah, good." Anna glanced at the clock and started for

the door. "I'll tell my mamm that I'll be a little late again tomorrow, yah?"

Dorcas nodded, her thoughts already racing to the completion of the project. The kinder would be so eager to start practicing, at least at first, and it would use up some of their extra energy.

She was just glad that Thomas hadn't shown up today. Maybe she'd have a few days' respite before he started intruding on her school.

When they stepped out onto the porch, she realized she'd thought too soon. Thomas, driving a wagon filled with lumber, raised his hand in greeting and drove past them toward the stable.

Anna gave her an inquiring look.

"You go ahead, Anna. I'll stay a few minutes and speak to Thomas about Esther. We'd best deal with that before it starts or there'll be trouble."

Nodding, Anna headed for the lane that led to the Stoltzfus farm, while Dorcas followed Thomas, mentally composing the quickest way of dealing with the situation. She'd best not hang around long, giving Betsy an opportunity to worry about her reputation any further. Rolling her eyes at the thought of her sister-in-law, she approached Thomas, who was unloading.

He paused and looked at her. "What about Esther?"

She blinked. "Did you hear what I said to Anna clear back here?" She'd assumed he was out of earshot.

"I have sharp ears," he said. "So what is my little sister up to that she shouldn't be?"

"Nothing yet." She softened the words with a smile. "I'm worried about what she's talking about doing. She's been bragging a bit about you working on the stable, and she says she's going to help you."

"You didn't think I'd let her climb around on the rafters, did you?" He raised his eyebrows.

"No, of course not. But I'm responsible for all of the kinder when they're on school grounds, and the idea of her doing any such thing—"

Thomas leaned against the wagon, arms folded over his chest. "Do you want to know what I really said when she asked if she could help me?"

"Please." She couldn't tell if he was annoyed or not.

"I said, 'We'll see.' Seems like Esther heard what she wanted to hear."

He sounded so frustrated that she had to hold back a laugh. "I'm afraid they all do that sometimes. We probably did, too."

"I guess. I just wasn't ready to find my baby sister so . . . well, different. She's not grown up yet, but she's surely not the child I remember."

Now Dorcas did laugh. "Wilkom to the group. At this age, kinder are impossible to predict. They don't know themselves whether they're kids or grown-ups. Or even which they want to be."

"I guess that's true." He looked rueful. "Funny. I thought I'd come back and find everything the same. I mean, I knew in my head that the young ones would be growing—it's my heart that's having problems with it. Truth is, I just didn't realize how hard it would be to find my place again."

"I'm sorry." She realized that now, at least, he wasn't teasing or joking. He really was a bit baffled. "Just . . . give it time. You can't catch up in a week. It will come."

Thomas studied her face for so long that she was afraid she was blushing. "You're a gut example for those kinder, Dorcas. You've grown up, too."

"I'm not so sure about the example part of it." She felt stuck, knowing that she needed to thank him for what he'd done for her and yet unable to find the words to start. "But I do care about them, and I want to give them the very best I can."

His face crinkled in a way that was such an echo of the past that she felt her heart thump.

Stop it. You can't lose your head, not where Thomas is concerned. Remember he has the power to mess up your life completely, just through a careless word.

"I do believe you've grown up, Dorcas."

"Not enough." She took a deep breath and then blew it out, trying to say what she needed to. "I owe you something, Thomas." She looked down at his hands, braced against the wagon. "I never thanked you for what you did. You ended up carrying the blame and being sent away, and I got off free."

It felt as if she'd thrown off a heavy burden. But then he didn't speak, and her tension began to build. What was he thinking? When he did speak, it was the last thing she could have expected.

"Remember the story of Joseph and his brothers? How they sold him into slavery in Egypt, but years later he was able to save them and a whole country because of it?"

"I remember." *But I don't understand,* she might as well have added.

Thomas's lips curled in that teasing smile. "Then you must remember what he said . . . how they meant it for evil, but God meant it for good."

She wrestled with that for a moment, wondering if he was equating her with the jealous brothers. "I didn't mean . . ."

"Ach, I know you weren't trying to do wrong to me. But it turned out the same in a funny way. I went out to live with my aunt and uncle, and I got a whole new way of looking at things. Unlike my father, my uncle didn't expect me to be a saint, but he did expect me to be useful. Thanks to him, I learned a craft that will keep me the rest of my life. So you don't need to thank me, Dorcas. I should thank you."

She shook her head, feeling tears sting her eyes and knowing she couldn't give way. She stared down at the ground, afraid to look at him.

She felt Thomas clasp her hand, just for a moment, and she was swept by a feeling she didn't want to recognize. She managed to step back, to find a smile.

"Maybe we're even. That night made me grow up, and I realized what terrible chances I'd been taking. But I was fortunate, because I had a friend like you." Dorcas fell silent, wondering how to get away from the unaccountable tenderness of the moment.

She tried to rally. Focusing on the lumber he'd been unloading instead of on his face, she shook her head.

"Mind you be careful when you're climbing around the stable. If you got hurt, I'd be responsible for you, too."

Thomas turned, pulling out another armload of boards. "You don't need to be. One thing I learned a long time ago is that we're each responsible for ourselves."

She waited for more, but that seemed to be all Thomas had to say. Was he implying that she hadn't taken responsibility for herself that night? That was true enough, but she didn't like the idea that he thought that about her.

Still, there wasn't a thing she could do about it. Dorcas turned to leave, only to discover that Lydia Gaus, mother of two of her scholars, was standing a few feet away, staring at them.

CHAPTER FIVE

Lydia." Did she sound guilty? She wasn't sure. She certainly shouldn't be, but she didn't care for the way Lydia was staring at her. "If you've come to pick up Hallie and Erna, they left with the rest of the children." She moved casually away from Thomas and toward Lydia.

"Ach, no, it was just that they told me about planning the end of school program. Erna is certain sure excited about it. After all, it's her last year."

"Of course." She walked toward the school building, compelling Lydia to follow. She was still wondering about the reason for this unexpected visit. "Erna has been a wonderful gut scholar. We'll miss her next year."

Lydia flushed a little with pleasure. "She got such a fine start with Teacher Ruth over at Oak Creek school."

"I'm sure she did." The Gaus family had moved from another church district when Zeb Gaus's father passed a couple of years ago. "Ruth Schutz is a fine teacher."

Ruth had been such a help to her when Dorcas started teaching that she could never repay her, except in doing for Anna what Ruth had done for her.

"Yah, she is. So wise, ain't so? She's just the right age for a teacher, I always say."

Dorcas blinked. She wondered what exactly Lydia considered the right age for a teacher, but decided it was best not to ask.

"Was there some reason in particular you stopped by?" she asked, hoping the woman wouldn't take offense at the direct question.

She'd turned slightly to look at Lydia, and from the corner of her eye she caught sight of Thomas, watching them. He looked as if for a penny he'd jump into the conversation and prayed he wouldn't.

"Ach, yah, I clean forgot why I came. This." She flourished a large envelope and then thrust it into Dorcas's hand. "This is the program Teacher Ruth did when our boy was leaving school. I kept a copy because we were so impressed with it. When Erna told me you were working on the program, I just decided to bring this right over."

Dorcas took the envelope a little unwillingly. "That's kind of you. Denke."

"It's no trouble. I just said to myself, why should you have to make up a whole new program when there's a perfect one right here that you can use. Teacher Ruth would be happy to share."

It was time she took control of the conversation before Lydia had the whole day planned.

"I'm sure Ruth would. In fact, when we had our teachers' gathering at the beginning of the school year, we already shared our programs with each other. Ruth and I always do that. It's very helpful to see what resources other teachers have."

Lydia looked a little taken aback at that, but she seemed to make a quick recovery. "Well, you won't need to get out your notes when you can just make copies of everything in that envelope."

They had moved inside the classroom as Dorcas spoke, and she belatedly thought that might be a mistake. Lydia might consider it an invitation to stay and talk, and she'd like to get home. Still, it was a teacher's duty to talk with parents, even when they had little to say.

"I'll think about that. Now I should finish cleaning up my classroom, so I won't be late for supper . . ."

Lydia was looking around the classroom and didn't seem to be paying much attention. "The Oak Creek school is a good bit bigger than this one, ain't so?"

"Yah, it is." Dorcas looked with affection at the room where she spent her days. "But we've always found it's sufficient for our needs."

"Because you have so few children," Lydia said. "It's a shame. I always say the kinder do better in a larger class where there are more people the same age, but you can't provide it when you have so few kinder available, can you?"

Dorcas stamped down impatience and annoyance, wondering if she'd found the person who wanted to send her scholars to the Oak Creek school. "Our numbers are a little down this year, but we'll have a larger group coming in next year, with so many kinder turning six. School numbers do go up and down."

Before Lydia could offer any more improvement suggestions, Dorcas hurried on. "Let me walk you to your buggy. And thank you again for this." She waved the envelope, wishing she could shove it right back in Lydia's hands. But that would seem rude to Teacher Ruth, whom she liked very much.

"If there's nothing else I can do for you . . ." Lydia let that trail off. Dorcas resisted the impulse to say that she'd done too much already.

They walked out to where Lydia's buggy sat waiting. Once again Lydia stopped, staring back toward the shed. "That's Thomas Fisher, ain't so? What did you say he was doing here?"

"I don't think I did say, but he's offered to do the needed

repairs to the stable and shed. The big storm caused a fair amount of damage, you know. It's very nice of him, ain't so?"

Lydia sniffed, looking as if she'd tasted a sour pickle. "That's all very well, but I didn't know he knew anything about construction. We shouldn't let someone work on the buildings without knowing what kind of job they'll do. I'm surprised at the school board."

"I don't think we need to worry about his qualifications. He's been working with his onkel's construction firm for several years." Dorcas could hear the forced patience in her voice and hoped Lydia didn't. "Abel knows about him. The onkel has a large business out in Ohio, and he thinks Thomas is ready to start his own construction company."

She wasn't positive Thomas had said exactly that about his uncle, but it had been implied.

Lydia didn't seem impressed, in any event. "Well, I just hope he won't run off in the middle of it. I was told he did that once already, running off to jump the fence and leaving his father with no one to help him on the farm."

Dorcas felt as if her head was about to blow off, but she made a huge effort to stay calm. "I'm afraid you were misinformed. When Thomas was a teenager, his parents sent him out to Ohio to live with his onkel and learn the trade. He never left the church."

Lydia climbed into her buggy and picked up the lines. "That's not what I heard." She drove away before Dorcas could answer, apparently determined to get in the last word.

Dorcas stamped back into the school, slamming the door to vent her feelings. And then was promptly ashamed of her lack of control.

One thing was certain—she didn't have to wonder any longer who was behind the pressure to combine her school with Oak Creek.

―――――

BY SATURDAY AFTERNOON, Dorcas had managed to stop worrying about Lydia Gaus and all her doings. Except when the thought of what she'd said about Thomas intruded. That still ruffled her. Whatever her own doubts and concerns about Thomas, he was having a difficult enough time without someone spreading false stories about him.

From her bedroom window, she could hear the sound of buggy wheels in the drive. Sarah was a little early. Grabbing her sweater, Dorcas hurried down the wooden staircase that was rounded by several generations of feet and on into the kitchen.

"Sarah's here to take me to the Mud Sale meeting, Mammi."

"Are you sure you have the list of the things I'm donating to the quilt auction?" Her mother turned from the stove, where she spent so much of her time. "Don't forget about it."

"I have it right here." She patted her bag.

"Are you sure? You'd better look." Mamm wore the worried expression that had become commonplace since Daadi's death.

To please her, Dorcas took out the list and showed her before tucking it away again. "I won't forget, Mamm. But why don't you come, too. You'd enjoy getting out, and I'm sure the committee would love your help."

Not only that, but it would do her mother good to talk to the other women from her age group. She so seldom went anywhere unless it was to visit family or to worship.

Mammi glanced at the door, and for an instant Dorcas thought she'd say yes. But then she shook her head.

"I'd best stay here. You know Betsy doesn't like being alone in the house. She might need my help."

Dorcas held back a number of things she'd like to say

and kissed her mother's cheek. "I'll be back in a couple of hours. Try to relax a bit."

Pulling her sweater on, she hurried out the door. Sarah had turned her buggy and pulled up at the porch, so Dorcas had only to climb in and they were off.

When they reached the road, Sarah made the turn before she gave Dorcas a questioning look. "You may as well let it out, whatever you're stewing about. Otherwise you might just explode."

Dorcas did explode then, but with laughter. "I can't hide anything from you, ain't so?" Although even as she said it, she thought of the one thing she'd never confided.

"Anyone up to noticing could see that. You'd best talk it out before we get to town, yah?"

"Do you want the whole list?" Dorcas said lightly.

"Just the immediate trouble will do to start. Is it your sister-in-law again?"

"Somewhat, I guess. And Mamm, too. I just thought it would be good for my mother to join us today. After all, the Mud Sale is coming up fast, and she always helps, besides donating to the quilt auction."

"I wish she would. Everyone would be wonderful glad to see her getting out more. And really, there's no reason why she has to stay home, is there?"

"She says that Betsy might need her help." Dorcas made a face that relieved her feelings somewhat. "And Betsy doesn't like to be alone there with the boppli."

Sarah, with her air of always trying to see both sides of any issue, shrugged. "Little Will isn't that old yet. I suppose every new mother is a little overly cautious with the first one." She smoothed her hand over her own still-flat belly, making Dorcas smile.

"I suppose. But Betsy hasn't made any effort to take her proper place in the household. The rest of us wanted to move into the daadi haus when they were married, but she wouldn't hear of it. She's just happy to let Mamm continue to run everything."

"She helps, doesn't she?"

"Yah," she admitted. "But not even that so much since the baby came." She looked at her friend. "All right, tell me I'm being too hard on her."

Sarah chuckled. "I wouldn't say that exactly. My cousin's wife settled into her place pretty quickly, but everyone is different. And Betsy is pretty young, ain't so?"

"You're right. And I'm probably turning into a crochety old maid. It's mainly that I'm worried about Mammi. Ever since Daad died, she hasn't wanted to go anywhere or do anything. She's so anxious all the time." Dorcas shook her head at the futility of trying to explain. "And then I worry about her."

"I know." Sarah reached across to pat her hand. "I know you want to help, but it may be that this is one of those things your mamm has to work out for herself. I'll tell you what—why don't I get my grandmother to stop in and see her? Grossmammi is wonderful gut at getting folks to open up to her."

Relieved at hearing a good suggestion, Dorcas smiled. "That would be perfect. Your grossmammi is just what she needs. She always makes me feel better just seeing her."

Sarah nodded. "She has a gift. Now—let's talk about this afternoon's meeting."

Accepting that her friend had contributed all she could to the situation, Dorcas zeroed in on the issue at hand. "I'm never sure why we have to have so many meetings about the Mud Sale. Everyone is still taking charge of the same things they always have, just wait and see."

"True enough," Sarah admitted. "But you should be there representing the school, and I thought we could help Dinah. It was nice of her to offer the use of the bakery space for the meeting, and I'm sure she plans to serve coffee and maybe something else besides."

Dorcas had to agree. "She's such a good person. She always makes me feel I should be doing something else to help people." Dorcas seemed to see the sweet face of the girl who'd gone through school and rumspringa with them. "And she's certain sure worked hard to make a go of things since her husband died."

Dorcas couldn't help but contrast Dinah's quiet determination to face life as a widow and make a go of the bakery she and her husband ran with her mother's withdrawal from life. But as Sarah had said, sometimes people had to work through things by themselves.

They were just pulling up to the building where the bakery shared space with the harness shop owned by Sarah's cousin, Jacob Miller, and Sarah went around the side to where buggies stood at the hitching rail. The harness shop was closer, so they went through it to the bakery, already filling up for the meeting. As always, the women were chatting together about families while the men clustered in the other corner for a chat about something that seemed to generate a lot of laughter.

With a grin at Sarah, Dorcas slipped behind the counter to join Dinah, who was already serving coffee and slices of a rich-looking coffeecake.

Dinah smiled her thanks when Dorcas took the tray to pass the coffee while Sarah started serving the coffeecake. There was a good turnout for the meeting since it was the last one before the event. Dorcas knew everyone, of course, and had a special greeting for the parents of her scholars. Spring was a busy time, especially for farmers, but the Mud Sale was important to the whole community, always netting a fine profit, which was split between the volunteer fire company and the school.

Once everyone had been served, it was time to get

down to business. Eli Younker, the church deacon, had been the driving force behind the spring Mud Sale for at least ten years. He seemed just as enthusiastic as ever when he called for reports on each aspect of the sale.

Smiling as she passed people, Dorcas went with her tray to slip behind the counter and join Sarah and Dinah, who silently handed her a mug of coffee and pushed a plate of crullers closer. Dorcas snatched one, well aware of the meltingly delicious quality of Dinah's crullers. She listened with half an ear to the various reports, thinking this would be a repeat of a long series of successful sales and everyone would go home afterward tired but happy. A good take might even allow her to buy some new books for the classroom beyond the usual expenditures.

She was mentally leafing through a catalog of children's books when she realized that Zeb Gaus was getting to his feet, obviously propelled by Lydia, his wife.

Dorcas set her coffee mug down with a thud, filled with apprehension. Something was about to happen that she wouldn't like—she sensed it.

But even as Zeb prepared to speak, her gaze was distracted by the door between the bakery and the harness shop opening. Thomas Fisher walked in, apparently to join the meeting. He glanced around the room until their eyes met. For an instant, she felt a connection that seemed to sizzle. Then, with an effort, she turned back to the meeting.

THOMAS YANKED HIS gaze away from Dorcas. Just because she was one of the few people he'd been in touch with since he'd returned, that didn't mean he ought to spend quite so much time looking at her. Although she certain sure was worth looking at, with her rosy cheeks and the sparkle in her brown eyes.

He pulled his attention back to the man who'd just begun to talk. It looked as if his wife was the woman who'd been prying around the school—the one who'd looked at him as if he were a stinkbug. They must be relative newcomers to the community. He'd remember them if he'd known them before he left.

". . . we . . . I . . . my wife and I thought we might change the division of the profits from the Mud Sale. Seems like the school doesn't have as many scholars this year, so it wouldn't need as much money. And the fire company needs new equipment."

He'd rushed his words as if to get them all out on a single breath and looked around, seeming to ask for approval. His wife frowned and nudged him. He looked at her blankly and then nodded.

"Yah, so what if we give seventy percent to the fire company and thirty percent to the school this year?"

He sat down abruptly. A low buzz of conversation broke out. Jacob, standing slightly behind Thomas, muttered in his ear.

"Nobody from the school board is even here. What does Zeb Gaus want to bring it up at the last minute for anyway?"

"Doesn't seem fair, does it?" Thomas didn't like the idea either. Especially not with Dorcas looking like somebody had come up behind her and shoved her.

Deacon Eli stood with an air of not knowing quite what to do but feeling sure he should do something. He looked around, seeming to search for an answer.

"Well." He cleared his throat. "Anybody have anything to say about that idea?"

Thomas nudged Jacob. "Go on," he muttered. "Speak up."

Jacob glared at him but took a step forward from where they stood against the wall. "Nobody from the school board is here," he said. "I don't think we ought to go changing things that affect the school when they're not around."

Elijah King, eighty if he was a day, shuffled his feet and shoved himself up to standing. "Lot of folks don't have kids in school, but everybody depends on the fire company. That's all." He sat down abruptly.

"The school benefits everybody, whether you have a child there right now or not. We all went to school, ain't so?" Given that he'd just been thinking he was too newly back to give an opinion, Thomas was surprised to hear his own voice.

"That's right," Jacob said, and Thomas could see a lot of heads nodding around the room.

Deacon Eli glanced around as if looking for help. "Anybody else? Somebody from the fire company want to speak?"

Nobody volunteered, and everyone began to look uncomfortable. Seemed like they'd gotten into a tangle, and there wasn't any way out without upsetting someone.

Jacob nudged Thomas. "Say something," he muttered.

"Why not you?" Thomas returned. Were they going to hang around for the rest of the afternoon because nobody wanted to argue with a brother in the church?

Finally he caught Deacon Eli's eye. "Thomas?"

"The sale is only a week away. It's getting late to make changes." He could see that his comment was going over. Plenty of people nodded now.

Deacon Eli gave him a look of relief. "That's right," he said quickly. "If somebody thinks a change is needed, take it to the committee in the fall. Agreed?"

His relief was echoed around the room. From the corner of his eyes he saw Lydia Gaus start to rise, only to be pulled back by her husband. She glared at him but subsided.

"We're done, then. Don't forget to be at the field next to the fire hall on Friday to start setting up." He turned his back on the room to thank Dinah, and people began getting up, catching their neighbors, and rehashing the meeting.

Thomas grinned, relaxing. Wasn't that always the way after a community meeting? All the people who hadn't spoken up would now tell their neighbors what they thought.

"Gut job, Thomas." Jacob clapped him on the shoulder. "I was right to shove you in here, ain't so?"

"I think you got me in bad with the Gaus family. Who are they anyway?"

"They moved here from over Fernville way to take over Hiram Stoltz's farm when he died. He was some relation, I guess."

Thomas nodded, dismissing the Gaus family from his mind. Dorcas undoubtedly knew what was going on. The woman had been bending her ear over at the school the other day. But what was she doing, wanting to take money away from the school her own kinder went to?

He had no desire to ask Lydia Gaus, but he wouldn't mind talking to Dorcas about it. He looked her way, but she didn't seem to want to meet his eyes. And then a couple of the men came up to tell him he'd said just the right thing, and the moment slipped away.

It wasn't until most people were leaving that he walked through into the bakery kitchen and found Dorcas packing leftover pastries into plastic bags. She didn't turn at once, so he stood where he was and watched her busy, efficient hands doing the task.

"Is there anything else I can help with, Dinah? These are about finished," she asked.

"It's not Dinah."

Dorcas spun around to face him. "I didn't realize . . . I mean . . ." She flushed slightly. "I should thank you for helping out in there."

She didn't sound as if it gave her much pleasure to say it, making him wonder what was in her mind.

"No problem." He shrugged. "What is it with that woman anyway? Her own kids go to your school. You'd think she'd want more money for the school, not less."

Dorcas wrinkled her nose, suddenly looking sixteen again. "She doesn't want her kinder at Orchard Hill. She wants to close the school and send all the scholars to the Oak Creek school."

"So she's the one behind that talk." He drew a little closer and leaned against the counter. "Why?"

"Who knows? That's where her kinder went before they moved over here. Apparently, she thinks it's a bigger and better school. Or maybe that Ruth is a better teacher."

"That's foolish." He felt like saying something stronger but suspected that would get him into trouble with Teacher Dorcas.

She shrugged, frowning down at the counter, bleached by countless washings. "I don't know how she got this bee in her bonnet. Her girls seem to be happy enough."

"Which ones are they?" He could only imagine the cluster of females gathered like so many clucking hens around his sister.

"Erna and Hallie. Erna's in her last year. Hallie is a friend of your sister, Esther."

"Maybe I should have a talk with Esther."

"Forget it," she said sharply. "I mean . . . well, don't bring the scholars into this issue. It wouldn't be right."

"If you say so." He frowned. "Isn't there something I can do to help?"

"You've done enough." Again, it sounded a little sharp. "Denke. Just . . ."

"Just leave you alone?"

"Sorry," she muttered. "Look, I'm grateful to you. Again."

He started to see a little daylight. Somehow this was tangled up with what had happened nearly eight years ago. And she clearly didn't want to talk about it. It bothered him a lot more than he would expect and annoyed him even more.

"Fine." He snapped the word. "I'll leave it alone. But let's be clear—I'm not looking for gratitude from you. Not for what happened in the past, and not for anything I do now."

He shoved himself away from the counter and pushed his way out of the door. He'd had enough.

But he had a strong suspicion that neither of them would be able to leave the subject alone. Sooner or later they'd have to be honest with each other, and it seemed Dorcas didn't want that.

But why? Was she afraid he was going to hold it over her? Or afraid he was going to let it out? Either way, he didn't think much of her attitude.

CHAPTER SIX

Dorcas found she was unconsciously slowing down as she got ready for worship the next morning. Giving herself a mental shake, she hurried through the last few things she had to do. She knew exactly what had caused her reluctance. Guilt. She had been rude to Thomas when he was trying to help her.

And why? Some serious soul-searching in the hours of the night had made it clear. She'd been rude because any kindness he did reminded her of how much she already owed him. Seeing that made her feel very small, to say nothing of unfit for worship.

That being the case, she knew worship was the best place for her, so she hurriedly finished getting ready. In the kitchen, Mammi was in a flutter because Betsy was going back to worship with the baby this week. Since the weather was lovely and the drive was a short one, she and Levi had decided, but the preparations suggested they were trekking across country.

Lemuel, patiently waiting with the buggy, exchanged smiles with Dorcas. Like her, he was sometimes amused by how much equipment one small baby required.

"Just wait until it's you," Dorcas whispered under

cover of Betsy's voice behind them, insisting that Levi check the diaper bag once more before they left.

"You're more likely to get there first," he said. "Even if you are my sister, you're too pretty to stay single for much longer."

A compliment from an older brother was so rare that Dorcas blushed. She tried to shake her head convincingly. "I'm an old maid, haven't you heard?"

"Wait until you see what comes along next for you." He said it with his best big brother voice. "It'll happen when you least expect it."

She shook her head but didn't try to argue since they were at last ready to leave. He clucked to the buggy horse, and they were off.

The spring air was a little cool this early, but the sun was thinning the light mist that hung in the valley. As it grew brighter, Dorcas imagined she saw the faintest tint of pale green surrounding the trees.

Her spirits lifted. Who could feel troubled on a morning like this? She would ask God's forgiveness and guidance. And then she would try to make things right with Thomas, even if something in her quailed at the thought of discussing what lay between them.

Worship was in a large storage shed cleaned out especially for the purpose. The Lapp family would have been at work all week in order to have it spotless, she knew, and that should reassure Betsy as to little Will's safety from any stray dust. The Leit moved toward the building in family groups and then separated to line up in their usual order . . . women on one side and men on the other.

As an unmarried woman, Dorcas belonged with the younger women, but she made her way to the end of the younger group so that she'd be seated where the married women started. That put Sarah next to her, just as they'd sat next to each other from the time they'd been able to sit apart from their families.

Sarah greeted her with a quiet smile and squeezed her hand. "All right?" she murmured.

So Sarah had known something was wrong when they'd parted the previous day. She wasn't really surprised. It was hard to put on an act with your closest friend.

She nodded. This wasn't the time or place to tell Sarah about it, but they'd probably have a chance to talk after worship. And also after worship, she'd try to find a moment for a quiet word or two with Thomas. Her pulse gave a little jump, and she closed her eyes in silent prayer before they went inside.

When she opened them, she found she was looking at Thomas, walking quietly behind his father toward the men's line. She glanced from father to son and looked away none the wiser. It seemed that the Fisher males had adopted the same stoic, expressionless face, like a blank door with no handle. Whatever they felt about Thomas's return, no one would know it by looking at them.

In a few minutes the lines began to move, women and girls first, and soon she was seated next to Sarah on the backless bench, looking down at her hands. Although she couldn't see them, she knew that Betsy would be seated farther back with Will on her lap and Mamm close at hand, ready to help.

She felt the movement when Sarah craned her neck to see the twins, seated on either side of their father across the way. She was sure they felt much too grown up to sit with their mammi.

If Dorcas looked, she might be able to spot Thomas, sitting much as she did, between the unmarried and the married men, so she carefully did not look. There might be a few furtive glances from others toward Thomas, since this was his first Sunday in worship since returning, but hers wouldn't be one of them.

One worship service after another, the same order was followed. No matter what the setting, one could count on being in the same position for worship. Your place was determined by your age from the time you were old enough to be apart from your mother.

Silence fell, and in the silence, Dorcas tried to order her thoughts for worship. It was never easy to prevent random thoughts and worries from popping up, and today it seemed harder than ever.

Before she could decide why, the voice of the Vorsinger lifted from the men's side in the beginning of the first hymn, and the rest of the Leit picked up the familiar German words. The slow echo of the hymn seemed to resonate through the storage building and the spirit of worship settled on Dorcas, calming her troubled thoughts.

The ministers went out, as usual, to consult as to who would preach this morning, and an unwelcome speculation slid into her mind. Would Thomas's father be chosen to speak today? And if so, would he talk about his son's return? The return of the prodigal might seem appropriate, but she suspected that neither Thomas nor his father would find that comforting.

In any event, she need not wonder any longer, as they came back. It seemed Minister Joseph Stoltzfus would give the long sermon, and a sense of relief enveloped her.

The kindness that had developed in Minister Joseph during nearly eighty years of loving and serving always permeated his words, and today they had the soothing that she needed so desperately. In the stillness her heart spoke of regret and repentance, and she found peace and forgiveness seeping into her heart in return.

When the three hours of worship came to an end, Dorcas felt ready. She would watch for an opportunity to speak to Thomas, and when she did, the words were simple enough. *I'm sorry. Thank you.* She'd tried to say that already, and then the first thing she knew, she'd said the wrong thing and offended Thomas, and they were worse off than ever. She had to try again and mean it this time.

"Are you all right?" Sarah asked again, and Dorcas realized she had been standing without moving. All around them, the men were making quick work of changing the benches into the tables where they'd lunch. Under the clatter, she leaned closer and spoke in an undertone.

"I need to say something to Thomas," she murmured. "Will you help me make an opportunity?"

There was a question in Sarah's eyes, but like the true friend she was, she didn't ask. "For sure. After folks eat would be the best chance."

Dorcas nodded, Sarah's twins came running up to them, and the moment passed, but she was content. This would work out, she felt sure, and then she and Thomas could go their separate ways without any shadow between them.

THOMAS WALKED OUT into the spring sunshine once the tables had been set up, surprised by his own reaction to the service. He'd worshipped regularly with his aunt and uncle, of course, so this shouldn't feel any different.

But it did. Despite the few curious glances he'd caught focused on him, he'd felt at home. It was as if, after a long exile, he was back where he belonged, and the warm sun just seemed to add another blessing to the day.

"Not so bad, ain't so?" Jacob nudged him. "Sitting next to you was just like old times."

"Very old." He couldn't help smiling when he saw Jacob's grin. "We must have been ten when we finally got to sit together in worship."

"Yah, right there in the front row under the ministers' eyes. I remember your daad glaring at me if I so much as looked at you." Jacob gave a mock shudder. "Sometimes I still feel as if he's watching me."

"You ought to be married, that's what he's thinking," Thomas said, a little maliciously. Still, he himself should be glad he wasn't the only man to reach his mid-twenties without acquiring a wife and a kid or two.

"Same for you." Jacob's good humor was unimpaired.

"You two plotting some trouble?" The question came from behind them. Thomas turned to find that Noah Raber had joined them, his twin boys hanging on to his hands.

"Way I remember it, you got into as much trouble as we did back in the day," Jacob said. "How about the milk snake you put in the teacher's desk?"

"Hush." Smiling, Noah put his hands over his boys' ears. "You want to give them ideas? Sarah would get after me if I incited any trouble for her great friend."

"That's for sure." Thomas had a vivid picture of Sarah and Dorcas at fifteen or so, giggling together at a singing, their gazes darting to him and away again.

While he was still smiling at the image, his brother Jonas came out of the storage building, edging his way around them as if they'd blocked his exit. Thomas opened his mouth to say something and was met by such a frowning glare that the words died on his tongue. What now? Didn't Jonas like to see him getting together with old friends?

When Jonas had moved away, Thomas turned back to find both Noah and Jacob staring after him. Noah glanced at him questioningly before speaking to his boys.

"You two go off and find your mamm. See if she needs any help."

Matthew looked as if he'd protest, but Mark grabbed his hand. "Come on, Matty. We can help." They ran off.

Jacob raised his eyebrows. "What's bothering Jonas? He looks like he just bit into a sour pickle."

Thomas shrugged, not wanting to get into his family problems. "Guess he's having a little trouble adjusting to having me back."

"Put his nose out of joint, did it? He'll get over it. Probably figured he was the eldest with you away." Jacob could dismiss it easily, since it wasn't his problem.

Noah moved restlessly, as if thinking this had gotten too personal. "So I hear you're doing the work on the school stable. If you need any help, give me a shout."

"Denke. You're probably busy with your furniture crafting, ain't so?"

Noah shrugged. "Not as busy as anyone who farms this time of year. I am trying to get ahead, so I have plenty of stock for summer visitors. Still, I can make time. I'll stop over one day. There's some work needs done enlarging my shop. We'll talk."

Noah had skirted lightly around the idea of talking business on the Sabbath, but what he'd said was enough to lift Thomas's spirits. This was what he'd hoped would happen. There was nothing like word of mouth to get a business going.

He nodded, and they moved out of the way as food began coming from the house toward the tables. Sunday lunch was underway. He caught a glimpse of Dorcas carrying a large bowl of schmier, the concoction of peanut butter and marshmallow cream that they'd all loved as children. The sunlight caught the smooth strands of soft brown hair, bringing out glints of gold.

Was she still as annoyed as she'd been the previous day? That had been a strange conversation for sure. Why did she act as if being grateful to him was the worst thing in the world? They'd been friends once, or didn't she remember?

He was distracted from this useless train of thought by the call to lunch. It was the usual array of food—meats, cheeses, salads, homemade bread, pies, and all of it more than anyone could eat. And the talk around the tables was familiar, too. In fact, he began to think it was the same conversation he'd heard after worship the Sunday before his life here collapsed.

Restless at the thought, Thomas took advantage of people picking up dessert to move away from the table. His daad was deep in conversation with one of the other ministers, so it didn't look as if he'd be ready to leave very soon. Knowing that Sam Lapp was noted for his fine Percheron team, Thomas wandered around behind the barn to have a look at them.

The team was in the field, grazing comfortably—two beautiful grays, as alike as could be. At the sight of him, they ambled over with the friendliness that seemed characteristic of draft horses. He leaned over the fence to stroke the neck of the nearest one, impressed by the breadth of the shoulders and the sleek, strong muscles under the skin. Sam must have a hard time not showing his pride in these beauties.

A challenging part of Amish culture—this business of pride. A person of faith was humble, not proud, aware that everything he had and was came from the Lord. Still, Sam could feel satisfaction that the pair he'd raised had turned out so well, just as Thomas could feel satisfaction with a job of work well done.

He gave the horses a final pat each and moved on around the barn. Funny that he'd never had an instinctive understanding of livestock. Daad had it, and Jonas did as well. Not he. Now, if he could just convince Jonas of that, maybe his brother could be a bit easier with his presence.

Understanding his siblings wasn't working out quite the way he'd anticipated. He'd been foolish, thinking that he'd return, and their relationship would pick up where it had left off. Not just foolish, he told himself. Stupid.

Catching movement from the corner of his eye, Thomas turned to look and spotted Sarah and Dorcas admiring an enormous clump of daffodils banked against the brick of an old, disused well by the side of the barn. He hesitated, not sure whether they'd seen him or not. Then Sarah met his glance, she smiled and gestured a welcome, so he went to them.

"I'm wonderful glad to see you, Thomas. I haven't had a minute to talk to you since you returned. It must be going well, because you look fine."

Sarah, he remembered, always had a motherly attitude toward anyone younger, even if it was only by less than a year.

"Yah, I'm happy to be here. Noah and those two boys are certain sure keeping you busy, ain't so?"

Her face glowed as if lit from within at the mention of her family. "They are that, and I'd best go and check on them. You'll keep Dorcas company, yah?"

Before either of them could respond, she'd whisked away.

Thomas stared after her for a moment and then turned back to Dorcas. "What was that all about?"

Dorcas's lips twitched. "That was Sarah being subtle. I asked her to help me find a chance to speak to you alone."

He leaned against the weathered barn siding, studying her face. It was turned downward, as if she looked for something on the ground, and every trace of that momentary smile had disappeared.

"I'm here, and for the moment, nobody else is around. What's troubling you?"

It was obvious that something was, since she'd lost the spark of laughter that was so much a part of her.

She took a deep breath, as if preparing for something huge. "Just . . . I'm sorry. And thank you."

NOW THAT SHE'D said the words, Dorcas knew that they were not enough. He didn't understand. Apparently, what had been haunting her wasn't even in his thoughts. She'd have to go into the whole story she'd thought buried seven years ago.

"If you're talking about your attitude yesterday, maybe we'd best let it drop." His expression had firmed. "You didn't like my interference. No reason why you should, that I can see."

She struggled to find the right words. "It wasn't that. You said what I hoped someone would say, so I wouldn't have to disagree with the parents of my students." A tiny smile hovered and was gone at the thought of Lydia Gaus. "You know very well I've owed you my thanks for over seven years. You never wanted to go to that foolish party to begin with."

Thomas's expression relaxed. "You were too stubborn for me."

"You should have refused to go at all." Suddenly they were talking like the friends they'd been then.

"And let you go off by yourself chasing that Englisch boy you were so sweet on?"

"I always thought you didn't know about him." She looked back, wondering, at the girl who'd thought she was so grown up.

"Troy Evans." He supplied the name. "How could I help noticing you looking at him as if he were a hero whenever you saw him?"

"He was about as far from that as he could be." She should be embarrassed, except that she knew she didn't have to be with Thomas. "He's the one who wanted me to come, and then when we heard the sirens, he just left me there and ran off."

His expression showed clearly what he'd thought of Troy. "I had a feeling the whole time that those parties were ripe to be raided. That was the summer the police said they were going to crack down on them, remember?"

"I don't think I ever heard that." She sent her mind back to that far-off summer. "I just knew that siren was the worst thing I ever heard." She seemed to feel like the scared girl again and rubbed her arms, chilled. "I started to run and then you grabbed me."

He'd caught her wrist, and somehow in all the confusion, she'd known it was him. And known, too, that Thomas would keep her safe.

"You were a pretty fast runner for a girl, as I remember." His face had eased into a smile, as if the memory that had haunted her actually amused him. "If we'd had another minute's start, we'd have gotten away."

She wasn't sure about that. It had seemed so impossible to be running through the thick grass with Thomas, thinking if only they could make it to the woods, they'd be okay. But they couldn't. She'd tripped, nearly fallen, and they'd both tumbled to the ground behind a downed tree.

They might still have made it, but the beam of a heavy-duty flashlight came piercing through the field, making it nearly as bright as day. "I know you're in there. Come on out now." The voice had been loud, but not unkind.

She'd been frozen. Thomas had pulled her close and whispered in her ear. "I'll distract them. Once they put the light on me, you run toward the woods and keep on going. You'll hit Kriner's lane and you can walk home from there."

When she didn't respond, he'd shaken her. "Understand?"

She forced herself to nod. "Yah."

"Do like I told you. Don't look back."

She'd felt his breath on her cheek, and then in an instant he was running the opposite way, shouting something. The light swung round and focused on him, away from her.

A frozen second later, she was doing as he'd said, running, choking back sobs, afraid to look and afraid not to. When she'd reached cover, she'd finally looked back, but it was too late to see anything but Thomas's back as an officer took him toward the waiting police car.

Without her realizing it, Thomas had come closer. "Stop it," he muttered. "No sense in reliving it. It's over and gone, and we never have to go through it again."

"I know." She tried to smile, but it was a poor effort. "I should have gone back. I let you go through it alone."

"Crazy." The word exploded out of him, and she realized he was actually angry at the suggestion. "What would have been the use of doing that? I wanted you to get away, and you did. End of story."

Her gaze searched his face. "Really? You weren't angry with me for running?"

"Silly." His flare of anger was gone as fast as it had come, and now his eyes held their familiar teasing look. "You let me think of myself as a hero. And going away was the best thing that could have happened to me. Honest."

"I was so sorry, and I never told you. And then when you came back, I was afraid . . ."

Thomas's face tightened. "Afraid of what? Did you think I'd tell on you now?"

"No, no, not exactly." But she had feared that, just for a moment. "But when you teased me, I thought maybe you didn't realize how important it was now."

"Teacher Dorcas," he said, with an inflection in his

voice that made it mocking. "I know. You don't need to be afraid. I'm not going to say anything. To anyone."

Now she'd hurt him. Was everything she said to him destined to be wrong? He started to turn away and she grasped his wrist, as he'd grabbed hers that night.

"Wait. I know. I knew all along that I could trust you, but I let doubt creep in. Forgive me."

He shrugged. "Nothing to forgive. You took care of yourself . . ." He stopped abruptly, and they both heard Sarah's voice, pitched a little louder than normal, coming from around the barn with someone else.

Before she could speak, Thomas was gone, slipping out of sight behind the barn and leaving her standing there by the daffodils. Saving her again, she thought wryly.

She'd said what she needed to say, but it didn't seem to have helped much. She'd managed to hurt him by her lack of trust, and she suddenly felt like that immature girl she'd been instead of the grown-up teacher she thought she was.

CHAPTER SEVEN

Dorcas turned toward the front of the barn, only to see Sarah and Lydia Gaus walking toward her. Of all the people to show up now—the woman seemed to be everywhere. Well, at least she understood why Sarah had spoken so loudly. She'd been trying to warn them. Dorcas could only hope they'd reacted in time. Given Lydia's attitude toward both Dorcas and her school, she'd probably put the worst possible interpretation on finding them alone together.

Trying to look as if she hadn't a care in the world, Dorcas went to meet them. "Here you are, Sarah." Not having any idea what Sarah had been saying, it seemed best not to make any definite statements.

"I'm sorry I was so long," Sarah said promptly. "I know I said I'd be right back, but I got talking to Lydia."

"That's fine. How are you, Lydia?" She started slowly toward the house, ensuring that they came with her.

"Fine, fine." Lydia looked as if she couldn't decide whether she was suspicious or ill at ease. Maybe both. "I . . . I didn't realize you were waiting back here all alone, or I wouldn't have delayed Sarah."

"That's fine. I was just admiring the daffodils. They

seem to like that spot by the old well. Ours aren't nearly as far along."

Had it seemed strange that she was standing here alone after lunch? She wouldn't think so, but she couldn't tell what Lydia was thinking. It was uncomfortable, to say the least, to have the mother of two of her scholars being so antagonistic to her.

Or was she exaggerating? Maybe Lydia was just overly involved in her children's education, wanting to control it. It wasn't necessarily personal.

"Well . . . well, I won't keep you standing here talking, but I did want to speak to you about the meeting yesterday."

"Yah?" Dorcas decided her smile must look frozen, because it certain sure felt that way.

Lydia's pale cheeks took on an unbecoming flush. "We . . . Zeb and me . . . we just thought that the fire company was a . . . had a . . . well, maybe needed the money more than the school right now."

"I see." She would not start an argument, right here in front of everyone, but she wasn't going to agree, either. Maybe the best thing wasn't to speak at all.

She saw Sarah draw in her breath, probably prepared to take issue with the idea that the fire company should take priority over the school. She caught Sarah's eye and shook her head very slightly. Sarah subsided, but she still looked annoyed.

Finding them nonresponsive, Lydia sniffed a little. "Next time we'll have to get started earlier. Maybe for the Harvest Festival."

If Dorcas ground her teeth any harder, her jaw would break. Before she could say something she'd regret, Esther came scurrying up to her.

"Teacher Dorcas, have you seen my bruder? Thomas,

I mean? I want him to let me drive on the way home. He promised he'd show me about driving the family buggy."

"Did he?" It seemed a little odd that Thomas would be doing it instead of her daad, and even odder that they'd do it on the way home from worship.

"Well, almost." She took on the look of discontent that seemed second nature to adolescent girls. "I thought he might be with you."

Dorcas saw Lydia's attention sharpen at that, and she could cheerfully have muffled Esther. Lydia didn't need any more ammunition for her battle.

"I'm afraid not." Not now anyway.

"You'd best hurry and find him," Sarah suggested. "People will be leaving soon."

"Yah, right. See you tomorrow." Esther hurried off at something just short of a run.

"I see Hallie looking for me, so I'll be going." Lydia gave them a meaningless smile and turned on her heel.

Dorcas let out a breath, grateful for the respite, but Sarah grimaced.

"That woman. I don't know why she has such a bee in her bonnet over the school. It's not as if anyone else wants to move the school. Well, except for one or two cross-grained people who don't have kin there and think they can save some money."

"Let it go," Dorcas said. "I have." Although she couldn't help a passing thought about the reaction if Lydia really was as determined as she seemed.

"You must be more forgiving than I am." Sarah squeezed her hand briefly. "But we want you to teach our kinder, right there where we went to school."

She couldn't help but feel better at her friend's swift defense of her. "I don't think that will change, not if I have anything to say about it." She hoped.

"We won't let it," Sarah said. She glanced at Dorcas's

face. "Did you get to say what you wanted to Thomas? I mean . . . I'm not asking what it was," she added quickly.

Dorcas grinned. "Yah, you are. It's all right. I just felt that I ought to thank him."

"For speaking up at the meeting? Yah, that was gut."

"For that, and . . ."

She hesitated. She'd never told Sarah the whole of what happened that night, and she should have. She'd told herself it wasn't fair to burden her friend with the knowledge, but was it that? Or was it her own shame?

Sarah was still looking at her.

"He helped me with something a long time ago, and I never really thanked him." She hesitated, thinking she should tell her the whole thing.

But they'd walked far enough to be enveloped in a crowd of people starting to gather their families to leave, and it clearly wasn't the time.

Lemuel elbowed his way through a clump of boys headed in the opposite direction, probably to set up for tonight's singing. He reached Dorcas and grasped her arm, nodding to Sarah.

"We'd better leave. Mamm says Betsy doesn't feel so well and wants to go home."

"I'm ready." She turned to Sarah. "I'll talk to you soon."

Sarah smiled, but she was already turning to search the crowd for her own family. And Lemuel was pulling on her arm, hurrying her toward the buggy.

At least that gave her time to think before she saw Sarah again.

Betsy was already in the buggy when they reached it, with Mamm beside her holding Will and Levi pacing back and forth. When he spotted them, he climbed in.

"It's about time," he snapped.

"Take it easy, Levi." Lemuel gave her a hand up. "Dorcas didn't know you wanted to leave already."

"All right. Sorry," he added as an afterthought. "Let's just get going."

Lemuel clicked to the horse, and the buggy jolted into motion. Betsy gasped and put her hand over her mouth.

"Are you all right?" Levi leaned over her, but she pushed him away, and he looked hurt. "Don't you want me to . . ."

"For goodness' sake," Dorcas said. "Can't you see she's nauseated? Give her a little air." She'd think anyone but apparently a doting husband could have seen the greenish tinge to poor Betsy's face.

"Here, you trade places with me. If she's going to be sick, she'd rather you were in the front."

Lemuel pulled to the side while they changed, and Betsy slid into the place nearest the side. Mamm reached under the seat with one hand to pull out the thermos of water kept there.

"Dampen your handkerchief so Betsy can bathe her face. That'll make her feel better."

Dorcas did as she was told, but several years' experience with small children having upset stomachs in school had taught her that nothing would make Betsy feel better at the moment. She pressed the cloth against Betsy's forehead and hoped for the best.

At least she could be sure she'd be busy enough not to spend the rest of the day fretting about Thomas, and that was just as well. Especially when she couldn't ever seem to find the right thing to say to him.

But she had a feeling she wouldn't be able to stop trying.

THOMAS HAD SEEN Dorcas and her family leaving for home shortly after they'd talked, and he'd been relieved. If she wasn't there, then he didn't have to keep thinking about her.

Unfortunately, out of sight wasn't exactly out of mind. He'd continued to mull it over all the way home, and even now, while he was removing the harness and brushing down the buggy horse, Dorcas refused to be chased out of his thoughts.

He understood that the grown-up Dorcas was now ashamed of her part in the events that had led to his arrest. What he couldn't take was her actually thinking that he might tell on her now. Just the notion had him fuming.

How long he'd have gone on, he didn't know, but he was yanked out of his thoughts by a loud quarrel between Jonas and Adam. Since Daad had already gone in the house, he wasn't here to put an end to it.

"It's not fair," Adam shouted, sounding the favorite refrain of little brothers everywhere. "I'll bet you didn't have to stay home from a singing just to help with the milking."

Jonas looked exasperated. "You don't have to stay home. But you also don't have to run off way early. After the milking there's plenty of time to get back to the singing."

"There's a volleyball game first," Adam snapped back. "I don't see why I should miss it. Nobody else has to."

"You don't know that!" Jonas raised his voice, whatever patience he had, and it wasn't much, running out. "You're needed here, and—"

"Wait a second." Thomas had told himself he wouldn't interfere between them, but this was foolish. "I'll be here, and by now I'm as fast as Adam is. I'll take his place for the milking. How about it?"

Adam looked as if he'd burst out, but Thomas frowned him to silence. "Okay, Jonas?"

Jonas didn't speak for a moment. Then he jerked a nod. "Yah, all right," he muttered, and walked off toward the house.

Adam looked at him and grinned. "He couldn't say no, but he wanted to."

"Don't talk like that about your bruder." Thomas added a frown for emphasis. He might think Adam was right about Jonas, but he wasn't going to take sides.

"Yah, right. No problem."

That lighthearted manner of Adam's made him smile. It also reminded him of himself at that age.

"You *are* going to the singing, right?"

Adam flashed him a look. "What do you think?"

In a way, he was kind of flattered that Adam, at least, didn't have a bone to pick with him. But he certain sure didn't want to be accused of conspiring if Adam was going to do something stupid.

"I mean it," he said. "You're going to the singing and nowhere else."

"Or what?" Adam seemed to be sounding him out. "Or you'll tell Jonas?"

"Or I'll come after you and drag you back in front of whoever you're with."

Adam glared at him. "I thought you understood. You broke the rules plenty when you were my age."

"Yah, I did." When Adam started to turn away, he put a hand on the boy's shoulder. "I've been there. The rules I broke weren't worth the price I had to pay."

He thought Adam would just shake him off, but after a moment, Adam shrugged. "Yah, well, there's nothing much going on anyway. I'll go to the singing. And nowhere else. You want me to sign a contract?" He gave Thomas a half-defiant, half-kidding look.

"Your word is good enough for me." He smiled and punched him lightly on the arm. "Better go slick yourself up if you're going to impress the girls."

Adam grinned, his mood dissolved, and he scurried away, leaving Thomas to put the horse in the field beyond the barn.

Shaking his head, Thomas did so. His return had upset the apple cart more than he'd ever anticipated. He thought again of Dorcas, then of his father and brothers. Maybe things would settle down. Maybe.

First Dorcas and now his brother Adam, reminding him again of the time he'd thought he could forget. Apparently his reputation as a wild teen was not going to be wiped away very easily.

He headed back to the house, thinking that all he needed was an encounter with his father to round out the day. But before he reached the house, Esther came running to latch herself on to his arm.

"You said you'd teach me to drive the buggy. How about now?"

"Hold on a minute. I said I would if Daad said it was all right. Did you ask him?"

He got a pout in return. "He'll just tell me no. But not if you ask him. If you ask him, he'll say yes."

Esther had a lot more faith in his relationship with Daad than he did.

"All right, I'll try. If he says yes, I'll get you started. But only if Daad is okay with it."

She hugged his arm, looking up at him as if he was some kind of hero. "I knew you would."

Just what made her so sure of him? She couldn't remember him that well, given how young she was when he left.

Maybe she'd been making up an image of him in her mind while he was gone. If she persisted in thinking he was some kind of super brother, she'd be disappointed. But for the moment, it felt good to have someone around who had faith in him. He couldn't say that about many people. He pushed the thought of Dorcas firmly out of his mind.

———

NORMALLY DORCAS ENJOYED a spring shower, encouraging the tender shoots of new plants to pop up from the damp earth. But a rainy school Monday was another thing. It had been pouring at lunch time, forcing her to keep her scholars inside, and by midafternoon, their restless spirits were starting to catch up with them.

At the moment, the younger children were supposed to be printing out their spelling words, while the older ones had a practice spelling bee under Anna's direction. But there was an undertone of whispering and a bit too much movement to make her believe they were concentrating.

She glanced out, noting that the clouds had moved off to the east, and a watery sun picked out sparkles of raindrops on the grass. Stopping where she was, in a midst of a row of first graders, she collected the children's attention.

"Since we weren't able to go outside for recess today, we're going to have a short recess in ten minutes' time." At the murmur of reaction, she continued. "But only if I see serious concentration on spelling for the next ten minutes."

She didn't bother saying what would happen if they didn't concentrate. They already knew, and after an exchange of glances, they applied themselves to their tasks.

Dorcas moved forward a step, which put her between the twins. His pink tongue sticking out of the corner of his mouth to aid his concentration, Matty was printing a wobbly B. Repressing a smile, she glanced at his brother. Mark was intent, his head bent over his work.

What was it about small boys that made them so irresistible? Maybe the combination of the vulnerable back of the neck combined with their fierce concentration? They weren't all that vulnerable, she knew, having seen them hop up without a tear from a fall that would have broken a bone in an adult. But they still needed care.

Her thoughts shifted to the previous day. Poor Betsy had been afflicted with one of those short-lived bugs that made the sufferer miserable for a day. So miserable, in Betsy's case, that she didn't seem to notice that Dorcas was the one to care for her baby while Mammi took care of her.

Betsy was much better this morning, of course, and Dorcas hoped that all the rest of them wouldn't pass the illness around. In any event, she'd truly enjoyed playing mammi to Will, cuddling him, rocking him, and tucking him into his cradle, where he slept intently, his small arms above his head.

She thought again of that moment when she'd lowered him gently into the cradle. She'd been swept by an overwhelming longing to have a child of her own to cherish. It had taken her completely by surprise, and she hadn't known what to do with the feeling. She'd thought that she was completely satisfied with her life, but that urge had been like a lightning bolt shattering a summer night.

Pushing it away didn't seem to be working very well, but she reminded herself firmly that she had her scholars. She didn't need anything else, did she?

Looking at the clock, she saw that the ten minutes were almost up. "All right, boys and girls. Put your papers neatly in your desks, and then you may line up for recess."

A few minutes later she strolled along one side of the playground area, alert as always for any sign that a calming word was needed. But the scholars all seemed so pleased with the surprise recess that they weren't in the mood to scrabble with one another.

Anna, having completed her own circuit of the playground, joined her. "The bigger girls are gabbing about the program again," she reported. "They want to do it outside."

"Spring fever," Dorcas said, smiling. "You know what would happen if we planned it outdoors."

"It would rain, I suppose." She sighed. "But they will be disappointed."

"We'll plan the picnic for outdoors, then." Dorcas knew Anna was close enough to her own schooldays to be disappointed, as well. "They would feel worse if their posters and decorations were ruined."

"Yah, they would." Anna glanced back at the barn, where they could hear the sound of sawing. Dorcas followed her gaze and was just in time to see Esther disappear around the corner.

"Esther!" She headed after the girl, fuming a little. She had just reminded the children that the barn and shed area was off limits.

Esther had turned back toward her, wearing an expression of innocence that didn't fool her in the least.

"I'm sure you heard me say that this area is off limits. What are you doing?" Beyond her, Dorcas could see that Thomas had stopped his sawing and was watching them. If he didn't like it . . . well, it didn't matter what he thought. This was her school.

"I want to talk to my brother." There was a hint of defiance in her voice that Dorcas hated to hear. All of the adolescent girls were likely to have moods, but Esther had always been respectful.

"The rules apply to you as well. You'll have to talk to your brother when you get home. Come along, now."

To her relief, Esther obeyed, but the petulant expression on her face was not appropriate and certainly not normal for her. Reminding herself that Thomas's return had undoubtedly caused some upheaval in the family, she didn't pursue it, hoping Esther's sunny disposition would soon return.

Nevertheless, when it was time to dismiss her scholars, she stood on the porch and watched to be sure that Esther headed off down the road with the other children and didn't make any detours to the barn.

Anna waited with her, but once they were all out of sight, she turned to Dorcas. "Is it all right if I leave now?"

"For sure," she said, a little surprised that Anna thought she had to ask. "Your time is your own. I'm just glad you feel like spending so much of it here. You're a huge help, you know."

Anna flushed with pleasure. "I do love it. It's just that today I promised I'd help with sorting and labeling the quilted items for the Mud Sale."

"You'd best go, then. Saturday will be here before you know it. Tell your mamm that I'll be there early to help."

"I will. Denke."

Anna hurried off like a dog that had been released from its pen. Dorcas smiled, knowing that events like the annual Mud Sale were important markers in the year at Anna's age. She only hoped the Mud Sale wouldn't live up to its name this year. They'd fit most of the booths and tents on the gravel around the fire hall, but inevitably some things would extend into the field—unpleasant for everyone if it was wet.

She'd gathered up everything she needed to take home and locked the schoolhouse when she turned and found Thomas waiting for her. The frown he wore didn't bode well for his mood.

"Do you need to talk with me?" Dorcas attempted to sound patient, even though she'd rather, like Anna, speed her way home.

"Did Esther get into trouble today?"

She hesitated. Thomas wasn't Esther's parent, and normally she wouldn't talk about a child's behavior with a sibling. But these circumstances weren't normal, since it was Thomas's presence that had caused the misbehavior.

Apparently thinking her silence had gone on too long, Thomas moved impatiently and seemed about to speak. Dorcas cut in before he could start.

"It's already taken care of," she said, hoping that would satisfy him. "These things happen."

"She was coming back to see me, wasn't she? Had you told the children not to?"

"Yah, I had. I reminded them just before recess." He was clearly upset with someone, and she wasn't sure whether it was Esther or herself.

"Sorry." He seemed to say the word with difficulty. "I'll talk to her about it."

"That's not necessary. As a teacher, it's my job to deal with, and I certainly wouldn't turn to the parents for something as minor as this."

He managed a twisted smile. "No, I guess you wouldn't. But this time it involves me. I'm beginning to think it would be better for everyone if I hadn't come back."

Dorcas was caught completely by surprise. What had been going on now?

"Ach, Thomas, don't think that way." She reached out instinctively to touch his hand in sympathy. "Everything will settle down. Give it time."

He didn't speak for a moment. Then he closed his hand over hers, holding it warmly. "Denke, Dorcas." His voice was husky, and it roused a feeling in her that she couldn't immediately identify. "Remind me once in a while."

Releasing her abruptly, he strode off.

When he was out of sight, Dorcas put her hand over the place he'd held. It was still warm from his touch, and it was affecting her entirely too much for comfort.

CHAPTER EIGHT

Thomas stood where he was and watched Dorcas disappear down the lane that wove through a patch of woods to her house. He probably shouldn't have said anything about Esther to her teacher. Esther wouldn't appreciate his interference, and Dorcas probably felt the same way. She had been kinder to him than he deserved.

What possessed him to show Dorcas so much of the turmoil he felt at trying to fit into his family again? Maybe, because he'd been away for the intervening years, he'd reverted to the relationship they'd had when he left.

They had been friends after eight years of schooling together, and that friendship had continued right into their rumspringa years. Maybe, if the disaster hadn't happened, that friendship would have grown into something stronger. Maybe they'd have married and had a few kinder by now.

And maybe not. Right now he'd best finish what he was doing, pack up, and head for home. And when he got there, he'd have a little talk with Esther about her behavior. She wouldn't like it, but she'd have to admit it was better than if he'd gone straight to Daad about her misdeeds.

Disobeying the teacher's orders, followed up by impertinence. When he was her age, Daad would have responded to a report like that with a licking. Probably he wouldn't resort to that extreme with Esther, but she certain sure wouldn't get off lightly.

But when he got home, he found Daad in a rage. From the milking shed came the sound of his raised voice. Esther? Had the news about Esther's behavior at school reached him already?

Then he spotted Esther coming around the house. She glanced at him, glanced in the direction of the milking shed, and seemed to decide to avoid both of them. Instead, she scurried off down the path that led to the creek.

Deciding he'd best find out what was going on before he did anything, Thomas headed into the house. Mamm would know. Daad was the disciplinarian, but Mamm always had her say.

Once inside, he followed the rhythmic hum of the sewing machine into the back room that was given over to Mamm's sewing and quilting. She bent over the machine, her feet working the treadle in a steady movement, face intent. In the moment before she noticed him, he was able to study her in a way he hadn't done since he'd returned.

Mamm's hair, once the same dark auburn as his, was sprinkled with gray, showing most strongly along the sides where it was drawn firmly back under her kapp. It seemed to him that she was smaller than she'd been when he left, or maybe it was just that he was bigger. Her hands were beginning to look like Grossmammi's . . . thin, strong, and showing the veins and bones beneath the skin more clearly.

The signs of age affected him more than he'd have thought, and he moved slightly, drawing her attention. She glanced up at him, nodded slightly, and whipped the fabric off when the needle came to the end of the row.

He nodded at the print fabric that wouldn't ever be used for Amish clothing. "Making a new quilt for the sale?" He moved toward her.

Shaking her head, she smoothed out the piece. "Not enough time for that, but I thought I could do another table runner. They sell pretty good, ain't so?"

"I never bought one, Mammi. It's not something I'd be likely to know."

He smiled when she swatted at him, glad she didn't seem unduly upset about whoever was in trouble with Daad.

"You ought to take an interest. You'll marry one day, and if your wife is a quilter, you'll have to know these things."

There was the first spoken hint. Now that he'd returned home where she felt he belonged, Mamm would start thinking about a daughter-in-law to provide her with grandbabies.

"That's jumping too far ahead," he said, putting his arm across her shoulder and hugging her. "What's going on out there?"

"Adam is in trouble." She looked both worried and exasperated, it seemed. "Why you young ones can't understand that whatever you do, someone will see, I don't know."

"Not only see, but apparently tell, in this case. How did Daad hear anyway?"

She shot him a sharp look. "You don't know anything about this, do you?"

"No, but I can guess it's something about the singing last night, since that's the only place he's gone lately." His mind switched off to the thought of Adam assuring him that he wouldn't go anywhere but the singing. Apparently he should have also insisted on proper behavior once he got there. "What did he do? Upset the punch? Quarrel with someone over a girl?"

"Nothing." Her lips formed a straight line. "He didn't show up at the singing at all. And there he was, getting home at eleven as bright as can be, letting on he'd been at the singing all evening."

Thomas's stomach clenched. So. It looked as if Adam's

promise wasn't worth much. And there he'd been, flattering himself that he was being a good guide to his little brother. He'd apparently just encouraged him to think Thomas easily fooled.

The disappointment was stronger than he would have anticipated. Maybe this was what it felt like to be Daad, not only ashamed that the whole community knew about your child's misdeeds, but also cut by the thought that his child couldn't be trusted.

Of course, as he remembered it, Daad never had trusted him. Maybe he'd changed with the younger ones. Maybe he'd trusted Adam and learned the trust was misplaced. If so, he probably felt just as bad as Thomas did right now. And that was a funny thing for Thomas to realize.

Mamm's head came up, and she seemed to be listening. "Your daad's coming in. Maybe best not to say anything."

He nodded. He didn't need to tell her that talking to Daad about his children's misdeeds was the last thing he'd consider doing.

Hearing Daad's footsteps coming down the hall toward the sewing room, he slipped out by the door that led through the pantry and on into the kitchen on the other side. Mamm was the best person to handle Daad right now.

Once he was outside, Thomas wasn't sure what he wanted to do. When he'd been living with his aunt and uncle, he'd grown fond of his younger cousins and been glad to help and guide them. But this was different, maybe because he hadn't felt a real sense of responsibility for them the way he did for his brothers and sister.

Now Esther had gone off the rails at school, and Adam . . . Adam, whom he'd trusted . . . had lied and broken his word. That was what hurt the most. He'd had plenty of experience with not being trusted. It had been painful, and so he'd been glad to trust his young brother.

One thing he knew for sure. He had to talk with Adam. Now. But where was he?

He walked toward the empty milking shed, where Adam and Daad had obviously had their set-to. But somehow his steps turned toward the barn, and then he knew why. When he'd been young and in trouble, needing to be alone, he'd found a spot in the farthest corner of the barn loft. Protected by a surrounding wall of hay bales, he'd been free to mull over his troubles.

No way of being sure that Adam had found the small safe spot, but it was worth a try.

He walked into the barn and approached the ladder. Quiet. Not a sound from above. But then he noticed wisps of hay fluttering down to the barn floor from the far corner of the loft. Moving quietly, he climbed the ladder.

Adam must have heard him coming across the loft, but he didn't move. He sat with his knees drawn up to his chin, his arms around his legs as if he wanted to make himself as small as possible. Thomas felt a pang of sympathy, but he couldn't allow it to control him. For an instant, he wondered if Daad had felt that with him.

"Got yourself in a mess, haven't you?" He kept his voice level with an effort.

"You don't need to start. I already heard it from Daad." Adam stared at the wide boards of the loft.

"Yah, but I'm the one you promised. I'm the one you lied to."

Adam slid a sidelong, shamefaced glance at him and then resumed his study of the floor. "Sorry."

"So, why? Why make a promise if you didn't mean to keep it?" He didn't know if he wanted to hug his brother or shake him.

Adam muttered into his knees. So far as Thomas could tell, he was saying that he didn't mean to.

"What was so important that you had to break your word?"

Adam flared up, glaring at him. "You're a good one to talk. Look at all the trouble you—" He stopped as fast as he'd started, flushing.

"Yah, I got into trouble." Thomas's voice was heavy. Consequences kept coming at him. "But I never broke my word."

Daad hadn't believed that, but it happened to be true.

"You did break your word," Thomas continued. "So I know I can't trust you." Swamped by a sense of the futility of it all, he turned away.

Before he reached the ladder, he heard a scramble behind him. Adam rushed across the loft and propelled himself into Thomas's arms, just as he had done when he was a child who looked up to his big brother.

Thomas held him, the ice inside his heart melting a little. He could cope with the consequences of the past, or he could leave again. Right now, he thought it might be worth the struggle to stay.

BY THURSDAY, DORCAS, with Anna's help, had prepared the speaking parts for the end-of-school program. This wasn't a matter of showing off individual talents, but a way of letting parents see the work the scholars had done throughout the year. And incidentally, to have some fun with parents and schoolmates before the summer break.

Not that her scholars wouldn't be working over the summer. They'd all have chores to do at home, and most of those would be learning experiences as well. She gestured to Anna, who was pitching the ball to some of the younger children during recess.

Turning the job over to one of the older girls, Anna came to join her. "Is it time to go in already?" She looked as if she'd been enjoying the game as much as the young ones did.

"Not quite, but I wanted to talk with you about the spring program. We'll give out the parts this afternoon, yah?"

Anna nodded. "They're ready to go. The kinder will be excited to have them."

"That's what I'm worried about," Dorcas said, smiling to show she wasn't serious. "We'll have to be ready for learning to slide as spring fever sets in."

Anna dimpled. "I remember."

"Yah, I'm sure you do. We'll do the best we can. I think we'd best wait until the last half hour of the day for working on it. Otherwise, they'll never be able to concentrate for the rest of the afternoon."

They stood together, watching their scholars, and Dorcas thought how much Anna had matured this year. She'd seen it before—those months when a girl turns from being a child to becoming a young woman, but it always surprised her how quickly it could come. In that, boys lagged behind, it seemed, even though many of them were doing men's work at that age.

"Esther has behaved since you spoke to her on Monday," Anna said, showing her awareness of any behavior problems. "She's still showing off a bit about her brother, though."

"I noticed." Dorcas glanced at Esther, wondering whether or not Thomas had spoken to her after their talk on Monday. She rather hoped he hadn't. "I hope he can cope with her hero worship until it wears off."

Checking the time, she reached for the bell rope. "Time to get back to work."

With the scholars reassembled, still flushed from running around outside, Dorcas switched to the schedule she'd developed for the last month of school. Reading aloud came after recess, to allow them time to cool off and settle down. Then a session of spelling and writing, another of arithmetic, and last the time devoted to working on the program.

As Anna started passing out the parts for the program, an irresistible wave of chatter swept through the classroom. "Let's try not to lose your parts this year," Dorcas reminded them. "Each day, we'll spend some time in the afternoon working on our posters and displays and practicing the parts and songs."

A hand began waving among the first graders. "Yah, Matthew." Inevitably, it was Sarah and Noah's older twin.

"Our daadi made the props for the Christmas program. I'll bet he'd make anything we need for this one, too."

"Matthew has reminded me that I want you to ask your families if they're willing to help with the picnic or the program." Several hands went up, and she shook her head. "We don't volunteer anyone without asking first, ain't so?" The hands went back down again. "You can tell me next week. Everyone is busy with the Mud Sale right now."

Heads nodded, and then was a certain amount of wiggling. Everyone liked the Mud Sale, from the youngest children to the great-grandparents. It was fun, but it was also distracting.

She and Anna divided the class into age groups and began working with each of them on what they'd do for the program. The rest of the afternoon passed quickly, with everyone engrossed. From what Dorcas could hear, they were still talking excitedly as they headed off for home. She realized, once they were gone, that she had forgotten to give her usual warning about avoiding the neighbor's property. But surely by this time they'd become used to staying on the verge of the road.

Dorcas still wasn't comfortable with that, but there seemed to be no alternative. Their neighbor hadn't given any sign of relenting, and certainly hadn't responded to any signs of friendliness. Shrugging it off, she finished her final chores.

When she emerged onto the porch, she could still hear the sounds of hammering coming from the stable. She turned that way, hesitated, and turned back again. Then she told herself that she ought to assure Thomas that his sister was back to her usual good behavior and headed off to the stable.

Dorcas reached the stable and had to lean back in order to see him up in the rafters. He had apparently not heard her come in. He was balancing seemingly effortlessly on a four-by-four rafter, reaching above his head to tap at something in the roof.

A chance to study him without notice didn't come along all that often. His position frightened her, although he seemed perfectly comfortable on his precarious perch. He'd been a tall, gangly teenager when he went away, but he'd filled out to match his height. He moved easily, the muscles of his back flexing as he reached and lowered.

Choosing a moment when he wasn't reaching up, she spoke. "I don't want to disturb you when you're working."

He looked down, smiling. "But you will."

When she began to speak, he shook his head. "Just kidding. I'm glad to take a break. What's up? Don't tell me my sister is acting up again."

"No, just the opposite." She watched him swing down, climb along the top of a stall, and drop to the floor. "I know you were concerned the other day, so I thought I'd assure you that all is well."

"That's good to hear." He took a step closer to her. "We don't need more of the family finding trouble."

Dorcas decided to ignore the slight bitterness in his voice. "Did you speak to her about it on Monday?"

"No." He looked slightly startled, as if he'd forgotten his intention. "Something . . . well, one of the others was in trouble with Mamm and Daad when I got home, and it didn't seem the time."

"I'm sure it wasn't. It's just as well, since she got over her problem on her own."

He must, she'd think, have meant Adam, but Thomas apparently didn't want to talk about it. Happy-go-lucky Adam had been a good student with a flair for mischief, much like Thomas.

"I guess that is better." He frowned. "But it shouldn't have happened in the first place. Mamm would be embarrassed if she knew."

"I'm sure your mamm knows enough about the moods of adolescent girls not to take it seriously. They change by the day . . . sometimes by the minute."

"Not like us guys," he teased, his worried look vanishing.

"The boys are just as bad, but it hits them later," she said, and wished she hadn't. It might seem a reference to his troubles, and she hadn't meant it that way.

But he just shrugged. "She does seem to have turned into a chameleon these days. But I'm glad to know she's behaving."

"Yah, well, I'll let you get back to your work. Sorry to interrupt."

"I'm always glad to see you, Dorcas," he said lightly, his eyes crinkling as always when he teased. He stepped up on a stall bar and then paused. "By the way, I probably won't be here tomorrow. It seems Mamm volunteered me to help build the stalls for the Mud Sale."

She couldn't help smiling. "I know the feeling. My mother volunteered me to help with the quilts. And I was just telling my scholars that they must not volunteer people to help with the spring program without asking first."

Thomas grinned in response. "I think maybe mothers are exempt from that rule. I guess I'll see you down at the fire hall then."

He turned to look down at her, missed his handhold, and hung by one hand for a perilous second. Dorcas dashed toward him with a confused thought of breaking his fall.

But there was no need. Just as quickly, his feet found a cross rail and he pulled himself up to perch on the timber above him. He smiled down into her face, which was likely the color of a sheet.

"Going to catch me, Dorcas?" His eyes sparkled.

Annoyed to find her hands shaking, Dorcas felt like throwing something at him. "You'd better not get too confident," she said. "Or next time I'll let you hit the ground."

She walked out of the barn with the sound of his laughter in her ears.

BY THE TIME she reached home, Dorcas had thought of a number of smart remarks she could have made to Thomas. Unfortunately, that would just have encouraged him. Underneath the grown-up seriousness she'd seen still lurked the boy who'd liked nothing better than teasing. Well, she wasn't going to play into his hands.

To her surprise, Betsy was busy at the stove when she walked in the house. As far as she could recall, Betsy hadn't fixed supper since little Will was born.

"It certain sure smells good in here," she said, hanging up the sweater she'd hardly needed today. "Is everyone all right?" She couldn't help wondering if Mammi was sick, given that she was always in the kitchen at this time of day.

"Denke, Dorcas. I'm making a pot roast." She raised the lid of the Dutch oven to peer at the contents. "Everyone's fine. Your mother is sewing, and she's listening for Will in case he wakes."

It probably wouldn't be tactful to express surprise, so

she contented herself with a nod. "Sorry I'm a little late."
She paused to wash her hands at the sink. "Tell me what
I can do to help."

Betsy glanced around the kitchen as if assessing her
progress. "I guess just set the table. It's almost ready." She
hesitated. "Denke."

Dorcas began pulling out plates and silverware. Whatever had brought about this change in Betsy, she was all
for it, but she couldn't ask.

"I hope Mammi's not working on something else for
the Mud Sale. We're supposed to sort everything tomorrow and set up for Saturday, and I hear there's plenty.
There's no need to rush anything else."

"I know. My mamm stopped by today to insist that I
bake something for the baked goods stand." Betsy hesitated a minute, not meeting her gaze. "She said it's time I
started doing my share, now that Will is a bit bigger."

So that was it. Betsy's mother was noted for organizing
everyone and everything she could. It sounded as if Betsy
had been on her list. What was the right thing to say? If
she agreed with Betsy's mamm, Betsy would probably be
upset.

"You know Mamm and I are always ready to help."
Dorcas put napkins at all the places, hoping Betsy hadn't
noticed her hesitation. "I do hope we can get Mamm to
come and help with the Mud Sale. Don't you think it
would be gut for her to get out more?"

Betsy looked surprised for a moment, as if she'd gotten
used to having Mamm at home all the time. "Yah, I guess
it would. I'll try to get her to go."

Levi came in the back door, wiping his shoes on the
mat. "Get who to go where?" he asked, giving his wife a
squeeze.

"We're hoping to get Mammi to go in and help set up
for the Mud Sale."

Levi shrugged. "Going to rain, I'm afraid."

"What? No, you must be wrong. Not another muddy Mud Sale."

Her brother grinned. "I don't control the weather, but it looks like rain coming tomorrow for sure."

Dorcas threw his napkin at him. "Don't say things like that."

He fielded the napkin easily. "Okay. But don't you say I didn't warn you."

Unfortunately, Levi turned out to be right. Dorcas woke in the morning to the sound of rain drumming on the roof and pouring down the windowpanes. Groaning, she pulled the quilt over her face. A rainy Friday. The children would be difficult, the playground soaked, and the field around the fire hall a sea of mud.

Rain or not, school must go on. Since the stable at school was unusable while Thomas was working on it, Lemuel drove her to school and agreed to pick her up afterward and take her to the fire hall. Goodness knew how they would all manage to get things ready inside.

She gave a passing thought to Thomas. At least she wouldn't run into him during setup. The men would probably have done what little they could during the day. Everyone would have to be there very early on Saturday to finish getting ready before the first customers came flooding in.

Thomas intruded into her thoughts again, and she pushed him out irritably. Given how she always came off the loser during their encounters, the less she saw of him the better.

CHAPTER NINE

Thomas dashed through showers from the house to the barn Friday afternoon. He'd said he'd help with the booths for the Mud Sale, and that would go on whether it was raining or not. Ducking into the barn was like entering a warm cave, and it seemed cozy with the rain drumming on the roof and the familiar smells of hay, straw, and animals.

Despite the dimness, he could see the buggy horses peering over their stall rails at him. No doubt each was hoping he wasn't picked to go out in the rain. They'd much rather stay in the warmth. Well, so would he, but it couldn't be helped.

"Sorry, but I've got to leave." He swung open the nearest stall door and patted the bay gelding. "You're not afraid of a little rain, are you?"

He heard movement above him, and Adam's face looked down at him much as the horses had. "Don't you know enough to stay out of the rain?" He smiled a little uncertainly, as if unsure whether Thomas would recognize it as a joke.

"Can't be helped. The Mud Sale goes on rain or shine, ain't so? I said I'd help set up today, not that we'll be able to put anything outside if this keeps on going. But I suppose we can put the stalls together and have them ready to move outside when the rain finally stops. If it does."

As Thomas spoke, Adam was sliding down the ladder, not bothering with the steps. "It doesn't look like it'll stop anytime soon."

They stood together looking out the open barn door at the sheets of rain pouring down, turning everything misty gray. It was the kind of rain that went on all day, but he wasn't going to admit that to Adam.

"Ach, it won't keep up this hard much longer. I'll get the harness on Jake and by then it'll slack off."

"I'll give you a hand," Adam offered. He lifted the harness from its hook while Thomas brought Jake out, the gelding stepping neatly and reluctantly from the stall. Adam hesitated, looking sidelong at Thomas. "I could come along and help with the setup. Okay?"

Thomas shrugged. "Fine by me, but you'll have to ask Daad." He knew better than to take anything for granted where Daad was concerned. Especially when it involved Adam.

"Thing is, Daad's not too happy with me right now." He reddened. "Guess that's fair. You probably aren't, either."

"We had all that out," Thomas said. "It's done with."

"So maybe you'd ask Daad. Please? I guess he doesn't trust me very much right now, but if I'm with you, I can't get into trouble."

Thomas winced at the word. Trust seemed to be in short supply around the Fisher place. Still, the boy deserved a second chance to do the right thing.

"Okay, I'll ask him. But whatever he says, goes." He looked out at the rain. "Soon as it eases up."

Adam smiled as he eased the headstall over Jake's head. "I don't think he'll object as long as I'm with you. I already told him how sorry I was. It wasn't worth it."

"What wasn't?" Did the boy mean apologizing wasn't worth it?

"Skipping the singing, I mean. But some of the guys asked me, and I didn't like to say no."

Thomas leaned against the stall, watching him. "Englisch guys?"

"Well, yah." He flushed again.

"So what was it? A drinking party?"

"I didn't have any," Adam said, too fast.

"Meaning they did?"

He nodded. "Not much. A couple cans of beer is all. One of the guys has a car, and we just drove around."

"If they were drinking and driving, and they were stopped, you'd be picked up, too." He tried to point it out in a colorless tone, not wanting to put the boy's back up. But riding with someone who'd been drinking was a dangerous thing to do, and Adam ought to realize it.

Adam looked startled. "I . . . I didn't think of that," he muttered.

Maybe it was best not to say anything more about it and trust that the point had gotten through. If he could make a difference for Adam, it could make up a little for all the other stuff he'd done.

"Looks like it's not so bad now," Thomas said. "I'll go see what Daad says." He darted out into a light drizzle.

Daad was sitting at the kitchen table with a mug of coffee. Mammi, at the counter, raised the coffeepot and looked at Thomas with a question. He shook his head.

"No, thanks, Mammi. I just wanted to ask Daad something."

"Yah?" Daad set the mug down.

"I'm headed for the fire hall to set up for the Mud Sale. Jacob asked me to help with putting the booths together. Mind if I take Adam? We could use the help."

He knew immediately that the answer was no. Daad

didn't even take the time to think about it. "The boy's being punished. He can't go anywhere."

Thomas tried to take it lightly. "I'd make sure he worked. No fooling around."

Daad didn't look impressed. "Like you did Sunday night?" The edge in his voice was sharp enough to cut yourself on.

Thomas could only stare at him for a moment. "I didn't have anything to do with Sunday night. I wasn't there."

"You encouraged him."

Thomas's temper spiked. "I did not. Why would I?"

Daad shoved away from the table and stood, glaring at him. "No way of knowing. But he never thought of such behavior until you came back."

He felt as if Daad had hit him in the face. Behind his father, Mammi stood with her hand to her lips, obviously shocked and pained. But she wouldn't say anything, not in front of him anyway.

His lips were numb, but he managed to spit the words out. "I see nothing's changed. You didn't trust me seven years ago, and you don't trust me now."

He spun and charged out the door. Nothing had changed. Nothing would change. So what was he doing here?

AFTER A SCHOOL day that would have tried the patience of a martyr, Dorcas finally reached the fire hall. Several buggies had been pulled into the only cover there was, a canopy stretched along the side of the hall for tomorrow's auction. The rain, after pouring down in the afternoon, decided to lessen into a steady, depressing gray shower that appeared to have no end.

Lemuel drew up by the door. "Here you are. Don't get wet. I'll come back for you later."

Dorcas hurried down and under the shelter of the small

roof over the door. "You don't have to come back for me. Someone will be going our way and drop me off."

He nodded, settling his shoulders against the steady raindrops that darkened his jacket. "See you at home. Stay dry." His smile flickered, and then he clucked to the gelding and drove off.

Dorcas ducked inside and was enveloped in an atmosphere of dampness, warmth, and chatter. On the far side, one of the engine bays had been emptied of its truck, and the men had obviously been busy putting the stands together. The materials had all been stored in the long shed behind the fire hall, where they lived from one event to another. They were ready to be brought out and assembled each time an event was held, and they got plenty of use with one thing and another.

Several of the men still worked on what were probably the last few stands. Her stomach seemed to do a complicated flip when she realized that Thomas was among them, standing on a stepladder to nail a top piece in place. He'd taken off his jacket, and suspenders crossed his broad shoulders.

Dorcas tore her gaze away before someone saw her, and she hurriedly focused on hanging her damp jacket on a wall hook where it could steam above the radiator.

Groups of women had appropriated some of the long tables that were used for community suppers. They worked around them, organizing materials for various booths, and the air was filled with the hum of their conversation, punctuated by an occasional laugh. A work frolic, that was what it was called, and these events always lived up to their names.

The longest table had been given over to sorting the many pieces that had been donated for the quilt auction. It was the biggest fund-raiser of the year, and every woman who did any quilting at all wanted to have her quilts in the auction. Full-size quilts, place mats, baby quilts, table runners, wall hangings, even potholders were donated and usually brought in generous prices.

Dorcas spotted Sarah among the woman working there, so Dorcas squeezed between tables toward her. At the moment, Sarah was pinning a small piece of paper to the corner of a quilted wall hanging. The paper contained an identifying number that could be checked against the master list. That would tell the auctioneer who the maker was, as well as an estimated value.

If the auctioneer felt the bidding wasn't high enough, he had his own methods of jollying the crowd along to push it up. Most people agreed that, with a good crowd, the items would bring a better price that way than any other method of selling them. The advantage of a good crowd for the auction was that people would get caught up in the excitement and spend more than they'd intended, even for small items like potholders.

Of course, more rain tomorrow would keep folks away, so there would be lots of prayers tonight for fair weather tomorrow. If the crowd was small, the take would be less. Some lucky buyer might get a handmade quilt for considerably less than its value. On the other hand, the school and the fire hall would be the losers.

She finally got around the last table, no easy feat as close together as they were, and reached Sarah.

"Wilkom." Sarah folded the hanging and put it on a separate stack with others of its kind and turned to give her a welcoming smile. "I was sure you'd come over as soon as school was out. Rain or no rain."

"I wouldn't miss it, no matter the weather." Dorcas pulled over the next item and set to work even as she spoke. "And I'm glad to escape the schoolroom on a day

like this. My students make even more noise than a hall
full of women. And labeling quilts is easier than keeping
my scholars occupied."

Sarah chuckled. "You don't need to tell me that. I left
Noah trying to finish what he could before the twins came
home. He knew he wouldn't have any peace when I was
gone."

"He should put them to work at something where they
can expend a lot of energy," Dorcas said. "But I don't suppose he wants them racing around his workshop. It's a
long day for the younger ones when they can't get outside.
Although I have to admit that some of the older scholars
can be just as pesky when it's raining, especially the boys.
They'd start wrestling in the cloakroom if I gave them a
chance."

"Which you don't, I'm sure. Yes, I remember those
days." Sarah glanced around the room. "Did you speak to
your mamm about coming to help?"

Dorcas nodded. "I hoped she'd come along with Lemuel when he picked me up at school and brought me in,
but she didn't show up. I guess the weather discouraged
her, or maybe Betsy needed her for something."

"I guess Betsy didn't need her too much, from what I
can see."

"What do you mean?"

Sarah gestured toward the door. To Dorcas's astonish-
ment, Mamm was coming in with Sarah's grandmother.
"Never underestimate the power of my grandmother to
get people to do what she thinks they should," she said
smugly. "I suggested this would be a good thing, and she
was happy to help."

Dorcas couldn't help laughing a little at herself. "I
guess your grandmother did it better than I did. Why is it
that older people will listen to their contemporaries when
they won't listen to us?"

"Aren't we the same?" Sarah asked. "I suspect I know some things about you that your mother doesn't. And the same is true of me."

"Yah, that's so." She had to agree. And there were some things even Sarah didn't know. She gave an inadvertent glance at Thomas, who was nailing a painted sign to the top of a booth.

Sarah followed her gaze, though her hands never stopped their work. "I guess you're seeing a good bit of Thomas Fisher these days, ain't so?"

"Too much," she said quickly, giving in to her thoughts and worries. That earned her a questioning look from Sarah.

"Why too much?" Sarah's eyebrows lifted. "There's nothing wrong with that, is there? After all, you're both free. And you were very close when you were teenagers. We all thought . . ."

Dorcas shrugged, deciding to ignore that last statement. She glanced around, but the buzz of talk and the sound of hammering made enough noise to cover a low-voiced conversation. But she'd best keep this talk light if she could.

"Thomas has enough on his mind with settling into his family again and starting his business. He doesn't have time for anything else. At least, he shouldn't," she amended. Sometimes she thought he was ready to forget all of that and let himself go, and then he'd become grave with what she supposed were memories and worries.

"And what about you? How do you feel about him?" Sarah wasn't one to let things go.

She focused on what was the least of her problems with Thomas. "I have enough trouble with people interfering with my school and trying to cause problems. I don't need Thomas around teasing me and making me feel like I'm sixteen again."

"So does he make you feel that way?" The light in
Sarah's eyes told her she'd said exactly the wrong thing if
she wanted to dampen Sarah's interest in what passed between her and Thomas.

"No, he—" She stopped, knowing it was no good trying
to make Sarah believe that. "Well, maybe some. Which
means I need to see as little of him as possible."

"I don't know about that," Sarah said, a teasing note in
her voice. "You're not that much of an old maid, ain't so?"

"You're just so happy now that you're married that you
want everyone else to feel the same," Dorcas retorted.

"Nothing wrong with that." Sarah was openly laughing
at her now.

"Not for me," she said firmly, and turned to the next
quilt.

Sarah, apparently deciding she'd teased enough, did the
same. They worked together in harmony, and Dorcas enjoyed watching the stacks of quilted products rise higher.

"Ach, it's even better than I hoped." Dorcas turned to
find her mother admiring the colorful stack of quilts. "I
knew we'd do well, but this is wonderful. We should bring
in a gut amount for the school, ain't so?"

"And the volunteer firemen," Dorcas added, smiling at
her mother. "Yah, I'm sure of it. Even if the weather isn't
perfect, people will turn up and bid with a display like this."

Mammi nodded agreement, and she looked livelier
than she had in weeks. Mammi's enthusiasm made her
feel hopeful about getting Mammi out and involved again.

"I thought you wouldn't have wanted to come in the
rain, or Lemuel could have brought both of us," she added.

"Yah, I did think I'd stay at home." Her mother actually flushed a bit. "But Sarah's grossmammi wouldn't let
me. She said I wouldn't melt if I got wet."

"And you didn't." Sarah's grandmother reached across
them to touch the stack of wall hangings, which promptly

collapsed in a colorful jumble. "Ach, I'm sorry. I didn't mean to do that. I'm no help, doing something to slow you down."

"It's fine." Sarah pulled a large box from under the table. "Time we started putting them in the boxes, ready for tomorrow. We can't leave them lying out."

"Should we leave the boxes here on the table?" Dorcas began stacking the wall hangings neatly in the carton. "I guess we'd best label the boxes so we can find things quickly for the auctioneer tomorrow."

"Yah, I brought a marker with me," Sarah said. "I think it was decided to put the boxes on the side wall near the door out to where the auction will be. We should put all the same things together in case Ben wants to auction them that way." Ben Schmidt was the auctioneer who volunteered every year. "He'll want to save pieces made for Englisch bidders for when the most people are there, so they should be boxed separately, I think."

Dorcas nodded. They both knew that some of the quilts had been made with prints and designs and colors to appeal to the taste of Englisch bidders. She'd seen Ben in action a number of times, and always marveled at how he managed to get the most out of any sale he did. She started to pick up the filled carton, but Mammi put out a hand and stopped her.

"Let someone else do the carrying while you go ahead with your work." She called out. "Here, Thomas. If you're not doing anything else just now, come and carry these boxes for us."

So much for Dorcas's resolve to stay well away from Thomas. Even Mammi was innocently throwing them together. At least, she supposed it was innocent on her part.

Thomas came, of course. He could hardly ignore a call for help. Would he think her mother was trying to bring them together?

It was what she was afraid of. Mammi hadn't given up on getting her daughter married, often pointing out that a daughter was a daughter, something she could hardly deny. She knew what that cryptic sentence meant. It meant a daughter was supposed to provide some granddaughters. And grandsons, of course.

Not that Dorcas would mind having a baby daughter one day. She remembered those moments when she'd held baby Will and once again she felt a longing she'd never known. But things were far too complicated when it came to Thomas.

Still, she managed to greet him cheerfully. She indicated the finished carton, which Sarah had labeled. "This goes over on the table by the wall, and there's another that'll be ready in a moment." Sarah was already putting quilts in place.

He nodded, his face even more expressionless than usual. "I'll wait and take them both at once."

"Gut." She hesitated. Something was wrong—it didn't take much insight to know that. The moment she'd seen him up close, she'd sensed there was a problem. Trouble with his family?

She couldn't help thinking that Thomas's return wasn't going as smoothly as his mother probably wished. Maybe she'd been too optimistic about how this would go.

Mammi had wandered off to help someone else, having done her spot of matchmaking, and Sarah was busy at the end of the table. She took advantage of their momentary isolation.

"Something is wrong, ain't so?"

His jaw tightened until it looked as if it would break. "You might say that." He spat out the words as if he were trying to find someone to vent his anger on.

"I'm sorry." There was probably little else to say. "If you want to talk about it . . ."

For a moment he stared at her as if he disliked her.

"Talking won't help. It never does." His bitterness made the words sting like a slap. "Sorry. I need to get out of here." Ignoring the carton, he charged through the milling crowd of women and out the door.

Dorcas picked up the carton and carried it over to the table herself, hoping no one had noticed what happened. She'd like to be angry at Thomas's behavior, but she couldn't. He was hurting, and that made him strike out, like an injured animal snarling at its rescuer. His pain made tears sting her eyes, and she wished she could disappear as well. But she couldn't. She had to stay here and pretend everything was all right.

TIME MOVED ON, and people began to leave as they finished their projects. Dorcas's mother left with a group of older women, and Dorcas stayed on to finish up preparations for the auction. Sarah would drop her at home when they were done.

As Sarah marked the last few boxes, Dorcas gathered up stray pieces of tissue and paper. "I'll take this out to the trash bin unless you need me to do something else."

Sarah straightened, putting her hands on her lower back and stretching. She glanced around the hall, seeming satisfied with what she saw. "That sounds gut. I'm almost finished with these, and then I'll be ready to leave. You must be starved."

Dorcas shook her head, her arms full. "Not too bad. Lemuel brought me a sandwich and a thermos of coffee, so I did have something before we started."

"Gut. We'll have to be here early tomorrow, ain't so?"

One glance told Dorcas just how tired her friend was. "There's no need for you to come early. Why don't you sleep in? Everything is organized for the auction, and there will be plenty of help here tomorrow, ain't so?"

"We'll see." Sarah was noncommittal, and Dorcas suspected that nothing would keep her from doing what she thought was her duty. Maybe she could get Noah and the twins to convince her.

Smiling a little at the thought, she headed out the door, pushing the bar with her hip to maneuver the armload through. She ducked automatically as she stepped outside and then realized it wasn't necessary. The rain had stopped, and the air was full of the scent of growth. She tipped her head back to see a star-filled sky.

Her spirits rose. It would be muddy for sure, but a sunny spring day meant a good sale.

Dorcas had put her load into the trash bin and turned back when she realized she wasn't alone. A figure moved in the darkness, giving her a momentary fright. Then she saw it was Thomas. He came toward her, one side of his face lit as he passed the glow from the window and then in shadow again.

"Mad at me, Dorcas?" His voice still had that tightly controlled sound, but at least he was talking.

She considered. "Not mad. Just wishing . . . well, that things were going better for you." She looked at his face and then away. "And that you had someone to talk to who could help."

"You think that would work?" He sounded unconvinced. "I can't see that it does much good."

"If it improved your mood, it'd be worth it."

He froze for an instant, and then his smile broke through. "Never afraid to say what you think—that's our Dorcas."

"Not always." Her thoughts fled to the time when she hadn't spoken out.

"Forget that," he said, his voice gruff. He seemed to read her thoughts with no effort at all. "I told you it worked out for the best."

"Still . . . I owe you, Thomas. If I can't help, at least I

can listen." Her hand went out to him, but then she drew it back, afraid of pushing.

For a moment his face was rigid in the dim light, as if he held out against her. Then he seemed to give in, all in an instant, his expression softening and his stiff shoulders relaxing.

"It's Daad," he muttered. "I don't know how my mother got him to say he wanted me back, but it's not true."

She felt the pain as if she'd been struck. "You must be wrong . . . he can't want you to leave again."

"No? You underestimate him." His mouth twisted wryly. "He didn't trust me when I was young, and he still doesn't. He managed to hide it for a time, but it came right back out again as soon as he had an excuse."

"But why? You haven't done anything to earn that attitude." She knew the man was rigid in his beliefs, but this seemed impossible.

"He thinks I'm to blame for Adam getting into mischief. Says Adam never thought of such a thing before I came back, giving him ideas."

"But that's ridiculous." If there was one thing she knew, it was kids Adam's age. "He's been prime for mischief since he was a six-year-old. I taught him, remember? I can easily predict which ones will go a little wild during rumspringa."

"Personal experience?" His voice lightened.

"For sure," she said. "But also it's from watching my scholars for all these years. This is about him missing the singing, I suppose."

"You knew about it?"

She shrugged. "My scholars talk all the time. You don't think Esther would miss an opportunity to tell her friends about it, do you?"

"I guess not. What he did wasn't all that bad, but Daad's carrying on like he broke all ten of the commandments. It's just making Adam resentful. Believe me, I know."

"Personal experience?" She repeated his words.

"Yah." The lines in his face deepened as he seemed to mull it over. "I remember the first time it happened to me. I told the truth about something that had happened, but he just yelled louder." He grimaced. "I soon learned. Daad wouldn't believe me no matter what I said, so I figured if I was still going to get punished, I might as well get some fun out of it."

He said the words lightly, but she could hear the pain beneath them, buried so deep that Thomas probably didn't recognize it himself until he saw it happening to Adam.

"And that was nothing compared to the way he acted when the police got in touch the night of the party." His voice grated now, the pain coming closer to the surface. "He didn't come to pick me up, did you know that? All the other kids were picked up by their parents, but he left me sitting there in the police station until morning. And when he did come, he acted as if I were a stranger—a stranger who'd outworn his welcome. I was a disappointment, he said. If I stayed around, I'd just be a bad example to the younger ones. So I had to leave." He came to a stop, sounding as if his breath had run out.

"I'm sorry." Her voice broke with the tears that weren't far off. "So sorry." This time she reached out, grasping his arm, longing to comfort him and not caring about anything else.

"Dorcas." He said her name, very softly, and reached up to touch her cheek. His face twisted, and then she was in his arms and he was holding her as if he'd never let go . . . kissing her as if there was nothing beyond this moment.

There wasn't. Her mind stopped functioning, and the world narrowed down to this moment with his lips on hers and her body close against his. This was what she'd wanted. This was what she'd been waiting for.

Then it was over. Thomas pushed her away, and the cool air where his lips had been chilled her to the bone.

"No. We can't." He threw the words at her. "I shouldn't have. It was my fault."

She couldn't let him think that. She reached for him, but he struck her hands away.

"Don't." His voice went deep with pain. "I can't, don't you see? I can't stay. Not with my father the way he is. I should never have come back."

For the briefest of moments, his hand cupped her cheek again, but this time it felt like good-bye. And then he was gone.

He was gone, and in that instant she knew she loved him. That was what had been happening all along—she'd been falling in love with him. And now it was over.

CHAPTER TEN

When Dorcas arrived at the sale grounds the next morning shortly after sunrise, it was already a hive of activity. Booths had sprung up in the area around the fire hall as if they'd been planted there, and a crew of Amish and Englisch worked rapidly to set up the remaining ones.

Turning her horse and buggy over to one of her older scholars, who seemed pleased with his job for the day, she headed to the auction canopy. That was probably where help was needed most right now. Besides, given the way Mammi kept volunteering her to help, she'd best find out what she'd been signed up to do now.

A quick glance around showed her that at least Sarah wasn't there yet. She certainly hoped that meant Sarah had followed her advice and slept in this morning. Sarah's fatigue had been very obvious the previous evening.

"Dorcas, glad you're here." The hail came from Jacob, who was working on the popcorn and lemonade stand. "Are your bruders coming? We could use some more help with setup."

"They'll be here as soon as the milking is done. Be sure you put them to work," she called back.

Jacob grinned. "No worries."

Dorcas had to smile. She'd noticed that people who worked where they were in daily contact with the Englisch picked up those phrases easily and used them almost without thinking. Englisch phrases and words were dropped into their dialect and stayed, coming into common use.

It made sense. Language changed all the time, and Deutsch had otherwise not changed since the first settlers came to America hundreds of years ago.

At the auction canopy, a crew of young people were wiping off wet folding chairs and setting them up, managing to nudge each other and giggle while they did it. These kids were a bit under the semi-official dating age of sixteen, but that didn't mean they weren't sizing each other up. It was beyond the power of teachers and parents to prevent that, she knew.

Ben Schmidt, the wiry, energetic auctioneer, tinkered with the speakers that would allow him to be heard once the auction began. Nola King, organizer of the quilt collection, hovered over him, looking worried. When she saw Dorcas, her face cleared.

"Ach, Dorcas, you're just the person we need. Your mamm said you'd be here early to help."

Certain this meant Nola wanted her to do something she didn't want to do herself, Dorcas approached warily, nodding at the auctioneer. "Good to see you, Ben."

He looked up and grinned, nodding back at Dorcas as Nola clutched her arm.

"Ben needs some help, and you're just the right person for the job, being a teacher and all." Nola spoke quickly, as eager to pass the job along as if it were a hot potato.

Resigned, Dorcas nodded. "What do I need to do?"

"Be my assistant," Ben said, straightening. "I need somebody to keep track of what's coming up, bring things out to me, and mostly be quick enough to switch stuff around if I have to make a change once I get the feel of the crowd. Figure out the prime items so you can bring them when I feel the crowd is ready, yah?"

"That doesn't sound bad." It'd mean running back and forth, but she'd rather be busy. "I helped set them up last night, so I know where everything is. And we already separated out the things we thought would bring the highest prices."

Ben grinned broadly. "Ach, I knew you were the perfect auction assistant. Anytime you get tired of teaching, you come to me. I'll have a job for you."

She shook her head, smiling. "I think I'll stick to teaching."

"Too bad, too bad. You don't know what you're missing." Ben's teasing accounted for a lot of his popularity as an auctioneer. "Be sure you're ready to join in the patter if I need you to help jolly the bidders along. Some folks need coaxing to warm up and bid on things."

There it was—the thing Nola didn't want to do. She'd known there'd be something. She raised her eyebrows and saw that Nola was avoiding her gaze.

"I'm not much of a comedian," Dorcas said. Especially not today, when her heart felt like lead in her chest.

He grinned. "Don't worry. You'll do fine. Just follow my lead."

Skeptical, she nodded, and Nola hustled back into the conversation now that she had what she wanted. "Gut, gut. You'll do fine. Now you go along in and grab some breakfast or coffee—whatever you need."

Food for early volunteers was always available, and knowing that, Dorcas hadn't had breakfast at home.

"Yah, I will. And I'll go through the quilts and put them in a tentative order. We've already sorted out the things that should be put up when a lot of Englisch are here."

Ben nodded approvingly, and with a quick look around

the grounds, Dorcas slipped into the building through the door by the canopy.

Her searching look around the area had shown her that Thomas wasn't there. She had hoped . . .

But it was no use hoping. After what he'd said last night, it wouldn't surprise her if he'd taken off already. But she had to know, one way or the other.

People would start noticing if she just stood there looking at nothing. Dorcas forced herself to move—to walk over to the stacked boxes of quilted products and pretend she was looking through them.

At one point during her sleepless night, she thought she'd come to accept the situation as it was. Now she knew she'd been wrong. Maybe, one day, she'd get over feeling as if her heart had turned to stone. But it was going to take a long time. If only she'd realized sooner what she felt for Thomas. If only.

Forcing herself to concentrate, she found herself remembering something her grossmammi used to say whenever trouble loomed. *Just do the next thing in front of you and pray. Trust the Lord for the rest.*

Dorcas wasn't left alone to stare blindly at the quilts for long. Dinah came up behind her and handed her a mug of coffee. "One sugar, yah?"

"Denke, Dinah. I didn't know you were going to be here early."

Dinah sipped her own coffee, studying Dorcas's face as if something were written there.

"Yah, I came thinking I'd be wanted at the bake sale counter, but they have enough for that, so they asked me to do the popcorn and lemonade. Until they finish setting up the stand, I'm free, so I can help you, if you want."

Since she couldn't go into a corner and cry, it seemed Dorcas would have to take her grossmammi's advice. Maybe Dinah would distract her enough not to brood.

She quickly explained what she was about, and together they began sorting through the various offerings, creating a separate stack of what they considered to be the best of the best. Although no one would ever claim to be the best quilter in the community, everyone knew whose work was extra special, either because of the artistry of the designs or the fineness of the sewing.

"We'd best not let anyone know what that stack means," Dinah said lightly, "or we might find ourselves in trouble."

Dorcas actually managed to smile. "True enough. That's our secret."

Dinah looked for a moment as if she'd ask something, but then she began chatting about the auction. Dorcas could only be grateful. Dinah, bless her, was almost too sensitive to other people's feelings. She'd guessed that something was wrong, but she'd gone further and known that Dorcas didn't want to talk about it. Dorcas could listen to her peaceful chatter with half her mind while the other half worked to suppress any thoughts about her loss.

As they finished, Dorcas spotted Noah and the twins heading toward her, but Sarah was nowhere in sight. When they reached her, she gave a quick greeting to the twins while raising her eyebrows at Noah. "Sarah?" she mouthed.

He clapped the boys on the shoulder. "We thought Mammi should sleep in this morning, so we got our own breakfast, didn't we, boys?"

"We did. I poured the milk," Matty said importantly.

Noah's eye twitched in what was probably a slight wink, making her feel sure that he'd spilled it, too. "Tell Teacher Dorcas what you did, Mark," he urged the shy one of the pair.

"I made toast and put butter on it," he murmured. "And it didn't burn, either."

"I'm sure it didn't. Sounds as if you two did a fine job, but I'll bet you could use a little something more in your tummies. I think there's coffeecake and shoofly pie over on the counter for helpers."

Matty's eyes lit up. "Can we, Daadi?" He tugged at his father's hand.

"I guess so." He glanced back at Dorcas as his sons tugged him away. "Denke. I hear you convinced her not to work so hard."

"I tried," she said, and then was distracted by Ben Schmidt beckoning to her. It looked as if he was ready for her help.

As she went out and saw the numbers of folks who'd already gathered, the business of the day threatened to overwhelm her. But against that pressure the need to see Thomas swept over her strongly. If only she could talk to him, maybe she could persuade him to give it more time.

Unless he'd gone already. One way or another, she had to find out.

As soon as the milking was done and breakfast over, Thomas began loading his tools in the buggy. Yesterday had been a loss as far as progress on the stable was concerned, but he could catch up today. The quicker he finished the job, the sooner he could leave.

"Thomas?" Mamm, pulling on her black sweater, was behind him. "I saw you from the window. You're going to the Mud Sale with us, ain't so?"

She must already know the answer to that if she'd seen what he was doing. He didn't want to disappoint her, but he certain sure wasn't up to a family outing today.

"No." His tone had been too sharp, and he immediately regretted it. "Sorry, but I can't miss the chance at putting in a full day's work at the school."

"You shouldn't be working all alone. What if you were hurt and there was no one around to know?"

He tried to respond patiently. "If I promise I won't climb up to the roof, will you stop worrying? Please, Mamm. I'm not up for a family outing today."

Mammi knew what was behind his refusal, but she didn't speak, any more than she'd spoken up to Daad.

Esther had come out behind Mamm, and she piped up. "Gut idea. I don't care about any old Mud Sale. I'll come and help you."

"Not today." He saw instantly that he'd hurt her feelings, and once again wished he'd been more careful. He managed a smile for his little sister. "What's this about not wanting to go to the Mud Sale? You know how much fun they are." He pulled out a ten-dollar bill and handed it to her. "Bad enough that I can't go. You go and bring me a caramel apple or a bag of popcorn when you come home, yah? And get one for yourself."

That seemed to mollify her. "Okay. Can I spend the whole thing?" She eyed the bill.

"Sure. That's our contribution to the sale, ain't so?"

Esther grinned back and raced off to the family buggy.

Mamm stood there a moment longer. Then she patted his arm wordlessly and turned back to the house.

He'd hit a new record in disappointing people this morning already, he figured. Still, the best thing for everyone right now was for him to be alone. At least then he wouldn't take his bad mood out on anyone.

Like Dorcas, for instance. He swung himself into the buggy and headed out the lane. He'd spent most of the night berating himself for what had happened with Dorcas. He shouldn't have told her what he did, and he certain sure shouldn't have kissed her.

How had he come to kiss her? He hadn't meant to. But there she'd been, looking at him with her eyes filled with sympathy and caring, standing so close he could hear her slightest breath, and it had happened.

Never again. Still, however much he might tell himself he'd been wrong, he couldn't really regret having done it. At another time, if things had been different, they might have made a match of it. For just a second he seemed to see a little girl with Dorcas's beguiling smile and dimples. But it wasn't to be.

The schoolhouse came in view ahead of him, reminding Thomas of the job at hand. Whatever happened, he'd finish the work on the stable and shed. He wasn't in the habit of breaking his word, whatever Daad might think. And he certainly wouldn't go off with the job not done, leaving Dorcas in the lurch and giving the people who wanted to close the school another reason to get their way.

He set to work. Usually, once started on a day of work, he concentrated on it to the exclusion of everything else. But not today. Something kept pricking at the back of his mind, making it hard to focus.

It wasn't until he'd gotten through about an hour's work that he knew what troubled him so much. It was the memory of last night, coupled with worrying what Dorcas was thinking right now. Did she imagine that he was gone already? That he'd left without finishing the work he'd promised?

It became unbearable to think that she might be fretting and unhappy over the work he'd promised to do. He owed it to Dorcas to reassure her about it. Given what he'd blurted out to her last night, she might be thinking the worst. Suddenly he couldn't bear the idea that she was brooding over the feeling he'd deserted her.

He knew where she'd be all day—at the Mud Sale. The least he could do when he'd finished work was to drive to the fire hall and tell her himself.

With that decision made, Thomas turned back to the job with a will. He worked steadily, not stopping for lunch, until he'd completed the job of work he'd set out in

his mind for today. Another day's work should have the
stable waterproof, and then he'd be able to focus on the
inside work so that Dorcas would have someplace to put
her buggy horse. The shed rebuilding could wait until the
stable was complete.

With his tools packed up and everything secure, he set
off for the Mud Sale, his thoughts completely occupied
with the need to explain to Dorcas. As he neared the fire
hall, he passed a fair amount of traffic, both buggies and
cars, coming out of the fire hall lane. At this hour people
would be heading for home to take care of their animals
or start supper.

He turned into the lane once it was clear, and the area
spread out before him. The fire hall sat in the valley with
a ridge rising behind it, a squat, cement-block building
that served the needs of the whole township. The field
around it was trampled and muddy, but a few nice days
would dry it out. He pulled into the first available space
along the hitching rail and jumped down.

From what he'd heard the previous night, Dorcas
would be helping with the quilt auction, so he wandered
in that direction. If she was inside where they'd stacked
the auction items, he might steal a few minutes alone with
her. It wouldn't take more than that to say what he had to.

But as he neared the crowd around the improvised
stand, he spotted Dorcas, obviously delivering whatever
Ben was going to auction next. Ben was still going strong
after all these hours, his voice chanting in the singsong
rhythm of the experienced auctioneer, pushing up the
price for the quilt displayed beside him, coaxing, teasing,
sometimes using Dorcas as a foil for his chatter.

And Dorcas gave back as good as she got, poised and
smiling as if this were an everyday event. If anything
about last night troubled her, she wasn't letting it show.

Well, why would she? She was in the place where she belonged, where everyone knew and liked her.

Unlike him. He was the outsider . . . the one who didn't belong.

Since it was clear she wouldn't be available for a private conversation for some time, this wasn't going to work. No matter how much he wanted to get it over with, he'd have to wait until Monday to have his chance to talk to her.

He'd nearly reached the rows of metal folding chairs, so he veered and headed back the way he'd come. Thomas hadn't gotten more than a few feet when Jacob grabbed his arm.

"Gut," he exclaimed. "I'd almost given up on you. Where have you been? I've seen the rest of your family."

He hoped Jacob hadn't asked them where he was. "I had to finish up some work at the school. Making up for the rain day yesterday. How has it been going?"

"Even better than we thought." Jacob beamed with satisfaction. "After all that rain, I was sure we wouldn't get a crowd, but they came. The sun came out, and people showed up from all over the place. The quilt auction is a draw for the Englisch, especially."

It seemed logical to say something about Dorcas, didn't it? "Looks like Dorcas is the auctioneer's assistant this year."

"Best he's ever had, according to Ben," Jacob said promptly. "She's used to being in front of people, I guess, being a schoolteacher. You should hear her sass Ben. She knows how to play up to him. They've been terrific together."

He didn't have any right to be upset at the thought of Dorcas getting along so well with someone else, especially Ben, long married and with a passel of grown kids. So why did he feel it?

Apparently taking his silence for assent, Jacob nudged him. "Glad you're here now anyway. You're just the person to help us tear down. Everybody wants to set up, but there are plenty of excuses for not staying to tear down when it's all over."

In the face of Jacob's words, he could hardly come out with the excuses that leaped to mind at the words.

"Yah, sure. What comes first?" He glanced around the field, determined not to look back toward Dorcas.

"Looks like Dinah is finishing up at the popcorn and lemonade stand." Jacob's gaze rested on the young widow for a moment. "We can start there."

Despite Jacob's reservations, they had plenty of helpers, and in another hour and a half, everything had been torn down and returned to its proper place.

Maybe it had been for the best that he hadn't had a chance to talk with Dorcas today, when he was still roiling inside. By Monday, he'd have a better handle on what to say, and he could easily catch her either before or after school.

With a farewell wave to Jacob, he headed for the buggy. He rounded the corner of the building, and nearly walked into Dorcas, whose eyes widened in shock.

DORCAS TOOK AN involuntary step backward at Thomas's unexpected appearance when she'd been picturing him far away. Her stomach turned over. "Thomas. But . . . I heard you weren't coming. I thought you were gone."

She had hoped to talk to him again . . . to try to convince him to give it more time. But Esther had mentioned that he wasn't coming. Now that he was here, all she wanted to do was be alone long enough to get her feelings under control.

"I wasn't. I mean, I wanted to get some work done on the stable, since yesterday was a washout."

She nodded, wondering what that meant for his plans to leave. And whether she dared to ask.

"I guess you've finished up what you were working on today."

"Yah, pretty much." Thomas frowned at the ground under his feet. "I felt . . . well, I knew I had to talk to you. To let you know that I'll complete the work at the schoolhouse before I leave. I wouldn't go back on my word."

So that was why he was still here. Not because he'd changed his mind about leaving. Not because of any feelings he had for her, but because he was scrupulous about doing what he'd said he would. Too bad his father couldn't see that.

"Denke." She managed to get the word out. Didn't he have anything to say about what else had passed between them? Apparently not.

And she wasn't sure she could have handled it anyway. "I had better go in and be sure everything is cleared up." She waved her hand vaguely at the building. Unable to stand facing him any longer, she spun and hurried to the door. She'd pressed the latch several times before she realized the truth. The fire hall was locked, and most everyone had gone home.

She pulled uselessly at the door again and realized how foolish she must look. Behind her, Thomas cleared his throat. "Seems like everyone has gone. Do you have a ride home?"

"Lemuel left the small buggy for me." She would not call the two-seater the courting buggy, not when she was talking to Thomas.

Thomas planted his hand against the door, and she stared at it . . . strong, capable, callused with the work he did. "Look, I wanted to say something else." He took a breath, and she wanted to block her ears to shut out what she knew he was going to say.

"I don't know what possessed me last night. I had no right. I shouldn't have kissed you. I'm sorry."

I'm not. That was what she wanted to say, but she couldn't. She fought for composure.

"It's all right. It was just a flashback to when we were teenagers. I understand."

"I didn't kiss you back then," he said, and she couldn't tell whether that was regret in his voice or not.

Why hadn't he? She couldn't ask the question, because she knew the answer. He hadn't kissed her then because she'd been too wrapped up in thinking about someone who was unattainable. Someone she wouldn't have wanted if she'd gotten him. Maybe she hadn't been any more foolish than most girls, but it had had dire consequences.

She'd spoken more surely than she knew. Last night's kiss had been a makeup for the kisses they hadn't shared long ago. If she had seen then what was close at hand, things might have turned out very differently for both of them.

She forced herself to block out that kiss for the moment. There'd be plenty of time over the coming weeks and years to think about it and to mourn what might have been.

Concentrate on him. The pain Thomas felt was so obvious to her. It was in every word, every look in his eyes. Didn't anyone else see it? Thomas wanted to stay, to belong here again, but he was convinced he couldn't.

"Please." The word came from her heart. "Give it a little more time. Maybe your father will come around—"

"No." A mixture of anger and pride flared in his face. "He doesn't believe in me, and nothing will change that."

"Something might. If I told him the truth about what happened back then—"

"I already told you." Now his anger was aimed at her. "I'm not going to crawl back to my father. I'm not going to have you begging him to understand. Forget it."

Did he realize that it was his pride speaking? Probably not.

Any more than she'd recognized her own cowardice in failing to come forward at the time. She looked at herself and didn't like what she saw.

CHAPTER ELEVEN

Dorcas awoke on Monday morning to the sound of her brothers' footsteps and the soft closing of the back door in the kitchen below her room. The pale light outside her window warmed as the sun made its way over the ridge.

She stretched, relishing her warm bed and the luxury of that moment between waking and sleeping. She'd almost closed her eyes again when the tide of memory swept over her, bringing with it a flood of grief and pain.

Pushing herself upright, Dorcas pressed her palms over her eyes, trying to retreat into darkness, but it was no use. She couldn't. She had to get up, to go through her morning chores and get off to school, all while putting on a cheerful face that betrayed nothing of her inner pain.

It seemed all the worse to be unable to share her feelings even with those who were closest to her. But she couldn't tolerate the thought of people talking about it and feeling sorry for her. She had no choice but to bury what had happened. If only it wouldn't keep rearing up again, tightening her throat and making tears sting her eyes.

Throwing back the covers, Dorcas swung herself around

and planted her bare feet on the rag rug next to her bed. Get moving. As long as she was moving, she could manage.

She dressed quickly, alert for any sounds from below. Levi and Lemuel were doing the milking, and she could hear the distant sounds of pails clanking if she tried. They'd be back, hungry for breakfast, before she knew it. In theory, Mamm and Betsy made breakfast, but Mamm had looked so tired last night that she'd urged her to sleep in.

And Betsy . . . she'd had high hopes after Betsy had reported her talk with her mother, but the fact that she didn't hear any sounds from the kitchen discouraged her. Hurrying with her hair and her kapp, she went quickly and quietly downstairs, stepping over the third tread from the top, which creaked no matter what was done to it.

The kitchen was empty, as she'd assumed, and she started oatmeal on the stove and began heating the cast iron skillet for eggs. Before she could do any more, Mamm came in, taking the container of eggs from her hand.

She shook her head. "I thought you were going to sleep in this morning, Mammi."

"I can't help waking when I hear the boys move." She elbowed Dorcas away from the stove. "You set the table and start the coffee. Besides, I heard the boppli in the night, so it's best Betsy sleep while she has a chance."

Mammi gave her a look that said plainly she ought not to criticize, so Dorcas held back whatever she might have said. It was just as well—she certainly had enough faults of her own without pointing out other people's.

Unfortunately, setting the table didn't occupy her mind enough to keep it from straying to the day ahead. Thomas would be at the school. She'd hear him working in the stable, even if he didn't want to talk to her.

That was probably best, although she doubted she could resist the temptation to have a quick look at him, at least. How many more could she count on?

If only his father could see his oldest son for the person he was now. If only Thomas would try again to make peace with him.

If only. Her lips twisted. How sad that phrase was. And how useless.

The boys came clattering in just as Mamm was forking sausage onto a plate, and Dorcas poured coffee.

"Denke." Lemuel drained half the mug in a single steaming gulp. "I needed that."

"It's a wonder you don't scald your insides," Mammi scolded.

"He's already turned them to iron," Dorcas teased, re-filling his mug.

"They're insulated," he said smugly. He glanced around the kitchen. "Betsy not down yet?"

"She was up with the baby in the night," Levi said, making it sound as if no one had ever done that before.

Before Lemuel could make the retort that Dorcas saw hovering on his tongue, Betsy's footsteps sounded on the stairs, and she hurried in.

"Sorry I'm late," she murmured. She clasped the wooden spoon with which Mamm was stirring oatmeal. "I'll do that. You sit down and eat."

Levi started to get up. "I'll help you."

Dorcas and Lemuel exchanged glances. "That's a first," he murmured.

"Shh." She tried to stop a smile and saw her mother doing the same. Levi's new father glow had certainly had an effect on his behavior. The fact that he was dripping oatmeal all over the stove was a minor annoyance in the scheme of things, she guessed.

Her amusement carried her along to school, where a room full of scholars should certain sure keep her from brooding.

She and Anna had barely finished talking over the day's plans when the children came trooping in, hanging up jackets and clattering lunch pails. The ones who walked along the road rushed in, talking excitedly, and she eyed them sharply.

"All right. Someone tell me what's wrong."

The older scholars exchanged looks, and then Esther seemed to appoint herself to speak for them.

"It was the neighbor, Teacher Dorcas. He came out and yelled at us again. Honest, we weren't doing anything," she added before Dorcas could ask the obvious question.

Joseph looked at Esther and then stared intently at his shoes. Clearly there was more to be said.

"Joseph?" she asked.

He tried not to meet her gaze. "Well, I . . . I . . . I guess maybe some of us ran across the edge of his lawn. We didn't mean any harm, but Mr. Haggerty saw us."

She could fill in the blanks without any difficulty. "Somebody dared somebody else to do it, ain't so?" She looked from one face to the other. Most of them didn't meet her eyes.

"All of you will stay in for recess." As a punishment, it was far harder on her than on the scholars, but of course they wouldn't see it that way. "That will help you remember how to behave another time."

She thought there might be a protest from those who weren't guilty, but they accepted it. Except for Esther, whose face flared with temper. Before she could say anything, Dorcas fixed her with the stern look that had wilted hardier souls than she was. Esther didn't speak, but there was a slight pout on her face as she went to her seat.

Dorcas gave an inward sigh. Sometimes she thought the pouting was even worse than sassing, but the only effective thing was to ignore it.

Anna joined her. "I wish they hadn't." She shook her head. "I'd hate to have a stranger yell at me."

"It's too bad the kinder didn't think of that before they got so silly. I'll have to speak to Mr. Haggerty after school and apologize. Again."

Anna's eyes widened. Clearly that was an aspect of teaching that hadn't occurred to her. "Do you . . . do you want me to go with you?"

The offer touched Dorcas, and she clasped Anna's hand for a moment. "Denke, Anna. I'd best go alone, but it's gut of you to offer."

Anna, clearly relieved, nodded, and Dorcas had a fleeting wish that she had a way out for herself.

Once lessons were underway, the classroom settled down to normal. Esther's pout disappeared fairly quickly, for which Dorcas could only be thankful. Girls that age sometimes carried on for days over something so small you'd need a magnifying glass to see it. She hoped she hadn't been like that but feared she probably had been.

The day moved on and staying inside during the sunny recess was torture for her as well as for the erring scholars. More than once she was tempted to let them off, but that would hardly teach the lesson.

The periodic sound of Thomas's hammer didn't help matters any. If she'd been outside, she might have seen him, at least. Maybe it was better this way, but she couldn't convince herself of that.

The afternoon dragged on until Dorcas felt as restless as the smallest of her first graders. When she finally dismissed them, with a final warning to stay off the neighbor's property, she felt like throwing her books in the air.

When the scholars were well on their way, she straightened her kapp and picked up her sweater and book bag. It was time for her apologies.

But when she walked out of the schoolhouse, Dorcas saw that she wouldn't have to go to Mr. Haggerty. He was coming toward her, and he looked as if there should be steam coming out of his ears.

"Mr. Haggerty." She forced a smile. "I was just—"

"I told you to keep those kids off my property!" His voice was loud enough to be heard in town, and she winced, her courage fading. "I warned you. I'm going to complain to the school board. And if that doesn't work, I'll call the police!"

THOMAS HAD JUST stepped back from the stall bar he'd been replacing when he heard the voice—loud, male, angry. Dropping the hammer, he ran toward the sound. Dorcas, the children . . .

He rounded the corner to see a man confronting Dorcas. His antagonism slipped down a notch. Whoever he was, he was oldish, probably sixties or seventies at a guess. Short, thin, with a peppery red face and a fringe of white hair. He might be loud, but he didn't look threatening.

Dorcas didn't seem frightened, but when he walked toward them, her expression turned to one of pure gratitude at his appearance.

"Was ist letz?" he said as soon as he was near enough to speak without shouting. "What's wrong? What happened?"

"Thomas, this is our neighbor in the house next to the lane, Mr. Haggerty. I'm afraid some of my scholars came across his lawn on their way to school this morning."

"That's right." He seemed to simmer down while Dorcas was speaking, but he flared back up again. "I warned you I wouldn't put up with it. A man moves out to the country to get some peace and quiet. Is that too much to expect?"

Taking his cue from Dorcas's calm demeanor, Thomas spoke easily. "I'm afraid you moved right next to a school, Mr. Haggerty. That's probably not the best place for quiet."

Thomas thought he detected an acknowledgment in the man's face, but he started to grumble. "In my day, the teacher had control of her students. Not like now."

Dorcas paled slightly, and Thomas knew she was thinking about the school board and the Gaus family's attempt to close the school. She seemed to try to speak calmly.

"Why don't you stop by sometime when school is in session? You might find it very similar to the school you attended."

"One-room school, is it?" For the first time, he seemed to be a little interested despite himself. "I went to a little two-room school." He paused, and then shook his head. "Never mind that. I don't want to see your students. I just want to be left alone and not have kids tramping over my yard."

"I'm truly sorry they disobeyed me. Apparently it had something to do with a dare. I punished the class for it, and I don't think it will happen again. I'd be glad to bring them to your house to apologize."

His face reddened again at that. "I don't want any kids at my house. See that it doesn't happen again, or I'll talk to the school board. And the police."

It appeared that was his last word. He turned and stamped back down the lane, the wind ruffling his fringe of hair and making it stand up like a rooster's comb.

She turned to Thomas, her whole body relaxing. "Denke, Thomas. I was glad to see you coming."

"You handled him all right without me, but he certain sure was unpleasant."

"Poor man." Dorcas's sympathy was as predictable as the sunrise. And just about as heartening. He was going to miss her.

"Why poor? He doesn't seem to want any sympathy, ain't so?"

"I don't know, and that's a problem. He's our neighbor, and I don't seem to know anything about him. Why did he move here? Does he have a family? What makes him so sensitive about his property?"

He shrugged. "What does it matter? You're worried about him going to the school board, aren't you?"

"I don't want that to happen on top of everything else, that's for sure. If I knew more about him, maybe I could help."

"And maybe he just wants to be left alone. That's what he says, ain't so?" It seemed to him that she had enough on her shoulders without worrying about what made the man the way he was.

She had a wry smile for that question. "People don't always mean what they say. Don't you know that?"

Clearly nothing he said was going to ease Dorcas's conscience about her neighbor. He made a silent promise to ask around and see what he could find out about this Mr. Haggerty.

His thoughts switched abruptly in another direction. "These kids who went on his property . . . was my sister one of them?"

Dorcas was silent for a moment, and he thought she didn't want to answer him. Then she smiled slightly. "I think we had this conversation before, didn't we? Just because you're here, that doesn't mean I should confide in you about one of my scholars."

"You should when the scholar in question is my sister, ain't so?"

"But not your daughter," she retorted, but he figured he knew the answer.

"Never mind. You can keep your teacher ethics intact. I know it was. She wouldn't lag behind when something was going on."

Her shrug was a tacit admission that he was right. "You know what kids are. If somebody dares you, you just have to do it to prove you're not afraid. You remember that, ain't so?"

"I do. But I don't think I want my sister following in my footsteps. Still, I have to say that if the man didn't make such a fuss about it, the young ones probably wouldn't even think of it. It's the challenge."

"That, and the fact that they can tell themselves he started it. No matter what caused it, this behavior has to stop. I just hope missing their recess today made an impression on them. It did on me." She made a face, laughing at herself a little.

"Yah, I can see that it would." He knew Dorcas wouldn't enjoy being stuck inside with a cross bunch of kids when the spring day beckoned.

Now she glanced toward the school. "I'd best lock up and be on my way home."

The afternoon sun caught her as she moved, gilding her hair and warming her cheeks. "One minute," he said before she could move away.

She looked at him questioningly. "Yah?"

"Why don't you want to tell my parents about what Esther's been up to?"

She paused, studying his face intently. At first he thought she wouldn't answer. Then she spoke, her expression serious.

"I think there's enough trouble at your house right now, ain't so? I don't want to add to it."

He could feel his face tighten. "Something else to add to my account. It would be better if I'd never come back."

"Thomas . . ." Her eyes darkened. "Don't think that." She reached out toward him pleadingly, palm up.

He took a step back, careful not to touch her. "Why not? It's true, and nothing anyone says will make it better."

CHAPTER TWELVE

By the time Dorcas reached home that afternoon, she felt as if she'd been trampled by a horse and run over by the plow. In every direction she turned, problems loomed like so many hills to be climbed. And even if she climbed them, she found no guarantee that there'd be any peace or comfort on the other side.

She was already pulling her sweater off as she walked into the kitchen, hoping she might have fifteen minutes to rest before plunging into a chore. The wish vanished when her mother hurried in from the hall, her bonnet on and her small suitcase held in one hand.

"What's wrong?" Dorcas dropped her school bag on the table. "What's happened?"

"Your cousin Jenny's Elijah has had an accident. The paramedics are there already, but there's no word yet. No one else is available to go right away."

Dorcas snapped to attention, her fatigue forgotten. Jenny's young husband . . . it must be bad, or they wouldn't have called the paramedics. And their little ones would be terrified.

"I can go with you——" she began, but Mammi shook her head.

"I'm all set, and Lemuel is going to drive me and take care of their animals. I don't know if I'll be staying the night, but I might. You'd best stay here and help Betsy."

That made sense, much as she'd like to rush to Jenny's aid. If it meant staying overnight, Mamm could do it much more easily than she could, with school in the morning. Still, she longed to be with her cousin. She hugged her mother.

"Tell Jenny I'm praying. Don't you worry about the rest of us. We'll be fine."

"I know you will." Mamm paused long enough to pat her cheek. "Don't let Betsy get all upset about it."

Dorcas nodded, although she thought she'd be more upset than Betsy would. After all, Jenny was her cousin.

Picking up Mamm's case, she walked outside with her, just as Lemuel pulled up in the buggy. She gave her mother a hand up and tucked the suitcase at her feet. Lemuel looked solemn, but he tried to smile. None of them knew what they'd be going into, but whatever it was, they'd help out as best they could.

And as the news spread, others from Jenny's church district would show up to help. Lemuel might be able to leave the outside work in the neighbors' capable care.

"Call as soon as you know anything. We'll keep checking the phone shanty." As was the custom, the phone shanty was a few yards from the back door, so the family could check for messages as they went past. Some Amish businesses had phones in them, and a cell phone was always charged and ready at the school in case of emergencies. The phone shanty was a compromise between convenience and necessity.

Mamm nodded. "When I can, yah."

Betsy came out onto the back step to join her in waving good-bye. She looked worried, making Dorcas think about what Mamm had said. Suddenly she realized why

Mamm had made a point of it. Betsy was likely picturing herself in Jenny's place, with her young husband perhaps leaving in an ambulance.

"It will be all right." She put her arm around Betsy's waist. A foolish thing to say, she supposed, but one always said that at such a time. Maybe the words contained some comfort. "We'd best get supper started before your husband comes in hungry."

Betsy went in with her willingly enough, but she was shaking her head. "Levi went down to the sawmill, so he most likely won't be home too soon. I'll put the chicken on—"

Before she got any more words out, they heard little Will's protesting wail. Dorcas smiled.

"Perfect timing. You tend to him, and I'll deal with the chicken."

Betsy nodded, heading for the stairs. At least she was no longer running the instant Will made a peep.

Mammi had planned chicken with homemade noodles tonight, and the noodles were already rolled out and ready to cut. She put the chicken pieces in the kettle to stew, considered the time, and decided to go ahead and cut the noodles.

If anything was designed to comfort her, it was this. Working with the noodle dough took her back to her earliest childhood. Mammi had taught her the simple steps in making noodles when she could just reach the table, giving her a bit of dough to roll out with her own tiny rolling pin.

But cutting the noodles . . . that was another story. She hadn't been allowed to do that until she showed that she could cut them into the fine, straight pieces that would absorb the chicken broth and turn a lovely golden color.

She smiled, remembering those days as she cut the noodles. So many ordinary things brought back memories to treasure. Did Thomas feel that as he worked around the farm where he'd grown up? Or were all his memories tainted by his father's distrust? It would be a terrible thing if that were so.

Trying not to think of it, she shook the cut noodles with her hands to be sure they weren't sticking together, and then scattered them on the floured board to dry a little more. It was when she was finishing them that she realized something odd. Little Will was still crying.

Odd. She washed the flour from her hands. Will was a placid baby, Mamm claimed, easily satisfied as soon as his food appeared.

She hesitated a moment. Would Betsy want her to come up, or would she resent any offer to help?

After a moment's hesitation, she decided that Mamm would have offered help at this point, so she went quickly up the stairs. Levi hadn't appeared yet, so he couldn't be of help, and if he were there . . . well, he doted on his small son, but he had even less experience with babies than she did.

When she reached the door to Levi and Betsy's room, Dorcas knew she'd been right to come up. Not only Will's face but his whole little head was bright red, and his shrieks could probably be heard clear to the barn. Betsy sat in the rocking chair holding him with tears flowing down her cheeks. She didn't know which one was unhappier.

"May I help?" she asked, wondering what help would be forthcoming, since she couldn't think of anything to do.

"I don't know what to do." Betsy's wail was nearly as loud as her son's. "He's been fed, and burped, and he has a dry diaper. Usually he goes right to sleep, but now he just screams, and nothing I do helps."

"He has a nice loud scream, too." She smiled, hoping to lighten the mood. "Why don't you let me take him for a

moment to give you a rest?" It couldn't be easy to try soothing an infant who reared back in your arms and screamed.

Betsy nodded in relief, and Dorcas lifted him, attempt-
ing to hold him against her shoulder. She immediately
found out just how hard it was. Her tiny nephew pushed
against her with a strength she found hard to believe.

"Strong, aren't you, little man," she said, hoping to distract
him. "but that's not making you feel any better, ain't so?"

It didn't have an impact on Will, but Betsy reacted immediately. "Oh, Dorcas, you don't think he's sick, do you?"

Dorcas needed both hands to keep Will from back-
flipping out of her arms, so she put her cheek against the
baby's forehead.

"He doesn't feel warm, so I don't think he has a fever."

Betsy came to touch his forehead for herself and then
nodded in relief. "You're right. But what else could make
him cry like that? I ought to know. I'm his mammi." Her
eyes filled with tears again. "I'm not a good mother."

The words were heartfelt. She actually meant that.
Dorcas had to say something to help.

"Ach, Betsy, don't be silly. You're a wonderful gut
mother. You know that, don't you?" She had to smile at
the contrast between Betsy's woeful face and Will's irate
one. "Anyway, he just looks like he's good and mad."

"If your mamm was here, she'd know what to do."
Betsy brushed away a tear.

"Well, I guess we just have to figure it out." She bounced
Will in her arms, moving from one foot to the other the
way she'd seen Mammi do.

For about thirty seconds, that actually seemed to help,
but then he got going again. She and Betsy exchanged looks.

"Maybe if you walked with him . . ." Betsy ventured.

"Gut idea." She looked into the tiny red face. "What do
you think, Will? Want to go for a walk with Aunt Dorcas?"

Deciding that his shriek meant yes, she carried him out

into the hallway, still bouncing. Still yelling, as far as Will was concerned. She paced down the hallway and back again, talking softly while Betsy watched.

"There now, you can see something different. See, from this window there's the barn, but if we go into my room, we can see to the east, the way the sun comes up." She paused by the window, and Will stopped in mid-yell, apparently attracted by the light through the panes.

Before she could congratulate herself, he started again. Bounce some more, walk some more, then sing a nonsense rhyme. And all over again. But by the time they'd reached the other end, the crying had gone down in volume, and he wasn't pushing back quite so much.

Betsy looked at her, her eyes seeming to light with hope. "Keep going," she whispered.

Dorcas hoisted him up on her shoulder into a more comfortable position and started patting his back as she walked. How much longer would it take? Should they be doing something else? Thoughts whirled through her head.

And then as if from nowhere, Will gave a gigantic burp, spitting up a little on her dress. Before she could realize what had happened, his little body relaxed like a punctured balloon. In another moment he was asleep against her shoulder. The silence was deafening.

She and Betsy exchanged glances. Was that it? Could that actually have worked? When he didn't stir, she moved very softly to the bassinet. Gently, inch by inch, she lowered him into the bed, afraid any movement might disturb him. At last she could slip her hands from under him and draw back. Still he slept. Betsy tucked a blanket around him, and all was silence.

They hovered over the bassinet for another moment, not wanting to move, and then backed away.

They were halfway to the door when Dorcas had an overwhelming urge to giggle. Putting her hand over her lips to stifle it, she hurried out to the hall, with Betsy a step behind her, trying equally hard not to laugh. Once the door was closed, they sank against the wall together, giggling helplessly.

Finally catching her breath, Dorcas managed to speak. "I haven't laughed like that since I was eleven. Imagine two grown women buffaloed by a tiny baby."

"I know." The strain had disappeared from Betsy's face and it brimmed with laughter. "Why was I so silly?"

"I don't know." She surveyed her sister-in-law. "What on earth made you decide you were a bad mother?"

Betsy looked surprised, as if she hadn't even thought about it. "I . . . I don't know. He wouldn't stop crying, and I felt so helpless. And my mamm . . . you know, she does everything so well."

Dorcas considered Annamae Mueller, Betsy's mother. Master quilter, master pie-maker, master canner, and organizer of a dozen good works. Come to think of it, she would be hard to live up to.

She put her arm around Betsy's waist. "You know what? She has quite a few years of experience on you. Just like Mammi does on me. We'll get there." She nudged Betsy toward the stairs. "Komm. Let's finish supper before Levi comes tramping in wanting to eat."

They walked downstairs together, and Dorcas realized she felt considerably lighter than she had an hour ago. It wasn't only that she had a new understanding of her sister-in-law. She felt better in herself. It seemed there was nothing like dealing with somebody else's trouble to ease the heartache of your own.

THOMAS COMPLETED A few outside chores and headed into the kitchen, wiping his feet on the mat outside the door. Mammi and Esther stood at the sink, finishing up the supper dishes. Mammi was clearly trying to make conversation, but Esther was turning it into an uphill battle.

Had he been that prickly when he was her age, or was it only girls who reacted to growing up in that way?

Esther, catching his eye, flared up in an instant. "Why are you looking at me?"

He raised an eyebrow, determined not to let her goad him into losing his temper. "You happen to be standing where I was looking, I guess."

Mammi dried her hands on the dish towel, looking from him to Esther and not seeming to like what she heard. "Esther, there's no reason that I can see for you to be rude to your brother."

Guilty conscience. He thought the words but didn't say them. No sense in making matters worse, was there?

"Sorry," Esther muttered under her breath. She shoved the pan she'd been drying toward the cupboard and missed, letting it hit the floor with a clatter.

"Esther!" Mammi bent and rescued the pan herself. "That's enough. What have you been up to that's making you so cross?"

For an instant Esther seemed to try to control herself, but she didn't succeed. "You tell Mammi." She threw the words at Thomas. "I suppose Teacher Dorcas told you all about it."

"Teacher Dorcas didn't tell me a thing about you," he said flatly. Not until he'd guessed it anyway. "I have eyes and ears, you know. I heard that neighbor you'd riled yelling at Teacher Dorcas and went to see what was going on. You didn't think of that, did you? That he'd blame her instead of you. At least, I hope you didn't."

"I . . . how would I know . . ." Esther began to stammer.

Mammi took her firmly by the shoulders and looked into her face. "Esther Grace, you'll tell me what you've done, and right now."

Whatever was left of Esther's defiance dissolved in an instant, and she sniffled. Mammi didn't seem impressed.

"Out with it," she commanded.

Esther rubbed her eyes and looked at him. "You tell," she murmured, tears spurting out, despite her efforts to control them.

Thomas began to wish he'd never come into the kitchen, but it was too late now. He'd have to explain.

"That new Englisch neighbor is really particular about the kids crossing his yard when they're on their way to school. Apparently Teacher Dorcas warned them to be careful about it, right?"

Esther nodded miserably.

"This morning it seems somebody dared someone else to cut across the yard, and the man's raising a fuss," he finished.

Mammi looked troubled. "You said he was blaming Teacher Dorcas for it."

"Yah. Yelling and threatening to tell the school board and the police and saying she ought to control her pupils. But how she could do that when they weren't at school yet, I don't know." He looked at his sister, who sniffled again.

Mamm zeroed in on her erring daughter. "It is bad enough to disobey. Worse to annoy someone else at his own home. And still worse yet to let someone else take the blame for what you did."

Mammi didn't talk that way very often, but Thomas remembered it. He'd remembered feeling as low as a worm, too, knowing that Mammi was disappointed in him.

Now Esther was experiencing it, and the flood of tears she produced was enough to water the whole garden, it seemed. Unimpressed, Mammi handed her a towel.

"What do you think you should do about this, Esther Grace?"

Esther tried to look at Mammi, failed, and stared at the floor instead. "Apologize," she whispered.

"That's right," Mammi said. "To Mr. Haggerty for going on his property. And to the other scholars, for daring them. And to Teacher Dorcas, for disobeying her and causing trouble for her."

Esther looked appalled at the retribution that was coming down on her, but she knew better than to argue. "I will," she whispered. "First thing tomorrow." She looked at Thomas, wilting a little. "I'm sorry. I don't know why I was mean to you."

He grinned. "I don't know either." He put his arm around her shoulders, giving her a hug and a little shake. "Just for that, you can play me in a game of Farms and Fields tonight, okay?" The board game, which he'd heard her call old-fashioned, had been a favorite when he was young.

She managed to produce a smile. "Okay. That's a deal." She brightened. "I'll go set up the board." She ran off toward the living room.

Mammi smiled, too, and patted Thomas's arm. "That was wonderful gut how you handled her."

Thomas shook his head. "I don't think I ever realized how hard it is to bring up kinder. Too hard for me, that's for sure."

"Ach, you'll feel different when they're your own kinder," she said. "You'll come and tell me you handled it just like I would have."

He was struck dumb for a moment. Despite everything that had happened with Daad, Mammi was so obviously envisioning a future when he'd be here. When he'd live in Promise Glen, get married, and have a houseful of grandchildren for her. Only none of it was going to happen.

He'd have to tell her he was leaving. In all his anger at Daad and his own hurt, he hadn't thought of her, and shame swept over him. This was going to hurt her maybe even worse than it had him.

And yet what else could he do? What he'd told Dorcas was true. Daad hadn't trusted him in the past, and he still didn't trust him. Staying around was just an invitation to see him do the same in the future.

"Mammi . . ." He hesitated, wishing he had a recipe for delivering sad news without pain.

"What is it, Thomas?" She looked at him, and in her face he read more than just a question. Her fear and concern hadn't gone away. They were still there, ready to jump out at any moment.

She knew as well as he did that things weren't going well with Daad, and she was probably waiting, minute by minute, for the situation to erupt again.

"I . . . I don't think it's going to work." He took her work-worn hand in his, wanting to protect her and knowing he couldn't. "I don't think Daad has changed. And I know he hasn't forgiven me."

She clutched his hand tightly. "Give it a little more time, Thomas. Please. Walls can't be broken down in a minute."

"Sometimes they can't be broken down at all," he said, picturing Daad's implacable face. He struggled to say something to ease her pain. "I won't leave tomorrow. I have to stay until I finish the work at the school. But then . . . well, then I'll have to go. I guess there's no going back."

He stood there and watched the hope fade from his mother's eyes. There was nothing he could do.

CHAPTER THIRTEEN

Feeling a little sorry for Esther, Thomas offered her a ride to school the next day. She accepted with a side-long glance, as if to be sure he meant it.

"Hop in, then." He gathered up the lines. "I want to make an early start today."

Esther tossed her lunch bag in the back and scrambled up to the seat next to him. "Denke," she murmured.

He smiled. "Don't worry. I'm not going to scold you."

"No, I didn't think that." She sucked in an audible breath. "Thomas, would you . . . would you stop at Mr. Haggerty's with me? Please?" She rushed the words out as if she wanted to get rid of them.

A twinge of sympathy softened the look he gave her. He remembered what it was like to tackle something he really didn't want to do.

"Sure. No problem."

The easy words seemed to reassure her. "I was really kind of scared of him, you know?"

"So that's why you started daring each other, right? When I was a kid, the old Miller place stood empty for a long time, and folks started saying it was haunted. So Jonas and I dared each other to go up on the porch."

Her eyes widened. "Did you? Did you see a ghost?"

"No ghosts, but Jonas cut his leg on a broken board, and I had to carry him home. And Mammi was worse than any ghost when she heard about it."

Esther giggled and then grew solemn. "Did she say she was disappointed in you?"

"Yah. Jonas started to cry, and I wasn't much better."

She nodded, and suddenly things were easy between them. "I know," she said.

Esther was quiet as they approached Mr. Haggerty's house. A quick look told him she was steeling herself for the ordeal, and he found himself stiffening, too. If the man started yelling at his little sister . . . well, he didn't think either of them would handle it as well as Dorcas had.

He stopped at the mailbox and ground-tied the horse, knowing he wouldn't go anywhere. "Komm. Let's get it over with."

Esther surprised him by marching straight up to the front door and knocking. He lingered at the bottom of the porch steps, ready for any kind of reaction.

The door opened. Haggerty glared at the sight of them. "I told you kids—"

"I'm sorry." Esther rushed the words out before he could get going. "It was my fault. I dared the others." She gulped. "It wasn't Teacher Dorcas's fault. She told us not to."

She seemed to have taken the wind out of his sails. For a moment he just stared at her. Then he cleared his throat.

"Yeah, well . . . don't do it again."

"I won't," she said quickly. "Denke."

"What does that mean?" His look was wary, as if he expected an insult.

Esther had turned away, but she looked back at him. "It means thank you."

He didn't go so far as to smile, but Thomas thought for

a minute he was amused. Then Esther raced back to the buggy. He nodded to the man and followed. His little sister had done the whole thing much better than he would have, and he felt irrationally proud to be a part of it.

Neither of them spoke until he pulled up at the stable. "Gut job," he said gruffly, and a smile lit her face.

"I'm wonderful glad you went with me." She hurried the words and then raced off to the schoolhouse.

Standing and watching, he saw her stop to speak to Dorcas and after a moment go on to the schoolyard. Dorcas looked toward him, and he walked over to meet her.

"Did she tell you she'd apologized to Mr. Haggerty?" he asked.

Dorcas nodded. "I wouldn't have asked her to do it, but I'm glad she did. It couldn't have been easy. I hope he didn't yell."

"I don't think he knew what to make of it." He grinned. "Maybe he's not used to kids."

"No." A shadow came over her face. "You know, I was wondering about him. About why he moved here, I mean. Levi says he heard at the hardware store that he had lived in Williamsport until his wife died. Seems like she'd been sick a long time, from what he heard. Still, it's surprising he'd move away from everyone he knew."

"Yah, it is." At least it was in comparison to the tightly woven fabric of Amish life, where every single strand touched another and another. "Maybe he won't be so hard on the kids now."

Dorcas shook her head, her eyes filling with compassion. "That doesn't matter. I just feel bad for him being all alone that way."

Dorcas, he thought, had an endless capacity for feeling empathy for others. He just hoped it didn't lead her into sorrow. He almost said as much when he reminded himself that it wasn't any business of his, not anymore.

"Better get to work," he muttered, and strode off toward the stable.

By the time he heard the school bell ringing, he was already deep into the work he'd planned for today. If he did what he intended, another week should be enough to finish the whole job.

And then it would be time to leave.

Almost at once he started finding reasons why he shouldn't do any such thing. Daad hadn't said anything more about his being a bad influence. In fact, he'd been downright mellow for the past day or so, probably because Mammi had soothed him down.

There was Esther. He'd just begun to get to know her all over again, and Adam, too. Even Jonas didn't seem to be looking so hard for something to argue about.

Give it time, Mammi had said. But if he did, he ran the risk of having it all come down on his head again. Until Daad found it in his heart to forgive him, his place here would never be secure.

There were no easy answers, and if he was honest with himself, he'd have to say that a large part of his need to find reasons to stay was Dorcas. He glanced involuntarily toward the school. He couldn't deny the attraction she held for him . . . no, something stronger than attraction.

Thinking this way wasn't helping matters any. He'd best just finish the job at hand and stop looking for a happy ending that wasn't going to come. Hooking his hammer in his waistband, he climbed up the stall bars. There was one crosspiece above his head that he wanted to double-check. If it had gotten soaked when the roof leaked, it might be just as well to replace it.

The stall bars didn't get him quite high enough, and he reached up for another handhold. Swinging his leg across, he felt for the ledge where his foot could go. He touched it, shoved his foot into place, shifting his weight. Something creaked, he felt himself slip, and he cried out as he plummeted toward the floor.

A CRASH AND a cry came through the open window in the schoolroom, freezing everyone in place for an instant. Even as Dorcas realized what it was—what it had to be—a rustle of awareness swept the room. Dorcas recovered herself immediately. No time to think about it, just to act.

"Stop this minute." The force of her voice stopped the rush toward the door. "Anna, you will take charge in here. Joseph and Benjamin, you come with me."

Before she reached the door, Esther grabbed her arm. "My brother—I have to come—"

"Come then." She grasped the girl's hand. "But you must listen to what I say."

Esther nodded, and with the two boys, they raced across to the stable, seeing the haze of dust in the air even from here. *Please, Lord, please, Lord . . .* The prayer filled her heart, even though she couldn't find the words. Thomas would be all right. Her heart clenched into a fist. He had to be.

They reached the door. Thomas lay on the floor, limp and unconscious, a couple of boards over his legs. As she hurried toward him, fragments of first aid jolted through her mind.

"Don't touch him," she ordered when Esther would have thrown herself toward Thomas. "We must see how bad it is first."

She knelt next to Thomas, barely able to breathe. Very gently she put her hand on his chest. Relief swept through her as she felt the steady beat of his heart.

"Is he . . ." Tears clogged Esther's voice.

"His heart is steady, and he's breathing all right." She touched his head, feeling for injury. Her fingers brushed a hard lump, rising by the moment.

She had to get medical help. A blow hard enough to knock him out could be serious. Concussion, fracture . . .

Putting the brakes on her racing thoughts, she turned to the children. "Esther, I want you to tell Anna to get the cell phone that is in the right bottom drawer of my desk. Tell her to call 911 and ask for paramedics and an ambulance. And tell her to call your parents, too. Can you do that?"

She nodded, scrambling to her feet. "Are you . . . is he hurt bad?"

"I can't tell how bad, so we need the ambulance. Hurry, now."

Choking back a sob, Esther raced toward the schoolhouse. Joseph moved slightly.

"Teacher Dorcas, I think we could lift the boards off him without jarring him."

She took a closer look. The boards weren't tangled with his legs, just pinning them down.

"All right. Let's try, slowly." She put her hands on Thomas's leg on either side of the board. "Each of you take an end and lift it when I say. I'm going to keep his leg from moving."

Joseph nodded, and the boys moved into position, each grasping an end.

"All right, now."

They lifted it. To her relief, Thomas didn't move, but his leg seemed to relax. The boys carried it out of the way and then came back for the other one. Now that they had done it once, it was easier. The process went smoothly, and she breathed a little easier.

He was still unconscious. How long had it been? This

wasn't a case of being stunned by a fall. Something was wrong.

But even as she thought it, Thomas's eyes flickered.

"Look," Joseph whispered. "He's waking up."

"Thomas." She spoke his name. "Thomas, can you hear me? You had a fall."

His eyes opened and he frowned, a line forming between his brows. "Fell," he murmured.

"That's right, you fell. Don't try to talk now. Help is on the way."

She wasn't sure he understood her, but he tried to move his head, turning it from side to side as if to be sure it still worked. "Fell," he murmured again.

"Yah." She slid her hand between the back of his head and the heavy planks that made up the floor, cradling it.

Running footsteps announced Esther's return. "She called, and they're coming. Mamm and Daad, too. She was by the phone shanty when Anna called. Is he better?"

"He's starting to wake a little." She looked at Esther's worried face. "It will be all right."

Esther seemed to believe her. Dorcas prayed she was right.

"You boys had better run out to the end of the lane and signal the ambulance when you see it. They might not know where the turn is."

"Right away." Joseph scrambled to his feet with Benjamin following a second later. They dashed off toward the lane.

"Can't I do something?" Esther reached out. "Maybe put him on a blanket?"

"We can't move him, but we might be able to slip something between his head and the floor. See if there's a blanket or something in the wagon."

"I'll find something." Esther hurried to the wagon.

Dorcas looked back at Thomas. His eyes had opened again, and he was frowning at her. "I fell," he repeated.

"That's right. You're in the stable, and you fell. You've got a lump on your head and I don't know what else."

She tried to speak lightly—to take it lightly.

"Feels like I landed on my head." He tried to move and grimaced.

"Just be still."

Esther hurried in with a thick brown carriage blanket in her hands. "What about this?"

"Just right. You get on the other side of him, and we'll slide it under his head." She focused on Thomas while Esther moved around him.

"We're going to put something under your head so you'll be more comfortable. Don't try to help us."

He didn't say anything, but he seemed to understand. Esther was folding the blanket and smoothing it into place.

"That's right." Dorcas put a hand on either side of his head. "You slide it under while I support his head."

When it was done, Thomas relaxed with a look of relief. "Better." He lay quietly for a minute, but then he frowned again. "I should get up." As he said the words, he attempted to lift his shoulders from the floor. Startled, she grasped him, and he sank back down, eyes closing.

"Maybe in a minute," he murmured.

"Not until we have you checked out," she said firmly. "You lie still until the paramedics come, or Esther and I will sit on you, won't we, Esther?"

That got a little smile from Esther. "That's right. You behave." She seemed to enjoy giving her big brother orders.

The distant wail of a siren penetrated. "Here they come," she said. "Esther, you'd best go out and wave them to the stable, so they don't try to go into the schoolhouse."

Nodding, she hurried out.

"Wish you hadn't called them," he muttered. "Everyone will know."

She patted him. "What difference does it make? Everyone always knows everything anyway."

He closed his eyes again. ". . . think I can't finish anything."

"Don't worry about it now. It will be fine." Was he concerned about finishing the stable? It would be done eventually.

The siren neared, and they heard the change in sound as the ambulance made the turn into the lane.

"You'll be fine," she murmured, and her heart seemed to be in her words. Unable to resist the temptation, she stroked his cheek. Without opening his eyes, he put his hand over hers, pressing her palm against his skin.

Esther spoke from the doorway. "They're here. They see me." In a moment the ambulance whined to a stop, and Dorcas began to feel she could breathe again.

The paramedics came in—quick and unruffled, probably used to scenes like this. Dorcas had to move away to give them space to work. Thomas released her hand slowly, his fingers drawing against her skin as if reluctant to part.

"Well, now, what have we here? Took quite a tumble, didn't you?" The older man scrutinized him while the younger one opened the case he'd carried in.

"Missed a step," Thomas said, seeming to need an effort to speak naturally. "I'm okay."

The younger man did a double take. "Thomas? I thought you'd moved away from here. Haven't seen you in years."

"Keith." He looked as if he'd fished the name up, frowning a little. "I'm back for a while, at least."

A while, Dorcas echoed silently. It was a time that would end before she was ready.

She backed away to the door, and to her surprise, Mr. Haggerty came hurrying over to her. He looked a little abashed as he spoke.

"The boys said that there'd been an accident. Anything I can do?"

"Thank you for coming." She tried to hide her surprise at his manner. "I guess no one can do anything until the paramedics finish." Her voice wobbled a little, and she took a firm grip on it. No one must know how affected she was. They might start wondering why.

"He's the carpenter, right?"

She nodded. "Thomas Fisher."

"He stopped by my house this morning with the girl . . ."

"His sister, Esther. Yah, she told me she'd stopped to apologize."

Maybe it would have been better to stay away from the grudge he had against the school, but he had brought it up. In any event, he just nodded, seeming to dismiss his anger in the midst of a crisis.

The sounds of buggies arriving distracted her. Someone would have seen the ambulance turn in at the school, and the news would have spread like the wind over the community. The first buggy belonged to Thomas and Esther's mother and father.

"Excuse me. I'll have to talk to the parents."

Haggerty nodded, but he showed no disposition to leave, just stepping back where he could watch the paramedics.

Dorcas saw Joseph and Benjamin still lingering and beckoned to them. "Joseph, will you stay close in case the paramedics need anything while I see to the parents? And Benjamin, just make sure that none of the buggies gets in the way of the ambulance."

They both nodded and hurried to do as she said. Slightly eased, she forced herself to walk away from the stable. From Thomas.

Thomas's parents were already hurrying toward the stable, leaving Benjamin to move their buggy. Esther threw herself into her mother's arms.

"He fell." Her voice was shrill. "Thomas fell and he was knocked clear out."

Dorcas reached them, looking from his mother, clearly apprehensive, to his father's impassive face. "We heard him cry out and found him right away. The paramedics are with him now. He's conscious and talking sensibly, so I don't think it's terribly serious." Again her voice wobbled despite her efforts.

Miriam clasped her hand warmly. "We'll go in."

Dorcas nodded, stepping away and letting her hand drop. Thomas's family was there now, and she had no place in taking care of him, or making decisions, or comforting him. But she couldn't stop herself from longing for that right.

Turning away resolutely, she went toward the schoolhouse, speaking to new arrivals as she went. Her place was with the children.

By the time parents who wanted to assure themselves that their young ones were all right had been satisfied, Dorcas saw that the paramedics were loading Thomas into the ambulance. Gesturing to Anna to take over, she fled. She had to get one more look at Thomas before he was carried away.

But when she reached the ambulance, Thomas was already loaded, and all she could do was smile at him. She turned to Miriam and Minister Lucas.

"Did the paramedics . . ." She stopped, realizing she was betraying herself.

Miriam clasped her hand again, her weathered face easing in a smile. "They don't think it's too serious, but he must go to the hospital to be sure. We want to go with him, but . . ." She paused, obviously thinking about how long it would take in the buggy to the hospital, especially when she longed to be with her son.

"We must get someone to drive you." Before Dorcas could begin to think of whom to contact, Haggerty spoke up.

"They'll want to go to the hospital. I'll drive them. Will you tell them that?"

In the stress of the moment, they had all been speaking in dialect, and of course he wouldn't know they could understand.

"Mr. Haggerty, this is Lucas and Miriam Fisher, Thomas's parents."

He nodded a little awkwardly, as if not sure what the appropriate greeting was.

"Denke, Mr. Haggerty." Lucas exchanged glances with Miriam, and whatever he saw there told him plainly that she would jump into the first available car. "We'd be grateful."

"Good, good." Haggerty's smile transformed his normally dour face. "My car's right behind the house. This way." He headed out the lane.

They started after him, but then Miriam turned back. "Denke, Dorcas. We'll let you know what happens."

"Yah, denke." Her husband nodded, looking a little surprised, and they hurried off.

Esther ran to them, obviously wanting to go.

"You go back to your class," her father snapped. "The hospital's no place for you."

For an instant, Dorcas thought Esther would erupt. Her face grew red, and there was a suspicion of tears in her eyes. She stamped her foot, then turned and fled.

It wasn't her business how the parents decided to handle their own children, but her heart ached. She didn't think Minister Lucas had meant to be so sharp. He was worried, but he might consider his daughter's feelings, too. As for Esther, she'd seize any excuse for anger now.

She just hoped Esther wouldn't decide that she was to blame.

The others who had hurried to the school to see what was wrong now gathered to watch the ambulance and then the car with Thomas's parents pull out. Joseph and his father went back to the stable, and she could see them straightening up the boards that had been knocked down.

There was nothing else she could do for Thomas, except to pray and trust. But maybe there was something she could do for his little sister.

When she returned to the classroom, the scholars were slowly getting back to work under Anna's direction. Except for Esther, who stood near the door, her face set, obviously trying not to cry.

Dorcas spoke softly, just for Esther's ears. "I'm sure your brother will be all right. He was awake and talking, and that's the best sign." She moved to put a comforting arm around the girl, but Esther shoved her arm away, hard enough to send her back a step.

"Just leave me alone." She stamped to her desk.

Dorcas could only stand and stare after her. Esther had been unpredictable lately, but she certain sure hadn't expected a reaction like this. It almost felt as if Esther was blaming her for Thomas's accident.

CHAPTER FOURTEEN

The rest of the school day wasn't an improvement, Dorcas decided. Worry about Thomas dragged at her, made worse by the fact that she couldn't show it.

Thomas's mother had said she'd let her know about Thomas, but what had she meant? That she would stop by or perhaps call the phone shanty later? For that matter, why had she said it? Did she suspect something between them?

Dorcas rejected that idea as soon as it came into her mind. She couldn't know anything because there was nothing to know. Involuntarily, Dorcas touched her lips, feeling them warm as they had for Thomas's kiss. She snatched her hand away and tried to focus on the children.

Fortunately they were outside for recess. Running around and playing vigorously should help get rid of whatever tension was left in them from the morning's accident.

None of the parents had even considered taking their children home for the rest of the day, for which she was grateful. Amish parents in general weren't overprotective. If her scholars had been upset by the accident, it was better for them to stay there and keep busy.

Except, perhaps, for Esther. She might have done better if she'd been allowed to go to the hospital with her parents, but it wasn't for Dorcas to say. She could understand why Esther's father had reacted as he had—he'd wanted to protect her. If only he could have found a gentler way to express himself . . .

Since it was highly unlikely that the minister would ask Dorcas's advice about his children, she'd best forget it.

Her gaze searched the busy play area for Esther. There she was, huddled with her closest friends, Erna and Hallie Gaus. Dorcas didn't have much trouble guessing what they were talking about. Esther seemed to speak vehemently, and all three of them cast frequent glances at Teacher Dorcas.

It was natural for Esther to be upset about her brother, but why was she suddenly so antagonistic toward her teacher? Did she imagine Dorcas should have done something to prevent the accident?

The sounds of raised voices jerked her attention away from the three girls. A quarrel had broken out over the seesaw between two of the third grade boys, flaring up in an instant. Try as she might to show her scholars that anger wasn't an answer to a disagreement, the going was slow, especially with boys of that age.

She started toward the spat and saw that Anna had reached the boys already. Stopping, she watched her young assistant. Anna was talking to them, and although it was too far to hear the words, she could see the calm and patience in Anna's face. Now she asked one of the boys a question, listening quietly to the answer.

Even from this distance, she could see the temperature of the quarrel going down under Anna's influence. And when the two combatants ran off together to the swings, she could have clapped. That was very well done on Anna's part. She had progressed immeasurably during the year.

Allowing the scholars a few extra minutes outside

seemed a good idea under the circumstances. By the time they'd returned to the classroom, most of them seemed back to normal.

Except for Esther. She continued to whisper to her friends until Anna went to them and stood pointedly next to them. Then they turned away and pretended to concentrate.

Dorcas frowned. She disliked having problems with any of her scholars, but with Esther it was especially hard. It shouldn't be, but it was.

They ended the school day with time spent on the spring program. Each age group was making a poster to illustrate some of what they'd learned during the year, and she went from amused to astonished to see what some of them thought was the most important accomplishment. Somehow she didn't think Mark's parents would be impressed that he'd learned to climb the tallest tree in the schoolyard.

As the children got ready to leave at the end of the school day, Dorcas opened the door. Surprised to find Mr. Haggerty standing there, she hurried to him, hoping nothing else was wrong.

"Afternoon, Teacher Dorcas." He smiled a little, as if pleased that he'd spoken to her as the Amish did. "I just got back from taking Thomas and his parents home. Said I'd make sure you and his sister got a report."

She smiled, relieved already. If Thomas was home, there couldn't be too much wrong, could there?

As the children filed past, she beckoned to Esther, who took one look at Mr. Haggerty and scurried over.

"Mr. Haggerty was kind enough to stop and let us know about your brother."

Eagerness flushed Esther's face as she turned to him. "Is he all right? What did they do to him at the hospital?"

"Nothing bad," he assured her. "Your mother told me

they said he had a slight concussion and some bruised ribs, but nothing worse. He has a headache and his ribs are strapped, but he was fit enough to go home."

Esther clasped her hands together as if she'd pray, and her eyes glowed with relief. "Denke, denke. I'm so glad."

"It's wonderful gut news, ain't so?" Dorcas said, trying not to let her own overwhelming happiness show. He'd be all right. She'd been trying to encourage herself with that thought for most of the day, and now she could believe it.

Esther nodded in agreement, but she lost her smile when she looked at Dorcas. "I can't wait to see him." She jumped down the three steps and ran full tilt down the lane.

"I guess she's happy," Haggerty said. "And you, too, I suppose. That was a scary thing."

She nodded, trying not to think of the moment when she'd run into the stable and seen Thomas lying there.

"He's always so careful. I don't know how he came to fall."

He shrugged. "Can happen to anybody. Anyway, I'm glad he's going to be okay." He hesitated, seeming to struggle with something he wanted to say. "You know, about the kids going in my yard . . ."

"You were quite right to be angry with them," she said quickly, not eager to start defending them and herself again.

"It's not so much them." Haggerty paused, frowning, his face drawing in. "Where we lived before . . . well, the neighborhood changed over the years. We should have moved, but my wife loved that old house. I didn't want to upset her, especially . . ."

He let that trail off, and she knew he was thinking of his wife's death.

"Anyway, the kids around there were pretty bad. Not just walking across the lawn but damaging anything they could lay their hands on." His lips pressed together, as if he didn't want to say more. Then the words poured out. "My wife loved her flowers. Said when she looked out and saw them, she forgot everything else. And those hoodlums—they ripped up the flower beds with their bikes, tore them all up and left them for us to find." He stopped then, reliving the past and fighting for control.

Tears welled in Dorcas's eyes. She touched his arm gently, longing to do something and knowing that nothing would make it better. "I'm so very sorry."

Haggerty gave a short nod, swallowing hard. "Didn't mean to say all that." The words were gruff, and he made an obvious effort to shake off his grief. "Anyway, I see now your kids aren't like that. Tell them I'm sorry for yelling, okay?"

"I will. Denke."

He smiled, and she saw what he must have looked like before he was ravaged by grief and pain. "Denke to you, too." He walked away quickly, and she realized he needed to be alone.

Alone for the moment, yes. But she prayed that he'd open his heart enough to let them make him feel welcome and at home here.

THOMAS HEARD THE back door slam and knew Esther was home. And shouting his name. He'd call back, but he'd already discovered that there were very few things he could do without making his ribs crunch in pain.

She came flying into the living room, where he was tucked up in the padded rocking chair and wedged into place with pillows. He'd had a painful try at every other piece of furniture before settling in Mamm's rocker. She had wanted him to retire to bed the minute they got home, but the thought of the steep stairs discouraged him.

"Thomas!" Esther surged toward him as if to hug him, and he raised his hand to fend her off.

"No touching," he said. "I'm as fragile as a piece of glass right now."

She grinned but backed up a pace. "You don't look it."

"Believe me, I feel it." He reached out to touch her hand. "Thanks for being such a help."

Esther looked as if she was holding back tears with an effort. "It was scary."

"You're telling me. I can't believe the floor was that hard. I feel like I've been kicked by a team of horses, at least."

That brought her smile back. "I've never ridden in an ambulance. Could you hear the siren? Did you have fun?"

He grimaced. "*Fun* isn't the word for it. Let's hope you never have to do it."

"I guess." Although she looked as if she still yearned to take a trip in an ambulance. She just didn't want to be hurt to do it. "Mammi says we have to take care of you for a couple of days. What do you want? Should I bring you some tea and toast?"

"Tea and toast?" He grimaced. "No, thanks."

"That's what Mammi always gives me when I'm sick."

"I remember. One time when I was sick, I talked Jonas into sneaking me a snickerdoodle. It made my stomach hurt, but it sure tasted good."

Esther smiled, but she looked disappointed at not being able to wait on him, so he tried to come up with something.

"If there's any ham left, you can make me a sandwich. With cheese and pickle."

"And tea?" she asked hopefully.

"Okay, tea," he agreed and was rewarded with a smile. When she'd gone off to the kitchen, he leaned back in the rocker, feeling exhausted. The next few days wouldn't be much fun, and the work wouldn't get done while he was laid up. He'd be glad to blame somebody else, but it was his own inattention that had caused this, unlike being sick, which nobody could help.

His thoughts drifted back to the day he'd told Esther about. It hadn't been hard to get Jonas to bring him that snickerdoodle. At that age, Jonas had looked up to his big brother, even wanted to be like him. Funny how much things had changed since then. No, *funny* was the wrong word. *Sad* was more like it.

Regret ate at him, but there was no cure. No one could go back and undo what had already been done.

What with all the fussing Mamm and Esther did, the day seemed longer than ever. All he could think was that he wanted to talk to Dorcas, to tell her . . .

To tell her what? Nothing had changed. But he couldn't erase the picture in his mind. He'd opened his eyes, stunned and hardly knowing who or where he was, and seen Dorcas's face, her eyes filled with love. He'd known, then. He couldn't deny any longer that they loved each other. But what kind of payment for her love would it be to ask her to leave her family behind and go off to who-knows-where with a man who couldn't even provide for her?

He couldn't talk to her, chained to the rocking chair as he was. He could only hope that someone had told her that he was all right.

But he should let her know that he fully intended to get back to work as soon as possible. Could he do that without straying into the dangerous territory of feelings? He'd have to; that was all.

Mamm wouldn't allow him to jaunt out to the phone shanty, even if he'd been able to. Still, he could send a note to her via Esther tomorrow, asking her to stop and see him after school. It wouldn't be private, but that was all for the best.

The evening dragged on, punctuated by Esther's attempts to amuse him. Finally, when she'd proposed dragging a table over to him so they could work a puzzle, Mamm intervened, declaring that that he must go to bed.

"I'm all grown up now, Mammi," he teased.

Mamm eased Esther and the table away from his chair. "Never you mind about that," she said firmly. "You're still my boy, and I know when you're tired, even if you don't."

"But I do," he protested, starting the process of getting out of the chair.

She put her hand on his shoulder and pressed him back gently. "Not by yourself. Jonas will help you."

Before he could argue, she was calling Jonas from the kitchen with orders to help him to bed. Jonas looked as reluctant as he'd anticipated, but he nodded.

"I can manage," Thomas said when his brother bent to take his arm.

"Best not to argue with Mammi." Jonas grasped his arm firmly. "Is this okay?"

He nodded. Jonas was right. Arguing would just draw attention to the breach between them.

With Jonas's strong arm supporting him, he managed to get out of the chair. He took a few steps, only to find the stairs confronting him, looking as scalable as a mountain.

"Whoa," he murmured.

Jonas looked from his strained face to the stairs. "If you sat on a straight chair, maybe Daad and I could carry it up."

He winced at the thought. "Like we used to do with Grossdaadi? I don't think so."

He thought he actually saw amusement in Jonas's face at that. "How about if you hold the railing on one side and I hold you on the other?"

"Since Mamm won't let me sleep in the chair, I guess we better try that." He reached for the railing.

"Okay, here we go." Jonas lifted, he pulled, and they got up one step, then another and another.

Funny. It was the first thing he and Jonas had actually done together since he'd come back. Wobbling and straining, they were finally up the steps and into the bedroom.

Jonas lowered him onto the bed in the room they had once shared, and Thomas knew he had to say something to break the uncomfortable silence between them.

"I was telling Esther about the time when I was sick, and you hid a cookie from Mammi and brought it to me."

Jonas managed a slight smile. "Gut thing she didn't catch me at it. I always thought she had eyes in the back of her head."

"She did," he said, smiling in return. "You risked a fine scolding for helping me. That was when you kept trying to be like me." His smile faded. "It's just as well you stopped trying after a while."

"I was just too scared of Daad, that's all." Jonas turned away before Thomas had time to consider that comment. But he knew there was something that should be said between them.

"Jonas, wait a second."

His brother paused, but he didn't turn back to face Thomas.

"Listen, I just want you to know that I didn't come back with the idea of taking your place here. I came because I wanted to be home. And I wanted to mend fences." He hesitated, not sure whether to go on. "I guess some fences are beyond repair," he said to Jonas's back.

He saw his brother's body tighten. Then just as quickly he relaxed, turning slightly toward him.

"I don't guess there's anything so bad it can't be fixed,"

he said. The words hung there between them for a moment. Before Thomas could find an answer, he'd gone.

Thomas lay back on the pillows and considered. Was that an olive branch? It sounded that way, and his heart warmed. He just wished he'd be there long enough to accept it.

WEDNESDAY SEEMED LIKE another very long day at school for Dorcas, even longer than the previous day, when she'd been waiting impatiently to hear how Thomas was. The familiar sounds of hammer and saw from the stable were silent now, and the school day seemed incomplete without them.

At least things had been calm at home. Mamm and Lemuel were back, with her cousin's neighbors taking over the work on the farm while others helped with the kinder. Best of all, Jenny's husband was home again. Dorcas felt a new bond with her cousin. She, too, had seen someone she loved taken away in an ambulance.

Shaking her head, she focused on the task at hand . . . namely, leading each grade level through its part in the spring program. It really had been coming together well, but for some reason today the scholars seemed infected by her own restlessness. The sixth graders stumbled over a recitation they'd done perfectly at the last practice, and the seventh graders could not stop rustling papers and whispering together. Only the primary children concentrated, saying their pieces with very little prompting.

She and Anna exchanged glances as the clock crawled toward dismissal time. "They'll be better tomorrow," Anna said, sounding as if she didn't believe it herself.

"They could hardly be worse." Dorcas smiled to show she didn't really mean that. "Let's see if you can get the seventh and eighth graders to try the ending once more."

Anna nodded and moved toward the group, but even as she did so, Esther broke away from them and marched toward Dorcas. She thrust a folded piece of paper toward Dorcas.

"This is for you."

Dorcas flipped it open, and her heart jolted when she realized it was from Thomas. Hoping she hadn't given herself away, she read through it quickly. Thomas hoped she would stop by the house after school today. He wanted to talk to her about the stable project.

Almost before she'd finished, Esther was speaking. "I s'pose you're coming."

She sounded so unwelcoming that Dorcas gave her a startled look.

"Yah, of course. Denke, Esther. I'll stop by after I've finished my work here."

Esther drifted off toward her group, and Dorcas looked after her thoughtfully. Odd, that's what it was. Esther must have brought the note with her when she came to school this morning. Why had she waited until now to give it to Dorcas?

She might have forgotten about it, but that didn't account for Esther's attitude. This seemed to be more pointed than simply forgetting.

Dorcas tried to brush it away. Esther's home life had been disrupted with Thomas's return, and from what Thomas had said about his father, it hadn't settled down yet. And given Thomas's accident on top of it, Esther might be excused for not handling things well.

It was nearly time to let the children go. She'd busy herself with work here so that she wouldn't have to walk to the Fisher place with Esther and the other scholars who lived in that direction. She felt as if she needed a small respite from them before she met with Thomas.

But once the scholars were on their way, Anna hurried

over to her, looking worried. "I . . . I have something to tell you."

Having said that much, Anna succumbed to reluctance, standing there twisting her fingers together and shifting from one foot to the other.

Dorcas forced herself to smile. "Whatever it is, tell me. I won't bite you."

"You'll feel like it." Anna's face eased a little. "It's Esther and her friends. I happened to overhear what they were saying when they should have been working." She lost the smile. "I felt . . . well, I knew you should hear it."

"Go ahead." Her thoughts raced. What could they have been chattering about that would have Anna so upset?

"It was Esther. She said that you . . . that you and Thomas . . . well, she said that you were trying to catch Thomas. To marry him, she meant."

Dorcas couldn't find words for a moment. What had happened that would suggest such a thing to Esther? Whatever there was between her and Thomas, she wasn't trying to catch him. And how would Esther know anything about their feelings? There had never been anything between them that she could have seen.

"I'm sorry," Anna said. "I was tempted to scold them for gossiping about you, but I didn't know if that was the right way to handle it or not."

She focused on Anna, who was looking apprehensive and needed to be reassured. "You did exactly the right thing. I'm glad you told me."

"Denke. I wasn't sure, but . . . anyway, I know it's ridiculous. You wouldn't be trying to trap Thomas into marriage, even if . . . well, even if the two of you . . ." She floundered into silence.

Dorcas patted her arm. "We certain sure haven't done anything wrong, and Esther should not be gossiping about us in any event." She shook her head. "I've been making

excuses for Esther, knowing that the family has been upset by Thomas's return, but this is going too far. I'm afraid
I'll have to speak to her parents."

And how on earth she was going to bring that up, she
didn't know. She came out of her absorption to realize
that Anna was still standing there, looking worried. "If
you want me to do anything . . . I mean, I'd do whatever
you said."

The unexpected offer brought tears to her eyes, and she
squeezed Anna's hand. "Denke, but there's nothing you
can do. You go on home. I'll go over there in a bit and talk
to them."

Anna nodded, clearly relieved that the burden didn't
fall on her. "I'll see you tomorrow, then." She hesitated.
"I hope it's all right." With that, she hurried away.

Dorcas wished she were going with her. Or anyplace
other than where she was. Esther was certain sure com-
plicating an already difficult situation.

Her thoughts stopped spinning and settled on the one
thing she definitely had to do. She had to tell Thomas
about it. If rumors about them were going around, Thomas
had a right to know it.

But she wished she didn't have to tell him.

CHAPTER FIFTEEN

Dorcas was still filled with regrets and apprehension when she reached the lane to the Fisher farm. And a bit of thankfulness, too, that she hadn't elected to walk home with Esther. That would have been much too difficult once she'd heard what Anna had to say.

She slowed down as she started toward the house, partly because she was tired of lugging her bag of schoolwork for this distance and partly to think again how to break this news to Thomas. The last thing she wanted was to disrupt the bond he seemed to be forming with his little sister.

Thomas must have hardly known Esther in those days leading up to his departure. She would have been a child then, and now she was approaching womanhood, with all the usual fits and starts along the way. Hers was a difficult age even under normal circumstances, and the family problems made it worse.

For the first time it occurred to her that Minister Lucas was not just hasty but actually wrong in his stubborn insistence on expecting such rigid adherence to the rules for his children. It seemed almost heretical to consider that, but she supposed a minister could be wrong about some things, just as any other person could be.

Children needed rules, of course. They couldn't be happy and good unless they had clear boundaries. She enforced that in her classroom. But justice had to be tempered with mercy, didn't it? Scripture said one should do justice and love mercy. Maybe it was the balance between the two that was difficult.

In any event, Thomas's father wasn't likely to accept advice from her. She'd have to be very careful how she spoke to him. Thank goodness she could ease it a little by talking privately to Thomas first.

A few minutes later, Dorcas was wondering exactly how private any conversation with Thomas would be. Miriam Fisher was in the kitchen as she'd expected, but Esther was there as well.

"Dorcas, it's wonderful gut to see you." Miriam beamed as she extended the warm greeting. "Will you have coffee? Or some cider? I just opened a quart."

"Maybe later." She noticed that Esther was looking everywhere but at her. "Esther brought me a note from Thomas, saying he needed to speak with me. How is he doing? If he's resting, I shouldn't interrupt him."

"Ach, goodness no. He's getting restless already at not doing anything. I had to practically tie him to the rocking chair to keep him from going out and helping with the cows."

"He certain sure shouldn't be doing that, but I don't suppose he likes to be idle." Most people didn't, finding an illness or injury a nuisance when there was much to be done.

Miriam glanced toward the living room. "He's fretting on getting behind with the work he's doing at the school." She had lowered her voice. "I told him a few days wouldn't make much difference, but he's so impatient."

Dorcas guessed by those words that Thomas hadn't told his mother yet that he intended to leave as soon as the work was done. Poor Miriam. There was sadness ahead for her. Maybe it was better this way. At least she could enjoy this time of having her whole family together.

"Shall I go in?" She nodded toward the living room.

"Ach, yes, what am I thinking? You didn't come here after a long day of school to stand around talking to me."

She linked arms with Dorcas and walked her to the front room. Esther, after a moment of apparent indecision, followed them. Now, how exactly was she to get rid of them? She couldn't have an audience to the conversation she had to have with Thomas.

Most of the clapboard farmhouses in the valley were built in the same style, and she could have found her way without a guide, but Miriam wouldn't think that polite.

"Thomas, here's Teacher Dorcas come to see you," Miriam called.

Thomas, leaning back in the padded rocker with his feet on a footstool, struggled as if to get up at their entrance.

"You stay right where you are," Miriam scolded, pushing him back gently. "Teacher Dorcas doesn't mind the least little bit."

"That's right." She smiled at him, hoping he knew how to persuade his family to leave them alone.

Miriam gestured to Esther, and together they pushed an upholstered chair nearer to the rocker. "There, now." Miriam patted it invitingly. "You sit right here, Dorcas, and be comfortable."

Obediently, Dorcas sat, plopping her school bag on the floor next to the chair. "I got your note," she told Thomas. "I was happy to stop over after school. How are you feeling?" *And how are we going to get your family to go away?*

"Much better. I should be back to work in a day or two." He gave his mother a defiant look.

"We'll see," Miriam said.

Dorcas could have told him that wouldn't work. No

matter how old he was, he was still Miriam's little boy. Her expression told Dorcas that Thomas wasn't going back to work until she said so.

"I'm glad you're doing better," she said quickly, interrupting what she feared would be an argument. "But that was a bad fall, and you mustn't come back too soon. The work will still be there."

She hoped she wasn't saying that just because it ensured that he'd be there a little longer.

Miriam was moving toward the door. "I'll leave you alone to talk about the job."

"Denke," Dorcas murmured, hoping her face didn't say how relieved she was.

Unfortunately, Esther lingered, leaning against the door frame and studying the planks beneath her feet.

When her mother reached her, however, she caught Esther by the arm. "Come along," she said, urging her out. "We need to go and get the laundry off the line. It should be dry by now."

Dorcas listened to their footsteps receding and felt a moment of dismay. Now she'd have to get on with telling him, and that wouldn't be easy.

"I wanted to be sure you knew I wouldn't go until I finished the job." Thomas was studying her intently. "But I see something else is on your mind."

"How did you know?" It would be better if he couldn't read her feelings so easily.

"You know," he said in an undertone.

She did. It was the same reason she could tell something was troubling him, sometimes even what he was thinking about. The bond between them had become so tight—how could Thomas think of breaking it?

"I'm afraid it's about Esther," she began, and then stopped, not really wanting to say the rest of it.

He looked resigned. "What has she done now?"

"I'm afraid," she repeated, and then shook her head. "I didn't mean that. The problem is that there's some trouble, and it involves us . . . you and me." She stopped to take a breath. He wouldn't understand unless she got it out. "Esther and her girlfriends were whispering when they were supposed to be working on a project."

"That's normal, isn't it?" She could see by his expression that he didn't want to hear this.

"It is, yah, but Anna overheard what they were saying. Esther was talking to the other girls about us. Gossiping about us. Anna heard Esther say that I was trying to trap you into marrying me."

Judging by the heat flaring under her skin, she was probably bright red by the time the words were out. Thomas just sat there. Then his anger spiked.

"That's ridiculous," he snapped.

She watched him steadily. "Do you mean it's ridiculous because she wouldn't say that, or ridiculous that anyone could think it?"

He shook his head irritably. "Either. Both. What have we done that would even put that idea into her head? Anna must have misunderstood."

"Do you really believe that Anna would tell me if she weren't sure?"

Thomas was silent for a long moment, obviously struggling with himself. When he spoke, he didn't really answer the question. "Esther must have seen something that made her jump to conclusions about us."

Dorcas felt a slight measure of relief. At least she didn't have to argue him into believing it.

"Yah, but what? She wasn't even there when you . . . when we . . ."

"When I kissed you," he finished for her. "No, she wasn't." And then, irrelevantly, he added, "I thought I regretted it, but I don't."

"I don't either," she had to admit. "Still, even though she can't have seen anything improper, she must have felt something . . . guessed something . . . just from seeing us together."

Thomas shook his head, getting a baffled, stubborn look. "I still say it's ridiculous. She'll have forgotten it tomorrow."

She'd never thought of the possibility that he'd dismiss it so lightly. It hurt, that he didn't see how dangerous this could be for her.

"Even if she does, and I don't think she will, the damage may already have been done. Don't you see what will happen if those girls pass that story on to someone else? You know how fast rumor can spread here. It would be all over the community by tomorrow."

"What if it is? I mean . . ." He stopped, obviously realizing he'd said the wrong thing.

"I see." She kept her voice calm and her expression neutral, but it wasn't easy. "You mean it can't hurt you, because you're going away. But it can hurt me. People aren't going to want a schoolteacher who . . . who sets her cap for someone who's working at the school." She felt the heat come into her face again.

He didn't speak for a moment. "Yah," he said finally. "I'm not thinking straight. It could hurt you."

It already has, she thought. He hadn't even considered her in his first reaction to the problem.

"All right," he said. "What do you think we should do?"

"I don't want to, but this is the sort of thing I normally would feel obligated to tell the parents. I can't handle it myself. It's too big for that."

"No!" He got the word out before she'd finished speaking. "You don't know how Daad will react. He'll be hard on Esther, and even harder on me. I don't matter. I'm leaving anyway. But it will destroy what I have with Esther, and Daad—he's not going to be gentle when it's a question of his own daughter spreading malicious gossip."

"Do you think I don't know that?" she burst out. "That's why I'm talking to you first. I hoped you might find some other way of handling it. But I can't just do nothing. It would be bad for Esther to get away with it, and much worse for me. I could lose my school."

"I know. I know." He reached out and grabbed her hand in a tight grip. She could feel his fierce concern through it. "Just . . . will you let me talk to her? Maybe I can get through to her. I'll make her see that the whole idea is ridiculous. If she tells the other girls she was mistaken, it will die out without any problems."

Maybe. She couldn't feel sure about that, even if Thomas got through to his sister. It might already be too late. He hadn't asked who the girls were.

Erna and Hallie . . . should she tell him they were Lydia Gaus's daughters? She wondered, not for the first time, what Lydia had against her and the school. In any event, if they had said anything about this, it was too late to repair.

Just as it was too late for them. *Ridiculous,* Thomas had said about the idea of the two of them together.

But even though all her senses were shouting at her that this was the wrong way to handle it, she couldn't deny Thomas this favor. It might be the last thing she could do for him.

"All right," she murmured, cherishing the feel of his hand on hers. "You talk to her. I won't tell your parents. Yet."

WHEN DORCAS HURRIED away, her face averted, Thomas knew that she was upset, probably regretting that she'd given in to him. Still, he couldn't believe the situation was as dire as she believed.

After all, they weren't teenagers. At their age, they might well be courting. The word gave him an odd feeling. Regret? If circumstances had been different, that might have been, but not with Daad so set against him. Daad didn't want him here, so how could he stay?

No, he had nothing to offer Dorcas. To be with him meant that he'd have to ask her to leave her people behind and go off into an uncertain future with him. He had his skill, but no job.

And even if she said yes, what then? What if her mother went into a depression the way she had when Dorcas's father was so ill? From what his mother had said, she was only now beginning to come out of it. Dorcas wouldn't be able to live with that. They couldn't build their happiness on other people's sorrow.

His only choice was to leave. Dorcas was young, even though she considered herself an old maid. She could still marry one day and have a family. He couldn't help wincing at the thought, but he had to be realistic for both of them.

Meanwhile, he had to deal with Esther. He'd have to find an opportunity to talk with her when no one was around. Once she knew what he wanted, she'd be only too glad to have it said in private. But he dreaded it.

The opportunity came after supper, when everyone else had gone outside, taking advantage of the longer daylight hours to get a few more chores done.

"You stay with your brother, in case he needs something." Mammi gave Esther a little pat. "Play a game or something, so he doesn't try doing things he shouldn't."

To his relief, Esther was happy with that idea. Smiling, she pulled a table over near his chair. "How about doing a puzzle? We have a bunch of them that you haven't seen."

"Okay. You pick one out." A puzzle was just right. It would keep their hands occupied, and he'd have time to figure out what to say to her. The trouble was that there was no good way to do it. He'd just have to avoid sounding like Daad in the midst of a lecture.

They started separating the edge pieces, linking them together where they could. He suspected she had deliberately hidden the picture from him, giving herself an unfair advantage.

"Putting a puzzle together isn't a competition," he observed mildly.

She looked a little startled, then realized what he meant and giggled. "I thought it would make it more interesting for you if you didn't know what it was."

He made a doubting sound. "We'll see about that."

Esther matched up a few more pieces and then linked them onto his. "There. I gave you a start. Can you tell what it is?"

"Sky," he said. "Lots of blue sky, by the looks of it." They worked together in silence for a few minutes, and he told himself it was time, before anyone else came in from outside. "I hear you've been talking about Teacher Dorcas."

Esther's fingers froze on the piece she was moving, and her lower lip came out. "I s'pose she told you that."

Esther's pouting look annoyed him, chipping at his goodwill. "You'd better be glad she talked to me instead of to Daad. Can you imagine what he'd say? You know how he feels about gossip."

She threw a piece down. "It's not gossip if it's true."

"It's not true," he retorted. "Teacher Dorcas and I have never done a single inappropriate thing."

Well, maybe that kiss had been inappropriate, but it hadn't been at the school, and anyway, no one knew.

"*You* didn't. You can't even see it, but she's trying to take you away from us." Her voice grew more impassioned. "You were gone so long, and then you came back and everything was nice. You paid attention to me, and we were friends. Until she tried to take you away. She's an old maid, and Erna says old maids always want to get married. She wants to marry you."

"Now listen, Esther, you have to stop talking that way." He knew which one Erna was . . . Lydia Gaus's older girl. "We're still friends—that hasn't changed. You're my little sister, and I love you. You know that, don't you?"

Esther's expression didn't change, but she nodded slowly, so he'd have to be content with that. He went on. "Even if there was something between me and Teacher Dorcas, it wouldn't be wrong. But there's not, and this could be serious for her. If you start spreading rumors around, Teacher Dorcas could lose her job."

Esther shrugged, taking on a look that reminded him of Erna. "Why should I care? Erna and Hallie say if she leaves, we'll all go over to the Oak Creek school. They used to go there, and they say it's a lot better than ours."

This had gotten into deep water in a hurry. He'd imagined himself saying a few well-chosen words to Esther, maybe resulting in a few tears. Then he'd comfort her to show that he didn't blame her, and she'd do her best to make the situation better.

Instead, Esther seemed to be someone he didn't know. That was it, wasn't it? Surely she couldn't really be as callous and uncaring as that sounded.

He took a firm hold on his patience. "I don't think you really believe any of that, do you? You're just repeating things that Erna Gaus says. And if you think any of the parents are going to want their kids going all the way over to Oak Creek, you'd better think again."

"I . . . Erna and Hallie say they will." She'd begun to sound uncertain.

"Erna and Hallie don't know as much as you think they do. And what do you suppose is going to happen to me if everybody starts talking about me and Teacher Dorcas?"

She looked at him, openmouthed. "Nothing . . . nothing will happen to you. Will it?"

"Maybe you should have asked your friends that." He'd like to tell them a few sharp things himself. "What do you think Daad will say? He'll blame me, and that will be the last straw. I'll have to leave again."

He was going to leave anyway, and he felt traitorous about not telling her that. Still, it would complicate everything if she knew.

"Well? Is that what you want?" he demanded.

Tears welled slowly in her eyes. "I didn't know. I didn't think."

"That's about the size of it. You didn't think. You just listened to other people's ideas and swallowed them, and now you've caused trouble for everyone."

"I didn't mean to cause trouble for you. I just wanted you to pay attention to me."

"Esther, I'll always pay attention to you, but that doesn't mean I can't talk to anyone else. And even if I'm not always here, I'm still your big brother. Nothing changes that."

Her mouth trembled. "I . . . I'm sorry."

He winced at the tears in her voice. Still, she had to learn. "Gossip gets out of control. Once something is spoken, you can't take it back. You don't know what damage it will do."

"But I don't want it to. I have to stop it." She shoved the pieces together on the table. "What can I do?"

That's where he'd thought they'd be a lot quicker. But at least now she saw, and he didn't think she'd be so eager to buy Erna's stories another time.

"You'd best do what you can to make it right. Tell Erna and Hallie you found out it's not true. Tell them if they talk about it, they'll bring terrible trouble not just to other people, but to themselves. I sure won't be quiet about them if the worst happens."

Esther shot to her feet. "I'll go call right now. I can leave a message not to say anything. And tomorrow I'll make sure they don't. I will, I promise."

She fled without waiting for a response. Just as well, because he didn't have anything reassuring to say. He thought she understood now, and it wasn't an easy lesson to learn. But what if it was already too late?

DORCAS TRUDGED UP the path leading home, tired and upset. Her inner self was telling her that she'd made the wrong decision in not going directly to Esther's parents, but she knew that if she had it to do over again, she'd do the same. Thomas had lost so much of his family already thanks to her cowardice. She couldn't ruin his fragile relationship with his little sister.

Thomas didn't seem to see what was really behind Esther's actions. It wasn't just a question of being indiscreet, or of eagerness to have important news to share. Esther was jealous of her.

Esther had all the teenage girl's awareness of romance in the air without the common sense to understand it. She'd sensed their feelings for each other even if she hadn't seen anything suggestive.

Poor Esther. She wanted to be important in her brother's life. She'd probably see anyone who drew his attention away from her as an enemy. The fact that Dorcas was her teacher simply made it even worse.

If there was a way out of this whole situation that wouldn't end up hurting anyone, Dorcas couldn't see it.

She'd reached the house by then, so she straightened her shoulders and walked more briskly. Raising concerned questions wasn't part of her plan. She could only try to behave normally and brace herself against the next blow to fall.

Unfortunately, Dorcas realized how little she'd succeeded when her mother took one look at her, put down the spatula she'd been using to turn the potato cakes, and hurried over to put her arm around Dorcas.

"What is it, Dorcas?" She gave her a quick hug. "Something has happened to disturb you. Is it Thomas? Is he more badly hurt than you thought?"

Mammi had an unerring knack for putting her finger on the right spot. Dorcas almost wished she'd go back to the inattention and withdrawal she'd shown when Daad was ill.

No, of course she didn't wish that. She was horrified at herself.

"His injuries are healing, at least from what Miriam says. I had to stop over there after school. Thomas wanted to talk to me about the work. He's determined to get back to it as soon as possible."

So he could leave Promise Glen. But she couldn't say that out loud.

"That's gut, but he mustn't rush it. I know it's important to get the work done. For the school, but for him, too." She drew Dorcas to a seat at the table and sat down next to her. "It will be a fine advertisement for the business he's starting."

There wasn't going to be a business, but she nodded. "Really, nothing's wrong. I'm just tired is all."

Mammi reached out to cup Dorcas's face between her palms, forcing her daughter to look at her. "Komm, now. We both know better than that. I don't want to pry, but . . ." Sorrow crossed her face and darkened her eyes. "For too long I didn't pay enough attention to you. Right at a crucial age when a girl needs her mammi the most. Let me make up for that now. Please."

"Mammi, you didn't . . ." She began, but her mother was already shaking her head.

She hadn't realized until now that her mother was aware of failing her. And that had been fine with Dorcas. She certain sure didn't want her mother to feel guilt on top of her grief. And it hadn't been her mother's fault if she had run a little wild in those days. She'd known what she was doing was wrong, and she'd done it anyway, with disastrous consequences for Thomas, if not for her.

One thing was certain. She couldn't confess to what she'd done back then, even to make herself feel better. It would just make her mother's pain worse and serve no good purpose.

But she could tell her about Esther. She'd promised not to give Esther away to her parents, but her own mother wasn't part of that.

The pressure was just too much. She nodded. "Something happened at school today that was upsetting. That's all."

Mammi took her hands from Dorcas's face and clasped them firmly on the table. "Tell me."

"It's Esther, Thomas's sister. She . . . she got the mistaken idea that Thomas . . . that I . . . well, she told her friends that I was out to trap Thomas into marrying me." She grimaced. "Apparently girls that age think that any maidal of my age is out to get a husband by fair means or foul."

"That's not so bad, is it?" Mammi patted her hands. "Even if it were true . . ." She let that die out, probably beginning to realize the possibilities. "Ach, what's going on with that child?"

"She's jealous of me, that's all it is. She'd be jealous of anything that would take Thomas's attention away from her. I can't blame her. She's missed out on a lot of years with him, and she's trying to make up for that in all the wrong ways. Still, I can't have her going around saying something inappropriate is going on at the school."

"Ach, no. You must talk to her at once. Or better still, tell Miriam and Lucas."

"That's what I should have done, I know. But when I went to the Fisher place, I saw Thomas first, and I told him. He was upset, that was certain sure. I think he felt that it was his fault, or at least his responsibility. He wanted to try talking with Esther himself, since it affects him. I agreed to let him handle it, but now I'm worried that I've done the wrong thing. If rumors start to spread around the community—well, it could affect my job."

"Ach, it's all such nonsense. As if you'd even do anything like that. It's not right for Thomas to put you in a situation where you don't tell the parents. Still, maybe Esther will listen to what he says better than to her parents. That happens with girls her age."

"Maybe."

Mammi patted her hands. "You mustn't worry so much about it. You haven't done anything wrong, and I don't think anyone would believe such ill-natured gossip. It will all blow over, you'll see. But Esther does need a gut talking-to, that's certain sure. Miriam would be embarrassed to think her daughter behaved that way."

Dorcas forced a chuckle. "I'm sure she's getting that talking-to from her big bruder right now. Maybe it's making an impression on her." She pulled her hands away. "Don't worry about it, Mammi. I just let it get me down because I was tired, but it's not worth fretting over." She glanced at the pan on the stove. "Anyway, your potato cakes need some attention."

"Ach, what's wrong with me?" Mammi sprang into action, everything else forgotten for the moment.

"I'll be back to help you as soon as I wash my hands." She'd use any excuse for a moment alone.

When she glanced at herself in the mirror over the sink, she understood why Mammi had reacted. Her face was drawn, and all her usual color had disappeared. Quickly splashing some cold water on her face, she tidied her hair and dried her hands.

As Dorcas went back to the kitchen she tried to stay occupied, but her worries wouldn't be ignored. She breathed a silent prayer. She hoped with all her heart that her mother was right, but she had her doubts. She didn't think they'd heard the end of this, not at all.

CHAPTER SIXTEEN

By Friday morning, Dorcas had stopped waiting for disaster to strike. She'd been so keyed up when she'd come to school the previous day, but nothing had happened all day, and Esther had been quiet and docile. Too quiet, in Dorcas's opinion. She considered saying something to her but decided not to risk making it worse. She didn't want the lively spirit stamped out of the girl, even though she'd behaved foolishly.

Still, whatever Thomas said to her seemed to have worked. From what Dorcas had seen of Esther in the past years, she should be resilient enough to bounce back from any scolding Thomas had given her, but it seemed she had taken this one hard, probably because it was from him. She cherished his good opinion as much as she wanted his attention.

Dorcas looked away from the mathematics lesson she was teaching to the eighth graders, surveying the classroom. No one was giggling or wiggling, and that was a cause for gratitude. Anna spun a globe as she challenged the middle grades to find various spots in the world. Her face was bright with interest, and the scholars' faces echoed her expression.

That was definitely the way to catch them. If you were interested, how could the children help but be? Anna had learned that lesson quickly.

Unfortunately Dorcas was finding it heavy going to keep the eighth graders focused on math. It was her fault, but today she couldn't work up enthusiasm about the subject herself. When she'd finally finished her lesson with the older scholars, Dorcas walked to the front and rapped on her desk. "Since it's such a warm day, how would you like to take your lunches outside?"

That idea was greeted with smiles and a few clapped hands.

"All right, then. Put your books away, and then you may get your lunches and line up at the door."

With an outburst of energy, the children scurried to do as she said. She'd been keeping half an eye on the Gaus girls, and she saw that now they were talking rapidly at Esther, who kept shaking her head.

About what? About Esther's brother and the teacher? Well, if so, they weren't making much impression on Esther. She shook her head again and walked away, picking up her lunch bag and getting in line at the door. The Gaus girls exchanged glances. Shrugging, they followed her.

She'd give a great deal to know what they were talking about, even if she didn't like the answer. But at least Esther didn't seem to mind turning them down. She couldn't help feeling that Erna, in particular, wasn't a good influence on the other girls. She was too precocious, for one thing. And maybe too like her mother, always convinced she was right.

Well, whatever it was, Esther had said no, so Dorcas would have to be content with her refusal.

Or did she? It had been on her mind all morning that she ought to talk to Esther herself, but she'd hung back, not wanting to chance disrupting the good work Thomas had done. Maybe during lunch period she'd have an opportunity to open a conversation, even on something completely unrelated. It might let her evaluate Esther's feelings, at any rate.

Dorcas picked up her own lunch and thermos and followed the children outside. She'd no more than stepped onto the porch when she saw a buggy coming down the lane toward the school. Jonas Fisher was driving with Thomas sitting next to him, while Adam leaned over the back of their seats.

Her heart gave an unexpected leap. She hadn't expected to see Thomas here before next week, at least. And judging by what she'd heard about Jonas's reaction to his brother's return, she definitely hadn't thought to see him sitting next to Thomas.

The brothers drove right around the school to the stable. Given the way her heart seemed to follow them, she decided that there really wasn't anything wrong with going back to the stable to check up on them.

Before she could move, Anna came hurrying toward her.

"I didn't think Thomas could possibly be back so soon. And his brothers, too. Do you suppose they're all going to work on the stable?"

Anna's eyes had an extra sparkle when she mentioned Thomas's brothers, making Dorcas wonder which one was the center of Anna's attention. Jonas was older than she was, but not enough to matter. And when a girl had her eye on someone, she didn't think of age. Adam seemed much younger, probably because he had that lively manner and a hint of recklessness in his smile.

Well, Anna would just have to wait if she wanted to talk to them.

"Will you take over here, please? I'll just go and see what they're going to do. I hope Thomas won't try to do too much. We don't want to go through that again, do we?"

Anna shook her head vehemently. "Please tell him I hope he's feeling better."

"I will." And she'd give him a strong lecture if he thought he was going to go climbing around the stable again.

Nodding to Anna, she slipped quickly around the schoolhouse and hurried toward the stable. Jonas was unloading something from the buggy, while Adam seemed determined to help Thomas get down.

When she reached them, Thomas seemed to be protesting about his efforts. "Let go, Adam. I can get down by myself."

"And injure your ribs all over again?" Dorcas gave Adam an encouraging nod. "You let your brother help you, or I'll kick the three of you off school property."

Her smile belied the sharp words. Adam grinned, and Jonas tried to hide a smile.

"You heard," Adam said, grasping his brother's arm. "Let me help you."

She saw Thomas wince at his grasp. "One moment," she said. "There's a bench just inside the stable door. If you get that, Thomas can step on it to get down. That way he won't risk jarring himself."

When Adam hesitated, Jonas came to give him a shove. "You heard. Do what Teacher Dorcas says." He nodded at Dorcas. "Thomas was determined to come. We're supposed to make sure he doesn't get into mischief."

"I'm right here," Thomas said. "I can speak for myself." But he was smiling.

Dorcas glanced from his face to Jonas's. It seemed the situation between the two of them had changed for the better, and she was glad. It wasn't right for brothers to be at odds the way they'd been.

Adam returned with the bench. Dorcas studied Thomas's face while the two of them bickered over getting it in the right place. He met her gaze and smiled a little. "Satisfied?"

"No, but I suppose you're too determined to listen to me. Why didn't you wait until Monday, at least?"

"Have a heart. One more day of Mammi and Esther fussing over me, and I'd be climbing the walls. I had to get out."

"At least have sense enough to go easy," she said. "And for goodness' sake, tell Adam how to help you before he breaks another rib."

Adam, caught in the moment of trying to lift his brother, looked startled and a little embarrassed.

"You heard," Thomas said. "Just stand right there so I can put my hand on your shoulder. That's the best way to help me."

Adam looked doubtful, but he did as he was told. Jonas took his place on the other side, and Thomas was soon on solid ground and no worse for wear, from what Dorcas could see.

She was about to go back to the children when she saw Esther peeking around the corner. Realizing she'd been seen, Esther waved.

"Teacher, can I come and say hi?"

Giving in to the inevitable, Dorcas nodded. "Just for a minute," she said. "And then we both have to get back to work."

Esther hurried over and touched her brother lightly on the arm, probably having been told not to hug him. "Everyone says to tell you hello. And they hope you feel better."

Thomas actually flushed a little. "Denke. You tell them I'm a lot better. I'll come over and talk to them at the end of school, if that's okay with Teacher Dorcas." He gave her a questioning look.

"Of course."

"I want to tell them I appreciate their good behavior when I had my accident," he added. He probably knew she wasn't likely to turn him down on anything, given how frightened she'd been by his fall. She could only hope she hadn't given away her feelings to anyone else. At that moment, she wouldn't have cared if the whole world knew, but she'd regained her sense since then.

"Come along, Esther." She touched the girl's arm, and this time she didn't pull away. "He's all right, and Adam and Jonas will make sure he doesn't overdo."

She anticipated the sulky look that had become habitual lately with Esther, but it didn't materialize. Instead, she seemed pleased to walk with Dorcas.

"Did you . . . do you know what Thomas said to me?" Esther gave her a shy, sideways glance and then dropped her gaze.

"No, I don't. He asked me to let him handle the problem instead of telling your parents, and I trusted him to say the right thing. Are we all right now?"

She nodded, still without meeting Dorcas's eyes. "I'm sorry," she murmured, her voice trembling a little. Then she darted ahead to the others.

Something that had been tense inside Dorcas seemed to relax. Whatever else came from this situation, it seemed to have made Esther more aware of her responsibility to others. That was an important step in growing up, and one she was still trying to master herself.

THOMAS TOLD HIMSELF firmly to concentrate on the job at hand and not watch Dorcas walking away from him. The trouble was, each time he saw her, it was harder and harder to hold to his resolution not to speak, and he had to. He wouldn't force her to choose between him and the people and place she loved. If love meant anything, it surely meant doing what was best for the loved one, no matter how much it hurt.

"What's first?" Jonas was looking above the stall toward the roof. "Looks like you had a fair amount to do on the roof. Is it all finished?"

"Yah, it is. And it was in worse shape than I thought at first." He moved toward them, quickly realizing that he couldn't go as fast as he'd expected.

It was all very well for the doctor to say he'd be uncomfortable for a few days. Uncomfortable, he could bear. The doctor should have gone on to say that Thomas wouldn't be moving much, either.

He stopped inside the stable, letting his eyes adjust to the relative dimness. "I didn't realize I'd brought that crosspiece down with me when I came. See, it belongs—"

He made an unwary movement to show them what he meant and fetched up grasping his ribs and breathless.

"Here, sit down." Jonas supported him while Adam dragged a bale of straw over for him to sit on. "You want to get us in trouble with Mammi?"

"You know who she'll blame if we bring you back all stove up," Adam added.

"All right, all right." He sank down on the bale and caught his breath. "You win. I'll talk, not move."

"Gut." Jonas had located the missing crosspiece. "You want us to start with this?"

"May as well. You see where it goes?"

"We see. It's pretty obvious that it came down when you fell. You must have hit it on the way down. Now don't move or I'll tell Teacher Dorcas on you." Jonas picked up hammer and nails. "You want to go up, Adam?"

"Sure thing." Adam started scrambling up the stall bars. "Mammi says I could climb like a monkey before I was out of my crib."

Jonas hoisted the end of the crosspiece up to him.

"What I remember is you trying to climb out of that crib and falling on your head. And me getting blamed for not stopping you."

"The older one always gets blamed," Thomas said. "That's life."

Jonas snorted. "You should have shared a room with him." He jerked a thumb toward Adam, perched high above. "I never even thought of most of the things he tried."

"You don't have enough imagination," Adam said, grinning and pleased with himself.

"Just keep quiet and nail that in place." Jonas handed the tools up to him and came back to Thomas. They both watched Adam walk nimbly along the top of the stall.

"He does have a head for heights," Thomas said, thinking about how long it had been since he'd done something with both of his brothers.

"The last barn-raising, he worked up on the roof without a second thought." Jonas was watching his younger brother with reluctant admiration.

"Wish I could see how he's setting that piece in." Thomas couldn't seem to help fretting. "No, what I really wish is that I could be doing it myself."

"He'll be okay." Jonas glanced at him. "I wouldn't have told him to go up otherwise."

Adam, probably overhearing, looked down at them. "Are you talking about me?" he asked suspiciously.

"Why not?" Thomas said. "Jonas says you're okay up there."

"He does?" Adam, sitting on a crosspiece with his legs dangling, actually looked surprised.

"I do, yah," Jonas said. "Just don't make a liar of me by doing something stupid."

Thomas nodded in agreement. "If you do, you'll have two big brothers jumping on you with both feet. Just remember it."

Adam grimaced. "That's what it is to be the youngest. I'll be good. Honest."

Watching him move around easily, Thomas had to admit that Adam probably did it better than he did. He shrugged. "He's good, I know. Don't think I'm not grateful to the two of you. It's just that this is my work. I don't want someone else doing my job."

Jonas's eyes seemed to narrow. "Our jobs are important to us. We get edgy if we think someone else might want them."

Thomas caught the meaning. "I told you. I don't want your job. I've got my own to do."

"Yah, I know that now. It shouldn't have taken me so long to see it."

Thomas realized that was as close to an apology as Jonas was able to come. But it was enough for him. He smiled at Jonas.

The color came up in his brother's face, and he seemed to be trying to find a way to change the subject.

"So how are the cousins? I haven't seen them in years. They must be getting grown up."

Thomas nodded, willing enough to talk about something else. "They're all good. You wouldn't know Emmy—she's sixteen and has half the boys in the church district crazy over her. She'll drive her daad crazy before she's done."

Jonas relaxed enough to grin. "She was flirting with everyone when she was only six at that wedding we went to. Guess I'm not surprised."

"No." He watched Adam for another moment. "You know, a kid who's a flirt doesn't change. And one who's daring in one thing might well be daring in another."

"I know." Jonas glanced at Adam, too. "He's not going to have as quiet a rumspringa as I did, that's certain sure." He frowned. "He needs someone to talk to, but I'm no good. We argue too much, and he probably thinks I'd go straight to Daad. He's talked to you, hasn't he? Adam, I mean."

"A little. Seems like he didn't listen very well. I've been away too long. That's the problem. If he knew me better, I could do more."

"You're not to blame for that. At least you can guide him away from the worst choices."

The hammering stopped just then, and Thomas lowered his voice. "No one who knows my history would think I was a good person to guide the young."

"He trusts you anyway. That's the most important."

He couldn't deny that it gave him pleasure to hear his brother say that. "Won't do any good if I'm not here."

Jonas looked genuinely surprised at that. "But you're staying, ain't so? I mean, Dorcas . . ."

So he thought that, too. Did everyone in the valley?

"I can't stay if Daad can't trust me. Or forgive me."

Jonas caught the point right away. He could see the recognition in his brother's eyes. Daad's high standards affected all of them, one way or another, and not always for the good.

DORCAS REMAINED CONSCIOUS of the noise from the barn for the rest of the afternoon. She hoped Thomas was being sensible and letting his brothers handle the work. Thomas was usually sensible, but when he thought something was his duty, he didn't care what risks he took. The way he had when he'd gone to that Englisch party with her.

It kept coming back to that in her mind. Thomas said that his father had stopped trusting long before that, but the truth was that it wouldn't have come to a head if it hadn't been for her foolishness combined with Thomas's mistaken chivalry. He should have let her take the consequences of her own actions.

She shivered at the thought. Thomas had been much braver than she was. In a crisis, she'd taken the easy way out. And Thomas had taken the blame.

Anna caught her gaze and looked meaningfully at the clock. Startled by the time, Dorcas pulled herself together.

"Let's clean up the materials from your posters now. Be sure the tops are secure on the glue bottles."

She and Anna would have to check them again, of course, but she was a believer in the value of continuing reminders. Children's attention was fleeting at times, especially when they were excited. There was a rustle of movement throughout the room as the cleanup began.

Joseph's hand went up, and she nodded to him. "May we go and speak to Thomas before we leave? Just to see how he is?"

She glanced out the window and smiled. "You won't have to. I see him coming now."

Sure enough, Thomas was approaching the front door. He probably wanted to be sure the children weren't tempted to go out to the stable and get in the way, which was definitely what they'd want to do.

She nodded to Joseph, who hurried to open the door. Grinning, he exchanged a few words with Thomas while Dorcas walked back to join him. Every face in the room swiveled toward Thomas.

"Let's be quiet for a moment, please, before you're dismissed. Thomas wants to say a few words to you." She gestured to Thomas, who rolled his eyes, probably at the thought of speaking in front of the class.

"I won't keep you. I just wanted to thank all of you for being so helpful when I had my accident this week." He paused, and a little voice piped up.

Matthew, of course, who was always ready to talk. "But we didn't do anything," he said, sounding disappointed.

"For sure you did. All of you cooperated with your teacher so she could do what had to be done. I'm sure Teacher Dorcas and Anna would agree that was a big help."

Matthew considered for a moment, and then he nodded.

"I don't remember what everyone did." Thomas made a face. "Mostly because I knocked myself silly. But thanks to Esther and Joseph and Benjamin, especially."

Joseph and Benjamin flushed and ducked their heads in embarrassment. But Esther . . . Esther's face glowed at the approval from her big brother. Dorcas nodded. He'd done that exactly right.

The scholars seemed to have a number of questions . . . everything from how it felt to ride in an ambulance to what he was doing when he fell. Thomas set about answering them, and Dorcas could let her thoughts follow their own track.

She saw again Esther's glowing smile. It was no secret that she adored her brother. If . . . when . . . he went away again, she would take it hard. Had Thomas thought about that? Most likely.

His brothers would be hurting at the idea, too. It had done her heart good to hear them laughing and joking with each other just as if Thomas's exile had never happened. Thomas had been mending fences with the rest of his family in the short time he'd been back.

But she knew Thomas wouldn't stay without his father's forgiveness. His father's opinion meant so much to him, and she wondered if Minister Lucas even knew how much. Thomas would leave again, and whatever the rights and wrongs of the first time, this time it would all be on his father.

How did Lucas rationalize that? Certainly many people in the community admired him for the way he tried to live up to the standards of his calling in his everyday life. But did they realize the cost of his standards?

Lucas was choosing one right thing over another right thing. How did anyone do that? How did a mere mortal choose between justice and mercy? *Do justice, love mercy, walk humbly with your God.*

Every Amish child had it drilled into him from an early age to be humble, not expecting praise for doing what he should or thinking more of himself than others. Minister Lucas must surely approve of that. But how did he balance justice and mercy when he was dealing with his own son?

Impossible to know, and she had no right to judge. But her heart was torn for all of them.

Thomas was leaning against one of the children's desks, looking tired. He'd been trying to do too much, and that didn't surprise her.

"All right, scholars. Thomas has answered enough questions for today. Go on out, please."

With a few murmured comments to Thomas, they filed out, talking and jostling one another as always. Esther went to Thomas and leaned against him. Dorcas saw him wince and had to bite her tongue to keep from speaking. It was up to Thomas, not her.

Thomas patted Esther's shoulder. "Will you run out to the stable and say I'll be ready in a couple of minutes? You may as well stay and ride home with us. It'll be a squash, but that's okay."

"I don't mind." Esther beamed. "I'll tell them." She hurried off.

Thomas gave a sigh of relief. "I'm wonderful glad we're friends again, but I wish she wasn't so heavy when she hangs on me."

Dorcas's worries dissolved in a chuckle. "That's the cost of being her favorite brother," she teased.

"Only for the moment. She'll switch off pretty soon, ain't so?"

She nodded, smiling. "I'm wonderful glad you took the time to talk with my scholars. The accident was the most exciting thing that had happened in school all month, so they're still talking about it."

He grimaced. "I'd rather forget it, but I understand. I remember how I was at that age. I just hope that's the end of it. Maybe you'd better put some more excitement on the calendar."

"All I have in the way of excitement is the spring program, I'm afraid. They'll have to be satisfied with that."

Dorcas stepped back, suddenly aware that they were alone together in the schoolhouse, probably not the wisest thing they could do. The voices of the children had died away outside, and they were probably off rushing home to tell their parents about seeing Thomas. "If you're ready to leave . . ."

"Not so fast." Thomas caught her wrist and held it, and she was sure he could feel her pulse pounding against his palm.

She tugged against it, but his grasp tightened. "If people are talking about us, this isn't wise," she pointed out.

"I know, but I've got to talk to you alone. What other chance do we have?"

The desperate note in his voice silenced anything else she might say. They had so little time . . . it couldn't be wrong to seize what few moments they had.

"It won't take much longer to finish the work here, especially with my brothers helping."

"It's wonderful good that they want to help you." But she was weeping inside at the way time was fleeing.

"Yah." He pondered for a moment, frowning, the vertical lines between his eyebrows deepening. "Everyone but Daad is coming around. But he's the one who counts." He took a deep breath. "As soon as the work is done, I'll go."

His grip slackened, but now it was her turn to clasp both of his hands in hers.

"Please, Thomas. Please listen. Won't you try talking to your father?"

The lines of bitterness carved themselves deeper. "Why? So he can tell me again what a bad influence I am? Maybe this time he'll come right out and tell me to leave."

"Don't." She couldn't help the pained outcry. "Can't you just try? Talk to him without anger and tell him how you feel. Even say that if he can't forgive you, you'll have to leave. At least give him a chance to consider what he's doing."

"More like giving him a chance to kick me out," he muttered.

She clasped his hands tightly, hoping he could feel her love flowing through them. "For the sake of your family, can't you try?"

"My family?" His gaze seemed to penetrate her skin, as if he saw right into her.

Feeling as if she held her heart in her hands, she added, "For me, then. Give us a chance."

He hesitated, and she could see the struggle inside him. If only he could . . .

He started to answer, but the schoolhouse door swung open. Lydia Gaus stood there, staring at them. Seeing them alone in the empty school, holding hands, looking at each other with their hearts in their eyes.

"Well!" Lydia put a wealth of meaning into the word. "That's just what I thought. This time you're not going to get away with it. We'll just see what Minister Lucas thinks about this."

She slammed the door, disappearing from their sight. "Wait. Let me explain—" Dorcas tried to go after her.

Thomas held her still. "It's no use, Dorcas. Nothing we say will matter to her." His face twisted in pain. "I'm sorry. I cause nothing but trouble for anyone who cares for me."

CHAPTER SEVENTEEN

Dorcas tried vainly to cope with this double disaster. Not only had Lydia Gaus found them in what she was sure to call a compromising situation, but Thomas had reverted to blaming himself for all of it. She couldn't bear the thought that he'd attempt to take the blame for this misfortune, just as he had all those years ago.

"You're not thinking straight." She forced herself to sound calm, even though she felt anything but. "Lydia is out to close the school, and she thinks she can do it by getting rid of me. You were just caught in it because you're here."

"If I weren't here . . . if I hadn't come back . . ."

"Then you wouldn't have healed your relationship with your mother and your sister and brothers. That's worth a great deal, isn't it?"

She wasn't getting through to him. She could see it in his face. He was as remote as if he'd already left Promise Glen behind.

Thomas took a step back from her. "That sounds like Esther and the boys. They're probably ready to leave. Don't say anything about it to them."

"But we have to. Lydia isn't going to let it drop. They'll find out anyway. Isn't it better if they hear it from us?"

He rubbed his forehead as if trying to clarify his thoughts. "Esther—she can't know. Don't you see?"

In his concern for his sister, he seemed to revert to himself again.

"You mean she'll think it's her gossip that brought this on." It was true in a way, but not in the way he thought. "She's just a bystander to Lydia. Like you, she's a tool to pry me out of the school. If it hadn't been this, it would be something else. If only she'd give some idea of why she feels that way, maybe I could deal with her. But it's not Esther's fault."

"Esther won't believe that. She'll blame herself."

Dorcas's temper flared unexpectedly. "It seems to me that people in your family are entirely too ready to blame themselves for everything that goes wrong." Except for Minister Lucas, and in her opinion, he had a lot to answer for.

Footsteps sounded on the porch, and Thomas took her hand in a fierce grip. It seemed she could feel the pounding of his heart through his touch.

"Don't say anything. Not now. I'll deal with it." Then he was turning toward the door, where Adam and Esther appeared.

"Jonas is bringing the buggy around. You want us to drop you at home, Teacher Dorcas? It'll be a squeeze, but we can manage."

"No, denke." She forced what she hoped looked like a smile, knowing it was probably a grimace. "I have to get some things together before I leave."

They didn't argue, probably eager to get Thomas home before their mother blamed them for keeping him too long. It was just as well, as she needed a little quiet to absorb the disaster that had fallen so quickly on her.

But Thomas paused long enough on his way out the door to give her a commanding look. He didn't have to speak to make his meaning clear. *Don't say anything.*

Dorcas waited until she'd heard the buggy go out the drive before she moved. Then, focusing on what she was doing, she got ready to go home.

Put the gradebook and the arithmetic papers in the bag. Pick it up, walk to the door. Don't look back, don't think that this might be the last time you do this. Lock the door, walk away.

Once she was no longer in sight of the school, Dorcas found she could think a little more clearly. What, really, had happened? Lydia had come unexpectedly into the schoolhouse and found her there with Thomas. Was that really so bad? Thomas was working on the outbuildings. There might be a dozen reasons why she had to talk to him after school hours.

Come to think of it, what had brought Lydia there after school hours? She hadn't come to pick up the girls, since she'd know they'd already gone home. Had they told her something that had brought her storming here to confront Dorcas?

She had assumed that if the Gaus girls had been going to spread the rumor Esther started, it would have been as soon as they'd heard it. But maybe Lydia had been busy mapping out her plans to get rid of Dorcas. Was it personal, or would she have felt the same no matter who the teacher was?

Whatever her reason, it had happened, and she'd found exactly what she'd hoped to find—Dorcas alone with Thomas. At least she hadn't been in Thomas's arms. She almost wished she had been. If Thomas were to leave immediately, she longed to have one last embrace to remember.

What would Lydia do first? Go to the school board? Well, that was probably on her agenda. But she'd said something about Minister Lucas. She'd said, "Wait until he hears about this," or words to that effect.

It didn't take a lot of imagination to figure out what Thomas's father would do. Blame Thomas. Blame her. Maybe go to the bishop and perhaps to the school board. It wouldn't occur to him that there might be another side to the story.

Thomas wouldn't explain, of course. He'd be angry. He'd be sure his father wouldn't believe him no matter what he said. No matter how she looked at that encounter, it couldn't be anything less than a disaster.

Thomas had told her to keep quiet. He'd said he'd take care of it. What did he imagine he could do?

Then she realized what he meant. He'd say it was all his fault. He'd tell his father, the bishop, the school board. He'd try to take the blame. Again.

She'd reached the farmhouse, but she didn't remember one single step of the walk home. She couldn't let that happen, but what could she do?

Hardly knowing what she was doing, she crossed the porch and went into the kitchen. Her mind vaguely registered that Betsy was there alone, pulling a pie from the oven. She set it on the rack, looking at it with pleasure. Turning to see Dorcas, her pleased look vanished, to be replaced by one of deep concern. Dropping the potholders, she rushed to Dorcas.

"Was ist letz? What's wrong? You look . . . terrible."

Dorcas pressed her hand to her forehead. "Mammi?" she asked, a question in her voice.

"I'm so sorry. She went to take supper to your cousin." She put her arm tentatively around Dorcas. "Can't you tell me? I'll help if I can."

"I know. It's just . . ." The need to tell someone overwhelmed her. "Lydia Gaus saw me alone with Thomas in the schoolroom, and she thought the worst. She'll probably tell everyone—the school board, Minister Lucas,

Mammi. And Thomas is trying to make it all his fault. I can't bear it." A sob choked her words.

"Ach, Dorcas, don't." Betsy hugged her. "It can't be that bad. Surely no one will believe anything wrong about you. And you're both free anyway."

She struggled to control herself. Betsy was too young and inexperienced to be burdened with Dorcas's problems. "Minister Lucas would believe anything bad about Thomas."

Betsy looked a little shocked, but she didn't draw back. "Even if he does, what could you do? If Thomas wants to try and save you the embarrassment . . ."

"I should let him?" A weight hung heavy on the words. "That's what I did before." Betsy wouldn't know what she was talking about, but that didn't matter now. What mattered was what she thought of herself.

She'd been a coward. She saw that now. She'd had a line of excuses that sounded genuine to her, and she'd let Thomas take all the blame. And she'd done it before because she was afraid. She'd given in to the fear and let him down.

Well, no more. She wouldn't let him do it again, no matter how much he insisted.

Dorcas straightened, managing a smile as she drew away from Betsy. "It's all right." She patted Betsy's cheek. "Thank you for listening. I know what I have to do now. Has anyone taken my buggy?"

Betsy shook her head. "I don't think so. But what should I tell Levi when he comes in?"

She considered saying it wasn't Levi's concern, but she couldn't do that. Not to Betsy.

"Just say I had to see Minister Lucas about something. I don't know when I'll be back."

She hurried out before Betsy could argue. She knew

now what she had to do, and she wouldn't let anyone talk her out of it.

THOMAS HAD HOPED to make it to the farm before Lydia showed up there, but when they turned into the lane, he spotted her horse and buggy pulled up to the hitching rail. That wasn't good. She'd had a chance to spew her poison before anyone could deny it.

"That's Lydia Gaus's rig. What's she doing here? She was just at the school." Adam leaned over the seat, his eyes alive with curiosity. "You and Dorcas looked kind of funny. Was Lydia giving you a hard time?"

He had no choice but to tell them. If Daad asked them any questions, it was only fair that they know why.

"Yah, she was at the school. She walked in and caught me holding Dorcas's hands and had a fit. I guess she's in there right now, complaining to Daad."

"That's foolishness." To his surprise, it was Jonas who spoke up first. "You're both free. What's it to her if you were holding hands?"

"Are you and Teacher Dorcas courting?" Adam nudged him, and he winced, as much from the pain in his response to the question as from the pain in his ribs.

"Not if doing so is going to make Teacher Dorcas lose her job and lead to closing the school." He couldn't help the bitterness in his voice. "I'd best get in there and do what I can." They'd come to a stop by then. "Give me a hand down, will you?"

"Sure thing." Adam hopped down and came to let Thomas lean on him to get down, absorbing some of the jolt.

"Denke," he muttered, focusing on the door. He had to get this done now. He had to find a way to keep Dorcas from being hurt by his toxic relationship with his father.

He mounted the steps slowly, hearing his brothers' low-voiced conversation behind him, and marched inside. It was just as he'd feared. Lydia Gaus was confronting his father, while Mammi stood by, her hands twisting together in obvious pain.

Lydia spun around at his entrance, and he could read the triumphant anger in her face. She must be confident that she was getting what she wanted, and he spared a moment to wonder how anyone could behave that way without an attack of conscience.

"You can't deny it." She addressed Thomas directly. "I saw with my own eyes—you and Teacher Dorcas making up to each other in the schoolhouse, of all places."

"School was over for the day," he pointed out, and then wondered why he was beginning with such a weak point. He needed something stronger than that if he were to protect Dorcas.

Daad frowned at him, his face set in the familiar lines of disapproval. "It's not your place to argue with Lydia when she's come to me as minister."

His father's words touched a match to his anger, and he fought to control it. "I surely have the right to defend myself, ain't so?"

"Thomas is right." Mammi spoke, and Daad looked at her in amazement—an amazement Thomas felt as well. He'd never in his life heard Mammi differ with his father in front of someone else, no matter what she might say in private.

"You must listen to your son as you would to any church member, ain't so?" she added.

Put on the spot, Daad had no choice but to nod. "Very well. What do you have to say to this accusation, Thomas?" His rigid expression didn't suggest that he would weigh it seriously, but at least he'd listen, and that alone was more than Thomas had expected.

"I don't know what Lydia thinks she saw, but the most she could have seen was me holding Dorcas's hands, because that was the most that happened."

"The way you were looking at each other—" Lydia burst out. "It made me certain sure that wasn't the first time. Besides, your own sister complained about you and Teacher Dorcas."

Mamm and Daad both looked startled. "Esther?" Mamm repeated, as if she couldn't believe what she heard.

"Esther!" Daad shouted her name. "Come down here."

Thomas's heart sank. He wouldn't have mentioned Esther's part in it, not for anything. But she was already coming in, and Daad swung on her.

"Have you something to say about your brother and Teacher Dorcas? Lydia Gaus says you have complained about their behavior."

"No!" Esther looked frightened, and his heart sank. "I didn't. I mean, I did say something to Erna and Hallie about them, but I didn't really mean it. They said they wouldn't tell, but they must have." She sent an unfriendly glance toward Lydia, and then she burst into tears.

Mammi went to her. "Stop crying now, my girl. You must tell us what you meant."

"But I didn't mean anything," Esther wailed. "I mean, I wanted Thomas to pay attention to me, and when he talked to Teacher Dorcas, I was . . . I was jealous."

"Esther . . ." Thomas took a step toward her, but a look from his father stopped him.

"Esther, are you saying you told a lie?"

"Not exactly. Well, yes. I didn't mean it, and afterwards I told Erna and Hallie it wasn't true and not to say anything. They promised, but they must have told their mother."

"That's not the point," Lydia broke in. "I know what I

saw. We don't want to have a teacher who behaves that way. It's not suitable."

"It wasn't Dorcas. It was me. I'm the one who insisted on talking to Dorcas at the school." He pushed back to the only thing that mattered.

"Why?" Daad shot the word at him, an angry edge to his voice. "What did you have to say that was so important that you had to say it in the schoolhouse?"

He stiffened, looking at his mother and knowing it would hurt her. "I had to tell her good-bye. I have to go away. I'm sorry," he added softly to her.

Tears welled in her eyes but didn't fall. Not yet.

Pain stabbed his heart at the sight. He was hurting his mother again. Hurting everyone. When would it end?

Before anyone could respond, footsteps were heard. Jonas opened the door and ushered Dorcas into the room.

A QUICK GLANCE at the audience waiting for her was enough to give Dorcas an inward quake, but she stiffened her spine and walked forward.

"I understand you're talking about something that affects me, so I think I should be here."

Lydia's expression said that she was taken aback by her appearance, and that gave Dorcas an odd sort of boost. Maybe Lydia wasn't as sure of herself as she pretended.

"Dorcas, this isn't necessary." Pain threaded Thomas's voice, and her heart twisted as she shook her head.

Minister Lucas looked from Dorcas to his son. Then, oddly enough, he looked at his wife. There was a moment's silence, and Dorcas seemed to see a message passing between them—a message she couldn't begin to interpret. Then, surprisingly, he pulled out a chair at the kitchen table.

"I don't know why we're all standing here. Let us sit down to talk about this."

The tension in Dorcas eased a little at the sight. He was going to listen, at least. Her greatest fear had been that he'd refuse to hear her. She'd already decided that, if so, she'd go to the bishop, little as she wanted to.

Lydia fidgeted with the back of the chair. Finally she sat, stiffly erect.

"Teacher Dorcas, Lydia Gaus has made a charge against you that—"

"I wouldn't exactly say a charge." Lydia's composure seemed to be slipping. Had she really expected that they wouldn't fight back? Minister Lucas ignored the interjection. "She said that you and Thomas were behaving improperly at the school. Is this true?"

Dorcas murmured a silent plea for the right words to say. "Since Thomas returned to Promise Glen, I have developed feelings for him, and I believe he has for me." That was the right beginning, she thought. But what next? "We saw each other often because he was working at the school, but nothing happened there that anyone in the community might not have seen and heard."

"Dorcas, this isn't right. You don't have to say anything." Thomas's strong hands clenched into fists on the table. "I've already said that any blame belongs to me."

Much as she wanted to look at him, to speak directly to him, she resisted the longing and focused on his father. The minister's face was lined and strong, a frown between his brows, but he was paying attention. He was hearing her, in a way that he didn't seem to hear his own children.

"Thomas is trying to protect me because he knows how much teaching means to me." She spoke directly to Minister Lucas. "He is a person who takes on responsibility for others."

Her eye caught a slight movement, and she realized

that Miriam was nodding. Their eyes met for just a moment, and she was heartened by what she saw.

So heartened, in fact, that she turned to Lydia. "Maybe you'd like to tell us why you're so eager to shut down the Orchard Hill school?"

All eyes turned to Lydia, and she stiffened. "I don't think it's proper to have so young a teacher. Look at her. How can she guide our young people? Now, Teacher Ruth has experience. My children did wonderfully well when they went to her school. It was good for them to be in a larger school with a mature, sensible teacher. It would be good for all the children, not just mine."

Dorcas couldn't hold her tongue any longer. "I don't believe you have the right to speak for the other parents. The children who live here have gone to our school for many years. Have you asked other parents what they think?"

Lydia seemed taken aback by the direct question. Her high color slowly faded. "I . . . well, of course I'm speaking for myself. And my husband. I have a right to express my opinion."

"Not when you try to get your way by accusing an innocent person of doing wrong." Thomas seemed to have full control of his temper now. He spoke firmly, but at least he wasn't showing the anger he had earlier.

"I know what I saw," Lydia said again, but she didn't sound quite as sure of herself this time. "Even if you're courting, it's not proper to do it at the school."

"Why?" Jonas's voice probably took everyone by surprise. They all turned to look at him, and Dorcas saw his gaze meet Thomas's for a moment. "The school had already closed for the day, and the scholars were gone. My brother and sister and I were there, just a few yards away. Do you think anyone else would agree to get rid of Teacher Dorcas when they know that?"

Dorcas could hardly believe it was Jonas coming to their defense. Jonas, who never seemed to stand up against anyone, and certainly never his father.

Maybe because of that, his words were having an impact. Minister Lucas's expression eased, and he nodded slightly. As for Lydia . . .

Lydia didn't have an answer to that question. She certain sure hadn't expected Thomas's family to come to his defense. Dorcas could almost see her mind working, turning this way and that, feeling what she wanted was slipping out of her hands.

Minister Lucas looked at her. "Well? That is a good question. What is your answer?"

Dorcas wasn't watching Lydia. Her gaze was caught by Thomas. His face had such a mix of emotions that she wondered how he could sort them out. Anxiety, surprise, and just a little, very cautious, relief.

""I'm sure if there's an explanation for what I saw, I'd be the last person who'd want to make trouble." Lydia cleared her throat. "I simply felt it my duty as a parent to . . . to question it."

"This is a serious matter." Minister Lucas looked very much as he did when he preached, and his eyes were fixed on Lydia. "To bear false witness against a sister and brother in the faith . . ."

"I didn't know." Lydia looked panic-stricken. "I mean, when Erna told me what Thomas's own sister had said . . ."

"And were you aware that Esther had told your daughters it wasn't true?"

Dorcas didn't know how Lydia felt, but she knew if one of the ministers spoke to her that way, she'd be cringing inside. A look at Lydia told her that was exactly what was happening.

The silence stretched. Lydia looked so desperate that Dorcas began to feel sorry for her in spite of what she'd done. When she couldn't handle it any longer, she had to speak.

"If Lydia realizes that she has made a mistake, I am satisfied," she said.

Lydia turned to her, seeming to search for words. Finally she nodded. "I didn't . . . I mean . . . If only we had . . . I'm sorry." Her voice wavered. Then, before anyone spoke, she pushed away from the table and scurried to the door as if afraid someone would stop her. Jonas opened it for her. She slipped through it and was gone.

A wave of relief surged through Dorcas, but she knew it was too soon for that. The heart of the issue lay between Thomas and his father, and unless that could be resolved, nothing she'd been through was worthwhile.

Still no one spoke. She rose from her chair, looking directly at Thomas, seeking to memorize every line of his face. "Tell your father why you've decided to leave. Please."

Unable to do anything else, she hurried out, feeling her throat tighten with unshed tears. She had done what she could. The rest was up to Thomas. If he chose to go away without her, she'd have to learn to live without him, no matter how hard it was.

CHAPTER EIGHTEEN

Once Dorcas was safely in her buggy and on the road, she was overwhelmed by the longing to be home—to feel comforted and safe. She could think of nothing else.

As if she were a child, she chided herself. But probably everyone, no matter how old, sometimes wanted to be a child at home, to lie in a warm bed and hear from downstairs the murmur of voices talking softly in dialect, forming a gentle lullaby to put one to sleep. If she could go back to those days . . . but she couldn't. No one could, but she still longed to feel that comfort.

A memory surfaced in her thoughts. She had sat beside Grossmammi's bed during the evening she had slipped quietly from this life to the next. Grossmammi had said only one thing. *Mammi*. Her hand had moved, groping, perhaps reaching for her mother's hand. Dorcas had taken the fragile weathered hand in her young grasp. Grossmammi hadn't spoken again, but she had smiled.

Mammi. That was who she wanted now. Without Thomas, Mammi was the only one who could give her what she needed. The comfort of home . . .

But when she walked into the kitchen, Dorcas realized

that no one here had any idea where she'd been or why she needed comfort. Supper was on the table, and Betsy was hustling everyone into their seats. Mammi, back from her errand, sat down with Will cradled in her arms, while Levi and Lemuel talked about the spring plowing and sowing.

She had been so keyed up, and now she had to pretend even longer. For a moment she felt a ridiculous resentment against all of them, and then she had to laugh at herself. How could they know what had happened unless she told them?

She'd have to wait until she could talk to Mammi. But as the moments went by, she found that just by sitting in her familiar place at the table, listening to the hum of talk among people who loved her, she had found what she needed. She was soothed, comforted, and at home.

Slowly, she started to think again about what might happen. So much depended upon what other people said and did. Lydia seemed to have been vanquished, but Minister Lucas and even Thomas himself had the power to make her happy or miserable. She couldn't affect it now. There was nothing for it but to wait. And hope.

Enough chatter went on during supper to cover her slight distraction. She could smile, and nod, and try to look her usual self. Betsy did give her a questioning look, but this wasn't the time or the place to reassure her.

Finally the boys had gone back to the barn. Betsy quickly scooped up the baby. "I'll take Will upstairs. You two have a nice talk."

Betsy might have been a little obvious, but she'd seen what Dorcas needed and given it to her.

"Now." Mammi reached out to clasp her hand. "Now you can tell me what's happening. Is it about Thomas?"

"How . . . how did you know?" Her throat was tightening already at the thought of talking about it.

"Ach, my sweet girl, haven't I seen you falling in love

ever since Thomas came back?" She patted the hand she held. "Tell me about it. Does he not feel the same?"

She wondered why she ever thought she could hide something like this from Mammi. "I love him. And I believe he loves me." She paused. Was she sure of it? She had to be. He wouldn't be so torn if he didn't love her. "But if he feels he has to leave here, he won't declare his love. He wouldn't ask me to leave."

Mammi shook her head. "I don't understand. Why would he have to go away again? I thought he'd come back to stay. Miriam certain sure thinks so."

The thought of Thomas's mother was a separate small pain. "I know. But his daad . . . Thomas thinks his daad has never really forgiven him. That he doesn't trust him. And now Lydia Gaus has been spreading stories about us and making everything worse. I don't think Minister Lucas believed her, but Thomas—"

Mammi's fingers tightened at the mention of Lydia. "That woman hasn't been happy since they came here. But I don't see why she needs to make others miserable. If Thomas won't speak, then you will have to. You'll have to tell him that you will go with him wherever he goes."

There was not a quiver in Mammi's voice when she said the words.

Dorcas blinked, trying to focus on Mammi's face. "But I thought . . . I thought you wouldn't want me to go."

"Ach, I don't, if there's another choice." Mammi shook her head. "It would be hard for us. But it would be the right thing to do. Where love leads, you must follow. Your grossmammi left all that she knew in Lancaster County to come here, and her great-grandmother left Germany to come halfway across the world. We can't be less brave than they were. If this is what happens, we will bear it."

Tears sprang into Dorcas's eyes, and she held her

mother's hand against her cheek. "Denke, Mammi," she whispered.

Before she could say anything else, Betsy hurried into the room, heading toward the back door. "It's Thomas," she whispered. "I'll let him in. You take him to the front porch, and we'll make sure Levi and Lemuel don't bother you."

Dorcas seemed to be shaking inside, and she took a deep breath. Mammi squeezed her hand. "You will know the right thing to do. Talk to him."

The next moment Betsy came in bringing Thomas. Before he could even greet anyone, Betsy was ushering the two of them out to the front porch.

Dorcas pressed her palm against her chest, where she felt her heart pounding. In a moment she'd know.

Betsy almost pushed them onto the porch and closed the door behind them. Dorcas felt herself blushing. "Betsy is trying to be helpful."

Thomas didn't answer, sending her anxiety up a notch. She led the way to the porch swing and sat down, gesturing to the place beside her and wondering if he'd want to stay farther away.

But he sat there, the swing moving with the pressure of his body. This close she should be able to read his expression. Sometimes she could even read his thoughts. But not now. Now, when it was crucial, he was closed to her. A chill slid down her back.

Thomas cleared his throat as if struggling to get words out. "I thought I should come and tell you what happened."

She controlled the urge to shake the words out of him. "Yah, of course you should. You must have known I would be waiting." Even someone who was just a friend would have been waiting.

"I didn't know what to expect after you went out." He turned to look at her. "Dorcas, you shouldn't have risked speaking. I don't want you to be hurt because of caring for me."

Her heart sank, and she lifted her chin. "That was about me. I'm a grown-up now, and I have to take responsibility for what I do." *And for what I feel,* she added silently.

"I know. You've told me before." His expression relaxed a tiny amount, and she felt better. "Daad . . . I expected a lecture. Or at least a description of all my faults. But instead . . ." He blinked, as if his eyes stung. "He asked me to forgive him. He said that he was sorry for the way he'd spoken to me about Adam." His voice roughened with emotion. "He said that Mammi told him that if he didn't change the way he thought about his sons, he would lose Adam just the way he'd lost me."

Dorcas heard the tears in his voice, and her own eyes grew wet. She touched his hand lightly, and his fingers closed around hers as if they were a lifeline.

"What did you say to him?" she whispered.

"What do you think?" His voice seemed to break between laughter and tears. "I said I was sorry, and he said he was sorry, and we both cried a little and hugged a lot." He was silent for a moment, and he seemed to look with surprise on what he'd just said. "I really believe he trusts me."

"Well, he should. You are very trustworthy." *And what about us?*

"I don't think you have to worry about Lydia," he went on, and she wanted to shake him. She didn't want to hear about Lydia. She wanted to know about them. But Thomas seemed intent on clearing everything up.

"Daad said that the bishop and the ministers have been thinking that they need to call on her. To talk about gossiping." He met her gaze, and the danger of Lydia's interference in the school faded away to nothing.

"So you won't lose your job, and the school won't be closed. But I was thinking . . ."

"What were you thinking?" She could read his face again now, and joy began to well up in her, wiping out the pain as if it had never been.

"That maybe you might like to take a few years off from teaching to have a family of your own." He reached up slowly to cup her cheek with his palm. "Dorcas, I have loved you ever since I can remember. I loved you when you were a mischievous child and when you were a wild teenager. And I love you even more as a beautiful, loving, giving woman. Please marry me. Share my life with me."

Joy welled in her like a never-failing spring. His words were everything she'd dreamed of hearing and feared she never would. The barriers between them were gone, and the future was opening up, filled with promise.

Dorcas smiled, feeling the movement of the smile against his hand. Her eyes were wet with happy tears. "You know the answer to that question, don't you? I think I have loved you just as long, but I didn't know it until you went away. And if you ever want to go somewhere else, I will come with you, no matter where it is, because where you are is home."

His lips punctuated her words, and she forgot everything she might say in the joy and love of his embrace.

"I will love you forever," he whispered against her ear, and then he kissed her again.

Home, she thought, snuggling against him and feeling the strength of his arms around her. Mammi was right. Where they were together, that was home.

EPILOGUE

What a difference a few short weeks made. Thomas paused by the schoolhouse steps, watching the crowd gathering around laden picnic tables in the schoolyard. He could walk up to Dorcas and talk intimately to her without prying eyes spying on them. In fact, any glances toward them would be tinged with the indulgent affection extended to courting couples who would soon be husband and wife.

His gaze sought out Dorcas, as it did whenever they'd been separated for more than a moment or two. She was at the picnic tables, helping the mothers set up the food they'd brought for the last day of school program.

As if she felt his gaze, Dorcas looked at him, smiling. A message passed between them as clearly as if they were alone together. A message of love and hope and anticipation. In a few short months, they would be man and wife.

Someone clattered down the steps behind him. He turned, reluctant to look away from Dorcas, to find his sister grinning at him.

"It's done," she announced, latching on to his arm. "No more school until September. And then I'll turn fourteen and be in my last year. I'll have one of the important parts in the program then. Can you believe it?"

"Are you sure?" he teased. "I thought Mammi said she made a mistake about how old you are, and then you could stay in school another year."

Esther gave him a mock punch on the shoulder. "I'll have you know that I'm getting all grown up."

He shook his head. "It's a scary thing, that's certain sure. Next thing we know, you'll be courting."

"Not me. I don't want to get sappy like you and Teacher Dorcas." She grinned and dashed off before he could retaliate, nearly running into Jonas.

Jonas shook his head as she rushed on toward the tables. "She's full of herself today." He jerked his head toward the edge of the crowd, where the teenagers had gathered. "Did you see Adam? He's making up to that cousin of Joseph's."

Thomas looked in time to see his youngest brother blushing and looking sideways at a pretty little brunette in a blue dress. "He'll have to actually talk to her if he wants to make any headway," he observed.

"Maybe he'll decide girls are more fun than running off to drinking parties and getting in trouble," Jonas said, and he nodded.

"Females do have a settling effect, don't they?" His eyes were drawn irresistibly back to Dorcas.

Jonas nudged him. "Ach, go on back to Dorcas. You know you want to."

Smiling at the truth of it, Thomas made his way through the crowd to her side. "Your scholars did you credit," he said softly.

"They did, didn't they? It was the best program yet, I think." Dorcas looked up, smiling, into his eyes. "And just about everyone has gone to look at the repairs you made to the stable and talked about what a fine job it was. I'd think you'd get some new work as a result."

"I already have. Two new jobs signed up just this afternoon." A wave of relief went through him. He could make a success of this after all. "So you don't need to worry that I won't be able to support you."

"I've never worried about that," she said, with a look of such trust on her face that it warmed his heart.

Someone asked her a question, and Dorcas turned to answer it. Thomas stood where he was, looking over the assembled community. They'd all come today, probably in an unspoken agreement to show that this was their school and they were going to support it.

Even Lydia Gaus and her husband were there, with Lydia looking uncharacteristically subdued. She'd had little to say in recent weeks, especially after being chastened by the bishop and the ministers. Daad had tactfully stayed away from that visit, but he knew all about it. According to him, there'd be no more trouble from that quarter. Lydia admitted that she had never wanted to move from the community where she was born. She'd thought that trouble with the school might convince her husband to move back. It looked as if he'd taken a firm line, so maybe she'd settle down and accept Promise Glen. It was a good place to be, as he had reason to know.

Mr. Haggerty was talking to Dorcas's brother Levi over a large wedge of pie, laughing at something he'd said. After his rocky beginning, Mr. Haggerty had turned out to be a wonderful gut neighbor to the school, and it seemed that he gained as much as he gave to the relationship.

Thomas felt Dorcas's presence as if they were touching, and his hand clasped hers under the level of the table. They stood together, hands linked, and he didn't have to look at her to know they belonged. They belonged together, and they also belonged here, with the families and the community they loved in Promise Glen.

GLOSSARY OF PENNSYLVANIA DUTCH WORDS AND PHRASES

ach. oh; used as an exclamation

agasinish. stubborn; self-willed

ain't so? A phrase commonly used at the end of a sentence to invite agreement.

alter. old man

anymore. Used as a substitute for "nowadays."

Ausbund. Amish hymnal. Used in the worship services, it contains traditional hymns, words only, to be sung without accompaniment. Many of the hymns date from the sixteenth century.

befuddled. mixed up

blabbermaul. talkative one

blaid. bashful

boppli. baby

bruder. brother

bu. boy

buwe. boys

daadi. daddy

Da Herr sei mit du. The Lord be with you.

denke. thanks (or *danki*)

Englischer. one who is not Plain

ferhoodled. upset; distracted

ferleicht. perhaps

frau. wife

fress. eat

gross. big

grossdaadi. grandfather

grossdaadi haus. An addition to the farmhouse, built for the grandparents to live in once they've "retired" from actively running the farm.

grossmammi. grandmother

gut. good

hatt. hard; difficult

haus. house

hinnersich. backward

ich. I

kapp. Prayer covering, worn in obedience to the biblical injunction that women should pray with their heads covered. Kapps are made of Swiss organdy and are white. (In some Amish communities, unmarried girls thirteen and older wear black kapps during worship service.)

kinder. kids (or *kinner*)

komm. come

komm schnell. come quick

Leit. the people; the Amish

lippy. sassy

maidal. old maid; spinster

mamm. mother

middaagesse. lunch

mind. remember

onkel. uncle

Ordnung. The agreed-upon rules by which the Amish community lives. When new practices become an issue, they are discussed at length among the leadership. The decision for or against innovation is generally made on the basis of maintaining the home and family as separate from the world. For instance, a telephone might be necessary in a shop in order to conduct business but would be banned from the home because it would intrude on family time.

Pennsylvania Dutch. The language is actually German in origin and is primarily a spoken language. Most Amish write in English, which results in many variations in spelling when the dialect is put into writing! The language probably originated in the south of Germany but is common also among the Swiss Mennonite and French Huguenot immigrants to Pennsylvania. The language was brought to America prior to the Revolution and is still in use today. High German is used for Scripture and church documents, while English is the language of commerce.

rumspringa. Running-around time. The late teen years when Amish youth taste some aspects of the outside world before deciding to be baptized into the church.

schnickelfritz. mischievous child

ser gut. very good

tastes like more. delicious

Was ist letz? What's the matter?

Wie bist du heit? How are you; said in greeting

wilkom. welcome

Wo bist du? Where are you?

yah. yes

Recipes

There's a soup for every season, and Amish cooks love collecting new recipes for hearty soups. Here are some of my favorites.

Chicken and Wild Rice Soup

½ cup butter
1 onion, finely chopped
½ cup celery, cleaned and minced
1 cup mushrooms, preferably fresh, sliced
½ cup carrots, grated
¾ cup flour
6 cups chicken broth
2 cups cooked wild rice
1½ cups boneless chicken, cooked, cut into bite-size
   pieces
½ teaspoon salt
½ teaspoon curry powder
½ teaspoon parsley
½ teaspoon black pepper

    2 cups half-and-half, milk, or a combination of the two

Melt the butter in a large saucepan. Stir in the onion, celery, mushrooms, and carrots, and cook slowly for about 5 minutes. Add the flour and stir well. Stir in the chicken broth. Bring to a boil, reduce the heat to low, and simmer for 5 minutes. Add the rice, chicken, salt, curry powder, parsley, and black pepper. Heat through, then slowly stir in the half-and-half or milk. Simmer for 1 to 2 hours, stirring from time to time.

Ham and Bean Chowder

    3 cups chicken broth
    1 can condensed cream of chicken soup
    2 potatoes, cubed
    1 cup cooked ham, cubed
    1 cup corn
    1 small onion, diced
    2 Tablespoons butter
    ¼ cup flour
    ½ cup warm water
    1 Tablespoon parsley
    1 can white beans, drained
    Salt and pepper, to taste

Heat the chicken broth and soup in a large saucepan. Stir in the potatoes, ham, corn, onion, and butter. Simmer on low heat for 2 hours.

Place the flour and water in a small container and stir or shake vigorously until smooth. Stir the mixture into the soup. Stir in the parsley and beans. Cook slowly for another 30 minutes. Season to taste with salt and pepper.

Broccoli and Cheese Soup

6 cups chicken broth
1 cup onion, chopped
1 cup celery, chopped
3 potatoes, diced
10 ounces frozen or fresh broccoli, chopped
10 ounces frozen or fresh cauliflower, chopped
2 cans cream of mushroom soup
1 pound Velveeta cheese, sliced
Salt and pepper, to taste

In a large saucepan, combine the chicken broth, onion, celery, and potatoes; bring to a boil. Simmer for 30 minutes. Add the broccoli and cauliflower; heat through. Add the soup and cheese, stirring until the cheese melts. Season with salt and pepper to taste. Simmer until the vegetables are cooked.

Dear Reader,

I hope you'll let me know if you enjoyed my book. You can reach me at marta@martaperry.com, and I'd be happy to send you a bookmark and my brochure of Pennsylvania Dutch recipes. You'll also find me at martaperry.com and on Facebook at MartaPerryBooks.

Happy reading,
Marta

Turn the page for an excerpt from

A CHRISTMAS HOME

A Promise Glen Novel

by Marta Perry

**Available now
from Berkley**

The buggy drew to a stop near the farmhouse porch, and Sarah Yoder climbed down slowly, her eyes on the scene before her. Here it was—the fulfillment of the dream she'd had for the past ten years. Home.

Her cousin, Eli Miller, paused in lifting her cases down from the buggy. "Everything all right?"

"Fine." *Wonderful.*

Sarah sucked in a breath and felt the tension that had ridden her for weeks ease. It hadn't been easy to break away from the life her father had mapped out for her, but she'd done it. The old frame farmhouse spread itself in the spot where it had stood since the first Amish settlers came over the mountains from Lancaster County and saw the place they considered their promised land. Promise Glen, that was what folks called it, this green valley tucked between sheltering ridges in central Pennsylvania. And that's what she hoped it would be for her.

The porch door thudded, and Grossmammi rushed out. Her hair was a little whiter than the last time Sarah had seen her, but her blue eyes were still bright and her skin as soft as a girl's. For an instant the thought of her mother pierced Sarah's heart. Mammi had looked like her own mother. If she'd lived . . . but she'd been gone ten years now. Sarah had been just eighteen when she'd taken charge of the family.

Before she could lose herself in regret, Grossmammi had reached her, and her grandmother's strong arms encircled her. The warmth of her hug chased every other thought away, and Sarah clung to her the way she had as a child, when Grossmammi had represented everything that was firm and secure in her life.

Her grandmother drew back finally, her blue eyes bright with tears. She took refuge in scolding, as she did when emotions threatened to overcome her.

"Ach, we've been waiting and waiting. I told Eli he should leave earlier. Did he keep you waiting there at the bus stop?"

Eli grinned, winking at Sarah. "Ask Cousin Sarah. I was there when she stepped off the bus."

And she'd seen him pull up just in time, but she wouldn't give him away. "That's right. I was wonderful surprised to see my little cousin—he grew, ain't so?"

"Taller than you now, Sarah, though that's not saying much." He indicated her five feet and a bit with a line in the air, his expression as impudent as it had been when he was a child.

"And you've not changed much, except in inches," she retorted, long since used to holding her own with younger siblings and cousins. "Same freckles, same smile, same sassiness."

"Ach, help!" He threw up his hands as if to protect himself. "Here's my sweet Ruthie coming. She'll save me from my cousin."

Ruthie, his wife of three years, came heavily down the back porch stairs, looking younger than her twenty-three years. She looked from him to Sarah, as if to make sure Sarah wasn't offended. "You are talking nonsense."

She swatted at him playfully. "Komm, carry those things to the grossdaadi haus for Sarah. Supper is almost ready."

"Sarah, this is Ruthie, you'll have figured out," Grossmammi said. "And here is their little Mary." The child who slipped out onto the porch looked about two, with huge blue eyes and soft wispy brown hair that curled, unruly, around her face.

And Ruthie couldn't have more than a month to go before the arrival of the new baby, Sarah could see, assessing her with a shrewd eye. When even the shapeless Amish dress didn't conceal the bump, a woman knew it wasn't far off.

Eli loaded himself up with Sarah's boxes, obviously intent on getting everything in one trip. "Surrounded by women, that's what I am," he said cheerfully. "And now there's another one."

He stopped long enough to give Sarah a one-armed hug, poking her in the side with one of her boxes as he did. "We're wonderful glad you're here at last, Cousin Sarah."

Sarah blinked back an errant tear. Eli hadn't lost his tender heart, that was certain sure. And Grossmammi looked as if she'd just been given the gift of a lifetime. As for Ruthie . . . well, she had a sense that Ruthie was withholding judgment for the moment. That was hardly surprising. She'd want to know what changes this strange cousin was going to make in their lives.

As little as possible, Sarah mentally assured her. All she wanted was a place to call home while she figured out what her new life was going to be.

Eli, finally laden with all her belongings, headed toward the grossdaadi haus, a wing built onto the main house and connected by a short hallway. Grossmammi had lived there since Grossdaadi's death, and when Sarah walked into the living room and saw the familiar rocking chairs and the framed family tree on the wall, she felt instantly at home.

"You're up here, Sarah." Eli bumped his way up the stairs until Sarah retrieved one of the boxes and carried it herself.

He flashed her that familiar grin. "What do you have in there? Rocks?"

"Books. I couldn't leave those behind. I just hope there's a bookcase I can use."

"If there isn't, we can pick one up at a sale. The auction house is still busy, even this late in the year. Almost December already."

"Grossdaadi used to say that any farmer worth the name had all his work done by the first of December."

"Ach, don't go comparing me to Grossdaadi," he said with mock fear. "Here we are. I hope you like it." He stacked everything at the foot of the old-fashioned sleigh bed. "Ruthie says supper is about ready, so komm eat. You can unpack later."

She'd rather have a few minutes to catch her breath and explore her new home, but Ruthie was her hostess. It wouldn't do to be late for their first supper together. With a pause in the hall bathroom to wash her hands, she hurried downstairs and joined Grossmammi to step the few feet across the hallway—the line that marked off their home from Eli and Ruthie's.

The hall led into the kitchen of the old farmhouse. Ruthie hurried them to their places at the table and began to dish up the food. Sarah glanced at her, opened her mouth to offer help, and caught Grossmammi's eye. Her grandmother shook her head, ever so slightly.

So something else lay behind the welcome she'd received. Best if she were quiet until she knew what it was.

This was a little disconcerting. She'd dreamed for so

long of being here, but those dreams hadn't included the possibility that someone might not want her.

Nonsense. Ruthie seemed shy, and probably she was anxious about this first meal she'd cooked for Sarah. The best course for Sarah was to keep quiet and blend in.

But once the silent prayer was over and everyone had been served pot roast with all the trimmings, it wasn't so easy to stay silent, since Eli seemed determined to hear everything about everything.

"So what was it like out in Idaho? I didn't even know there were any Amish there." Eli helped himself to a mound of mashed potatoes.

"Not many," she admitted. "It was a new settlement." She didn't bother to add that anything new was appealing to Daad—either they understood her father already, or they didn't need to know. "Ruthie, this pot roast is delicious. Denke." The beef was melt-in-your-mouth tender, the gravy rich and brown.

Ruthie's face relaxed in a smile, and she nodded in acknowledgment of the praise. "And your brothers and sister?" she modestly moved on. "How are they?"

"All married and settled now." They'd wisely given up finding a home with Daad and created homes of their own. "Nancy's husband is a farrier in Indiana, and the two boys are farming—Thomas in Ohio and David in Iowa."

"Far apart," Grossmammi murmured, and Sarah wondered what she was thinking. To say it was unusual to have an Amish family so widespread was putting it mildly.

"They all invited me to come to them," she said quickly, lest anyone think that the siblings she had raised were not grateful. "But I thought it was best for me to make a life of my own. I'm going to get a job."

Eli dropped his fork in surprise. "A job? You don't want to be working for strangers."

She had to smile at his offended expression. "Yah, a job. Some work I can do in order to pay my own way."

That wasn't all of it, of course. Her desire went deeper than that. She'd spent the past ten years raising her brothers and sister, and it had been a labor of love. What would have happened to all of them after Mammi died if she hadn't?

But that time had convinced her of what she didn't want. She didn't want to become the old maid that most large families had—the unmarried sister who hadn't anything of her own and spent her life helping to raise other people's children, tending to the elderly, and doing any other tasks that came along. She wanted a life of her own. That wasn't selfish, was it?

Even as she thought it, Eli was arguing. "You're family. You'll do lots of things to pay your own way. You can help Ruthie with looking after the kinder, and there's the garden, and the canning . . ."

He went on talking, but Sarah had stopped listening, because she'd caught an apprehensive expression on Ruthie's face. This, then, was what Ruthie was afraid of. She feared Sarah had come to take over—to run her house, to raise her babies . . .

Ruthie actually did have cause to be concerned, she supposed. She'd been in complete charge of the home for the past ten years, through almost as many moves and fresh starts. It wouldn't be easy to keep herself from jumping in—with the best will in the world, she might not be able to restrain herself unless she had something else to occupy her.

"I'll be happy to help Ruthie anytime she wants me," she said, using the firm voice that always made her younger siblings take notice. "But I need something else to keep me busy."

"And I know what," Grossmammi said, in a tone that suggested the discussion was over. "Noah Raber needs someone to keep the books and take care of the billing for his furniture business. I've already spoken to him about it." She turned to Sarah. "You can go over there tomorrow and set it up."

Sarah managed to keep her jaw from dropping, but barely. She'd intended to look for a job, but she hadn't expected to find herself being pushed into one as soon as she arrived.

"But . . . bookkeeping? I don't know if I can . . ."

"Nonsense," Grossmammi said briskly. "You took those bookkeeping classes a couple of years ago, didn't you?"

She nodded. She had done that, with the hope of finding something outside the home to do. But then Daad had gotten the idea of moving on again, and she had given it up. Did she really remember enough to take this on?

"Mostly Noah needs someone to handle the business side," Grossmammi went on. "The man loves to work with wood, but he has no idea how to send a bill. That's where you come in."

"But Noah Raber." Eli looked troubled. "Are you sure that's a gut idea? Noah's situation . . ."

"Noah's situation is that he needs to hire someone. Why shouldn't it be Sarah?" She got up quickly. "Now, I think we should do the supper cleanup so Sarah can go and unpack."

Grossmammi, as usual, had the last word. None of her children or grandchildren would dare to argue when she used that tone.

Carrying her dishes to the sink, Sarah tried to figure out how she felt about this turn of events. She certain sure didn't want to continue being in a place where she was only valued because she could take care of children.

But this job . . . what if she tried it and failed? What if she'd forgotten everything she'd once known? Noah Raber might feel she'd been foisted on him.

And what was it about his situation that so troubled
Eli? She tried to remember Noah, but her school years
memories had slipped away with all the changes in her
life since then. He was a couple of years older than she
was, and she had a vague picture of someone reserved,
someone who had pursued his own interests instead of
joining with the usual rumspringa foolishness. Was he
interested in offering her the job, or had Grossmammi
pushed him into it?

But she'd already made her decision in coming here—
coming home. She shivered a little as a cold breeze snaked
its way around the window over the sink and touched her
face. There was no turning back now.

"WHY DIDN'T YOU put your shoes together under the bed
like you're supposed to?" Noah Raber looked in exasper-
ation at six-year-old Mark, dressed for school except for
one important thing—his right shoe.

"I did, Daadi." Mark looked on the verge of tears, and
Noah was instantly sorry for his sharp tone. Mark was the
sensitive one of the twins, unlike Matthew. Scoldings
rolled off Matty like water off a duck's back.

"It's all right." He brushed a hand lightly over his son's
hair, pale as corn silk in the winter sunlight pouring in the
window. "You look in the bathroom while I check in here."

There weren't that many places where a small shoe
could hide, but the neighbor kids were already coming
down the drive, ready to walk to school with the twins.
With a quick gesture he pulled the chest of drawers away
from the wall. One sock, but no shoes.

From the kitchen below he heard Matty's voice, probably commenting on the fact that the King children were
coming. But a woman's voice, speaking in answer, star-

tled him out of that assumption. Who . . . ? Well, he had to find the shoe before anything.

When his mother had been here, this early-morning time had run smoothly—he hadn't realized how smoothly until he'd had to do it himself. Still, it had been high time Mamm had had a break from looking after his twins, and her longing to visit his sister Anna and her new baby was obvious. Naturally he'd encouraged her to go, insisting he and the boys would get along fine. If he'd known then . . .

"I found it!" Mark came running in, waving the shoe. "It was in the hamper."

He started to ask how it had gotten there and decided he didn't really need to know. The important thing was to get them out the door.

"Let's get it on." He picked up his son and plopped him on the bed, shoving the shoe on his foot and fastening it with quick movements. "There. Now scoot."

Mark darted out the door and clattered down the stairs, running for the kitchen. Noah followed in time to see Mark come to an abrupt halt in the kitchen doorway. He stopped, too, at the sight of a strange woman in his kitchen.

"Who—" He didn't get the question out before Matty broke in.

"This is Sarah. She's come to work for you, Daadi."

The woman put a hand lightly on Matthew's shoulder. "Only if your daadi hires me." She smiled. "Matthew and I were getting acquainted. This must be Mark." Her eyes focused on Mark, hanging on to Noah's pant leg, but she didn't venture to approach him.

"I'm sorry. I don't . . ." His mind was empty of everything but the need to get the boys off to school. "Just a minute." He turned to his sons. "Coats on, right this minute. And hats and mittens. It's cold out. Hurry."

Apparently realizing this was not the time to delay, they

both scrambled into their outer garments, and he shooed them toward the small mudroom that led to the back door. "Out you go."

"I think—" the woman began, following him.

"Just wait," he snapped. Couldn't she see he was busy? "Have a gut day, you two. Mind you listen to Teacher Dorcas."

He opened the door, letting in a brisk wind. A hand appeared in front of him, holding two small lunch boxes. The woman was standing right behind him.

"Aren't these meant to go?"

Instantly he felt like a fool. Or at least an inept father, chasing his sons out without their lunches. He grabbed them, handing them off to the boys, and saw to his relief that, by running, they reached the lane to the schoolhouse at the same time as the other children.

He gave one last wave, and then it was time to turn and apologize for his rudeness. The turn brought him within inches of the woman.

"Sorry," he muttered. "You must be Sarah, Etta's granddaughter. I didn't expect you so soon."

"No, I apologize. I shouldn't have come so early. My grandmother assumed you started work at eight, and I didn't want to interrupt."

Looking at her, Noah realized she wasn't quite so strange after all. Etta Miller had talked about her granddaughter coming, of course. He had said that he didn't remember her, but now it was coming back to him.

"You were a couple of years behind me in school, weren't you?"

She nodded, face crinkling in a quick smile. "That's right. By the time I was big enough to be noticed, you'd left school and started your apprenticeship, I guess."

"Sarah Yoder," he said, the last name coming to him. Her mother had been Etta Miller's middle girl, her father a newcomer from down in Chester County. If he didn't remember anything else, he should have remembered hair the color of honey and eyes of a deep, clear green. She was short and slight, but something about the way she stood and the assurance when she spoke made her hard to overlook.

He realized he was staring and took an awkward step back. It seemed suddenly intimate to be standing here in the narrow mudroom with a woman he hardly knew.

"You're here about the job." He reached past her to grab his wool jacket from the hook. "Let's go to the shop and talk. No need to be hanging out in here."

She nodded, buttoning her black coat as she stepped outside, then waiting for him to lead the way to the shop.

"Didn't your great-onkel used to live here?" He heard her voice behind him as they crossed the yard through frost-whitened grass.

"Yah, that's so. We moved in about eight years ago." When he and Janie had married. When he'd still believed marriage meant forever. "My great-onkel used this building as a workshop, so I started my business here."

He found himself looking at the building he called the shop, seeing it through a stranger's eyes. It wouldn't look like much to her—hardly more than a shed with a small addition on one end.

But when he looked at it, he saw the future—the future that was left to him after what Janie had done. He saw a thriving furniture business where his handcrafted furniture was made and sold. He saw his sons growing, working alongside him in the business they'd build together.

"I understand from my grandmother that you need someone to handle the paperwork so you're free to spend your time on creating the furniture."

He nodded, liking the way she put that—*creating*. Each piece of furniture he made was his own creation,

with his hard work and whatever gift he had pressed into
the very grain of the wood.

"I'd best show you the paperwork, since that's what
would concern you." *If I hire you,* he added mentally. But
who was he kidding? He hadn't exactly been swamped
with people longing to work for him, especially ones who
knew anything at all about running a business.

He held the door open and ushered her into the shop,
stopping to put up the shade on the window so that the winter sun poured in. Fortunately he'd started the stove earlier,
so the shop was warming already, and the sunlight would
help. He'd added windows all along one side of the shed,
because he needed all the light he could get for working.

"Over here, in the far corner." He gestured toward the
office area—a corner of the workroom with a desk, some
shelves, and a chair. At the moment the desk was piled
high with papers. "I haven't had time to get at it lately."

He wasn't sure why he was explaining to her. It was his
business. But he guessed it was obvious he needed help.
"You can take a look at it. See what you think."

Instead of commenting, Sarah walked, unhurried, to
the desk. He followed her, not sure how to conduct this
interview, if that's what it was. She began leafing through
the papers, seeming to sort them as she went. After a moment she looked up.

"Where do you keep the receipted bills?"

"Um, there should be a box . . . yah, that. The shoebox."

Sarah looked at it, still not commenting. Her very silence began to make him nervous. "It's not always such a
mess." Just most of the time. "My mother has been away
on a trip for several weeks, so I've had the boys to manage
as well as the business."

"I see. Sorry. That must be difficult. If you'd like me to
see what I can do with this . . ." She hesitated. "I take it
your wife doesn't help with the business?"

He froze, his stomach clenching. Didn't she know? Didn't she realize that was the worst thing she could possibly say to him?

SHE'D SAID SOMETHING wrong—very wrong. Noah looked as if she had hit him with a hammer. His strong-boned face was rigid, the firm jaw like a rock. His dark blue eyes had turned to ice. Remorse flooded her. If the poor man had lost his wife, why hadn't Grossmammi thought to tell her?

Standing here silent wasn't helping matters any. "Noah, I'm so sorry. I didn't know. I'd never have said that if . . . I suppose the family thought I knew your wife had passed away—"

"No." The word was a harsh bark. He swallowed, the strong muscles in his neck moving visibly. "Janie didn't die. She left us a few months after the twins were born. We haven't heard from her from that day to this."

Sarah struggled for words. "I . . ."

"There's no need for expressions of sympathy." His mouth clamped shut like a trap.

Whatever she did, she mustn't show pity. It wasn't easy, but she schooled her face to calm. "You are the fortunate one, then."

Noah gave a short nod, as if he understood her instantly. "Yah. I have the boys. They are worth anything."

He spun, turning away from her, and looked yearningly at his workbench. Clearly he didn't want to talk anymore. Did that mean he didn't want her around at all?

"What do you think?" he said, not looking at her. He gestured toward the desk with the papers on it.

Sarah touched the stack of papers in front of her, mentally measuring it. If Noah wanted to carry on as if nothing had happened, surely she could manage to go along with him.

"It might be best if I look through these and sort them. Then we'll have a better idea of where we are. If that's all right with you." She trod as carefully as if she were walking barefoot on broken glass.

"Yah, gut. Denke." He still didn't look her way. They were both being cautious and polite, trying to pretend nothing had happened. "However long it takes. I'll pay for the time it takes to decide if you want to do this or not."

"You don't need to—"

"The laborer is worthy of his hire." He flashed a smile. It was a feeble effort, but it was the first she'd seen from him. "That's what my daad always says."

She nodded, sitting down at the desk while Noah moved quickly to his workbench. Her family might have been better off if Daad had adopted that saying. His, unfortunately, had been more in the nature of *The grass is always greener on the other side of the fence.*

Somehow, no matter how often he had been proved wrong, Daad had clung to that belief. Still did, she supposed. But at least she wasn't going with him now, the way she'd had to for the sake of her brothers and sister.

They worked without talking, and the workshop was silent except for the gentle swish of fine sandpaper against wood. Sarah glanced around the room. It was well designed, she supposed, with that row of windows bringing in a lot of light so Noah didn't have to depend on gas lighting.

But there wasn't much space. The small addition, which she'd assumed was a showroom for his finished pieces, was instead filled with all the equipment he didn't have room for in here. She began mentally rearranging it, putting her desk and chair in the addition with a few display pieces and moving all the work into the larger space. It would still be crowded, but it would be a better use of the space.

Noah glanced up and caught her looking at him. "Did

you want to ask me something? You can interrupt, you know. Unless I've got my fingers near a saw blade."

The attempt at humor encouraged her. He wouldn't bother, she thought, unless he wanted to make this work.

"I haven't run across any tax papers." Sarah said the first thing that popped in her head. "I suppose you do keep tax records."

"If you can call it that." He rubbed the back of his hand across his forehead. "If you can figure out the taxes, you're better than I am. The file is in the house. I'll get it when we stop for lunch."

Sarah nodded, but before she could go back to sorting, he spoke.

"So what do you think? You've probably never met such a mess in any of your other jobs."

The expectation revealed in the comment startled her. Clearly he thought she'd been working as a bookkeeper. What exactly had Grossmammi told him?

"It . . . it's just what I would expect if you haven't had time to do anything with it in the past month or so."

Noah grimaced. "Make that three. Or four." He looked a little shamefaced. "Even when my mother was here, I didn't spend enough time on that side of the business."

She nodded, unsurprised. "So I see." She hesitated. "Just so we're clear—I don't know exactly what my grandmother told you, but I haven't actually had a job in bookkeeping." Before he could react, she hurried on. "I took all the classes, and I'd accepted a job, but then we moved before I could start work."

"You moved a lot, did you?" His voice had grown cool quite suddenly.

So it did make a difference to him. Disappointment swept over her. She could do this job, she thought, but not if he didn't give her a chance.

"I kept house for my daad and took care of my brothers

and sister. When Daad decided to move on, we went with him."

It wasn't as if she'd had a choice. So she ought to be used to disappointment by this time.

But she wasn't giving up on getting this job before she'd shown what she could do, so she continued.

"It looks as if it will take a week or so of full-time work just to get everything organized. Once a system is set up, you may only need to spend a few hours a day on it."

Sarah waited, giving him the opportunity to say that in that case, he wouldn't need her. Or to agree that he'd hire her. But he didn't say anything. He just nodded and turned back to his own work.

Well, she'd have to take silence as his permission to go on with the sorting, at least. Perhaps he was thinking that would buy him time to see how well it worked out, having her here.

Did her presence upset his work? She studied him covertly over a stack of receipts. His eyebrows, thick and straight, were drawn down a bit as if he were frowning at the curve he was sanding . . . the arm of a delicately turned rocking chair. The curves of the legs and the back were what many Amish would consider fancy, but the whole piece was so appealing that it seemed to urge one to sit and rock for a bit.

Maybe he wasn't disappointed in the work—that look might be one of deep concentration. His strong features could easily look stern, she supposed, even if that wasn't his feeling. The twins hadn't inherited that rock-solid jaw, or at least, it didn't show yet. Their faces were round and dimpled.

Did they look like their mother? She didn't even know if the woman was someone local or not. Obviously, Grossmammi had some explaining to do.

Thinking of the twins caused a pang in the area of her

heart. She shouldn't let herself start feeling anything for those two motherless boys. She knew herself too well—she'd fall into mothering them too easily, and that wouldn't do.

Presumably Noah's mother would take over again when she returned from her trip. Noah had been fortunate to have her available when his world had fallen apart.

Grossmammi had offered to take Sarah and her siblings when her mamm died, but Daadi hadn't wanted it. And Sarah, at eighteen, had been fully capable of looking after the younger ones—not only that, but she'd felt it her duty. She couldn't regret the years she'd spent raising them, but she didn't want to do it again, not unless it was with her own babies.

She stole another glance at Noah, his closed face giving nothing away, his dark brown hair curling rebelliously as he worked. He hadn't offered her the care of his children. He hadn't even offered her the bookkeeping job yet.

And if he did . . . well, given how difficult his situation was, she wasn't sure she should take it.

Ready to find
your next great read?

Let us help.

Visit prh.com/nextread

Penguin
Random
House